PRAISE FOR
THE ROPES THAT BIND

"Critical acclaim for this desperately needed type of love story. In my 40 years of work as a psychotherapist I often find myself advising patients to "treat themselves as if they were someone they loved." The response I frequently get is "how?" Tracy Stopler provides the model, or the "how to" in *The Ropes That Bind.* The focus in her debut novel is adult recovery from childhood sexual abuse. However, the path braved by the main character, Tali Stark, is one that can be followed by all those who struggle with any potentially crippling traumatic life event at any age. Written in a novel/memoir style in the first person, the story catches you on the first page and doesn't let go until the last sentence of the conclusion."

♦ **Dr. Ted Horowitz, DSW, Doctor of Social Work**

"*The Ropes That Bind* is an incredible story of its main character Tali Stark. Tracy Stopler begins with Tali's horribly traumatic childhood experience and crafts a wonderfully tender, caring, insightful and inspiring story of Tali's search for meaning, love and ultimately acceptance and forgiveness, without the sensationalism one might encounter given the subject matter. It's Tali's journey, but you as the reader are with Tali every step of the way. And what a journey it is. I feel enlightened and better for it."

♦ **Amazon Customer**

"This heartbreaking story of the emotional scars of child sexual abuse has the most troublesome and painful beginning. But as this artful tale unravels, the narrator takes the difficult and necessary journey toward healing, through romantic relationships and her curative work as a registered dietitian. Tracy Stopler's main character Tali Stark is memorable, and her story is narrated in the most compassionate way. *The Ropes That Bind* will leave you feeling inspired." ♦ **Marie Carter, Author of *The Trapeze Diaries***

"When Professor Stopler, asked me to read her book, I assumed it was an educational book on nutrition. Wrong! Instead, it was an inspirational book on life. I connected with Tali as a young girl, a student, a professional and a survivor. This book is about discovering your best self despite life's curveballs. To quote a line in the book, '*Applause, applause, applause.*'"

♦ **Survivor of Rape**

"The Ropes That Bind will break your heart and then rebuild it better than it was before. Stopler's moving story, one of transformation from childhood sexual abuse, reassures us that the human spirit is truly indestructible."

♦ **Rabbi Todd Chizner**

"Tracy Stopler's *The Ropes That Bind* is a provoking novel of a young girl's journey overcoming childhood sexual abuse. Once I started reading it, I could not put it down. Not only does Ms. Stopler portray the complexities of recovering one's identity after a traumatic event, she skillfully delves into issues of spirituality, of finding and maintaining romantic relationships, and the lifelong quest of finding peace with herself and the world around her. A captivating, brilliant read that will leave you better educated about the survivors of childhood sexual abuse and what it means to feel alive. As a licensed social worker, I would highly recommend any survivor, male or female, to read this novel."

◆ **Amy Angelone, LMSW, Enough Abuse Campaign Trainer**

"Tracy Stopler is a gifted writer, who makes her narrator, Tali Stark, come alive with a unique, tender and brave voice. The beginning is hard to read, yet, riveting – a nightmare to any mother. The middle is inspirational and true to life. It took me a week to read the last twenty pages because I didn't want it to end."

◆ **S.D., Mother of Survivor**

"*The Ropes That Bind* is a painfully realistic account of the day-to-day life of a survivor. There is a true connection between the main character, Tali, and the reader, as the story genuinely reveals the struggles and triumphs that are part of living life. It is a beautiful story, giving a voice to those who have remained silent."

◆ **Heather B. Gilmartin, LMSW**

"It has been an honor to read and experience *The Ropes That Bind*. This inspiring novel is beautifully written – filled with vivid details. I was there in every scene and felt every emotion. I cried, I laughed, and I was upset. I connected with my inner child and with my source of Power and Creation. I meditated. I reflected. I saw things that I wasn't aware of before. The most beautiful thing was observing Tali transform from a victim to a victorious, successful woman, bringing healing to others with her compassion and love. What an exciting ride it has been."

◆ **Patricia J., Survivor of Sexual Abuse and Domestic Violence**

"'Nobody wants to revisit a war zone,' yet in *The Ropes That Bind*, Tracy Stopler pays such a visit with the ultimate purpose of healing from the inner personal war of previously unspoken child sexual abuse. In doing so, the author has created a memorable story, a healing antidote, and a story filled with 'the courage and strength to break free from the shame.' This is a series of beautiful love stories... one of family, another of student/mentor, and most meaningfully, one of discovering love of self! Ms. Stopler has truly paved the way for all victims of life's tragedies to become survivors - in fact, thrivers of life's gifts. This book will touch your heart, break it wide open, and then place it back in your chest with added compassion, spirit and love."

◆ **Dr. Seena Russell Axel**

"*The Ropes That Bind* is very uplifting. I like Tracy Stopler's use of *Kabbalah* and meditation as ways of coping with life. This book can help to break the silence of child sex abuse, start the difficult conversation, and allow healing to begin." ◆ **Valeri Drach Weidmann, Coordinator of Circulation/Public Relations, Highland Park Public Library, Poet**

"Before I opened this book, I poured myself some wine. I knew there were life lessons waiting for me, and Tracy Stopler did not disappoint. She created a real-life character, Tali Stark, who struggled with a real-life problem, living with the secrecy and shame of childhood sex abuse. She also created in me a sense of hope and a feeling I had never experienced before – forgiveness to my younger self. Because we are all survivors of something, every person can connect with Tali. So, pour yourself some wine, but don't forget the tissues." ◆ **J.S., Female Survivor**

"Tracy Stopler's *The Ropes That Bind* is an amazing and richly detailed book that I could not put down. The narrator, Tali Stark, like many of us, struggles to find a new normal while living with the shame of a childhood secret. It was breathtaking to watch Tali transform from a victim to a victor. This empowering story is definitely worth reading." ◆ **Fabrizzia Vinhal**

"This is a glorious, heartbreaking and triumphant story. Tali Stark is a realistic, inspiring protagonist who reminds us that although we all live with invisible antagonists, *the ropes that bind*, the Light is always there." ◆ **Frances, 82-year-old Survivor**

"*The Ropes That Bind* is an inspirational, poignant and emotional portrayal of life after child sexual abuse. In her first novel, Tracy Stopler brings us from the depths of despair to the summit of love, light and accomplishment. This triumphant story has inspired me to be more introspective and to help others heal after paralyzing trauma. Tracy has given a voice to those who can no longer speak for themselves." ◆ **Susan Weiner, RD, MS, CDE**

"*The Ropes That Bind* is a meaningful story that follows the journey of a young girl into adulthood after experiencing child sexual abuse. Tracy Stopler gives voice to an issue people are uncomfortable discussing. She demonstrates the negative impact that child sexual abuse has on the main character, Tali Stark, but also enlightens us as to how someone can move from victim to healthy survivor. I applaud this work. It's a wonderful story." ◆ **Cynthia Scott, MA, Executive Director, The Safe Center, LI**

THE ROPES
THAT BIND

BASED ON A TRUE STORY
OF CHILD SEXUAL ABUSE

THE ROPES

THAT BIND

BASED ON A TRUE STORY

OF CHILD SEXUAL ABUSE

TRACY STOPLER

BINAH📖BOOKS

LIBRARY OF CONGRESS CATALOGING-IN-PUBLICATION DATA
Stopler, Tracy, author
The ropes that bind: based on a true story of child sexual abuse.
Includes appendix: child sexual abuse

ISBN-13: 978-1-53-338111-8
ISBN-10: 1533381119

Printed in the United States of America

THIS BOOK IS DEDICATED TO

Dana, Erika, Melanie, Seth,
Eric, Deborah, Gabriel, Samantha, Mikayla, Colby,
Daniel, Brandon, and Genna:

Holding each of you as newborns,
feeding you as infants,
playing with you as toddlers and
watching each of you continue to blossom
into magnificent individuals
has been my greatest joy.

I love you all deeply.

All My Love,
Aunt Tracy

WITH GRATITUDE

Thank you, God.

I am indebted to the following people who gave generously of their wisdom, knowledge, time and love.

- **Victor Herbert, M.D.,J.D.,** my mentor and now guardian angel. Your love, patience and understanding put me in the right direction – your energy keeps me there. I am privileged to have known you. My life has been changed by what you have taught me. You have provided me with so much light that I am no longer afraid of the dark. I miss you terribly.

- **Richard Faust**, my dear friend and colleague, who sat with me every week for five years pretending that this daunting task was fun. Thank you for your expertise and commitment and for redirecting my attention when my inner voice was silent. Without your support, this book never could have been completed. Your unexpected passing made it bittersweet finishing the final lap of this journey without you. Chapter twenty-five is a tribute to you and your gentle soul.

- **Barry and Michael Stopler**, my brothers who have devoted endless hours of time to reading and researching this book's content for accuracy. Thank you for your insight, tenacity, and self-sacrifice. Your sense of humor is priceless, and your lifetime of unconditional love and support is beyond words. Growing up with you has been a blessing. Growing old with you is a bonus. I love you.

- **Sandy Brenner**, my rock and personal Internet explorer, with whom I communicated daily about specific contents of this book. You truly understand what this book is about because you understand me. While writing parts of this book made me experience the dark side, my time spent with you pulled me back into the light. Thank you for your vital support and for always providing a shelter from the storm.

- **Caryn Nistico**, my dear friend and colleague, who read and edited many incarnations of this book. Your *Faith* made this project manageable and venturesome. I am forever grateful.

ACKNOWLEDGMENTS

Rajiv Mehta, *madad ke lie shukriya,tumane mujhe bachaaya*! Thank you, Sara Brenner, for your priceless, witty editing. Hope Ortiz, you are my soul-sister. Scott Kasdan, you are like no other.

Toda rabbah, Rabbi Todd Chizner, for your valuable contribution to the spirituality sections. Two thumbs up for Amy Shearn, my valuable and optimistic script doctor, and Deb Kuhlman, my amazing, hard-working, fast-acting, on-the-ball copy editor.

My gratitude to my friends and colleagues who sat for hours listening and reading this story with patience and devotion: Amy Angelone♥, Seena Russel Axel, Regina Breuer, Mary Conlin, Heather Gilmartin, Keri Guarino♥, Diane Harvey, Ted Horowitz, Patricia Jorquera, Janice Omstrom, Phylis Levine, Jeffrey Schwarz, Cindy Scott, Fabrizzia Vinhal, Valeri Drach Weidmann, Susan Weiner and Amy Hammel Zabin.

Thank you to the following people who added to this story in their own special way: Gary Andrews, Zvi Avigdor, Todd Bredehoft, Karsten Bundgaard, Kent C. Chan, Aaron Cohen, Loren Daitch, Margie and Tony Dezego, John DiGiorgio, Rick Fie, Robert Francis, Ellen Gasman, Rich Golden, Roseanne Gotterbarn, Josh Hanson, Marilynne, Alissa, Laura and Kathy Herbert, Katherine Hutchison, AnneMarie Jackson, Elaine and Don Kasdan, Kent Keyser, Stephanie and Theophania Kranias, Allen Kwang, Robin Meyers, Michele Mirabel, Maura Noel, Kent Norton, Bob Otto, Jerry Polansky, Susan Ribak, Howard and Annette Roth, Erik Schwimmer, Kent Seelig, Anthony Sepe, Craig Shaw, Bill and Marissa Sparke, Ron Streit, Mollie Sugarman, James Williams, Barbara Yanofsky, Matthew Yasmer, Ed Yuchowitz and Anthony Zenkus.

Thank you to my Gotham Writers' Workshop instructor, Marie Carter, whose support and constructive criticism was an essential ingredient in moving this project forward.

A special thank you to The Safe Center and The Enough Abuse Campaign for providing indispensible support and training.

Finally, a standing ovation to my family, my mom and dad, Ceil and Nat Stopler; Michael, Barry, Shari and Marina Stopler; Sandy, Norman, Jeffrey, Karen and Sara Brenner; Toby, Herbie, Stephanie, Pam and Brian Schneider. There are no words to express my appreciation for your endless love and support. I am blessed to share this lifetime with you all.

CHAPTER CONTENTS

CHAPTER CONTENTS

MY MIDDLE (Continued)

MY NEW BEGINNING

my beginning

"There are many heartfelt reasons
for pushing our childhood sexual abuse
to the edge of our lives
and one amazing reason
to embrace a healing journey;
It reunites us with our shining,
colorful, joyful spirit."

Jeanne McElvaney

one

April 15, 1974

I looked out from my bedroom window on the eighth floor. It was a rainy Monday morning in the Bronx. Cars were pulling out of the parking lot across the street and driving around the little traffic island with its big trees and flowers just beginning to bloom.

My Panasonic cassette radio echoed out Karen Carpenter singing the chorus of "Rainy Days and Mondays."

"Hangin' around
Nothin' to do but frown
Rainy days and Mondays always get me down."

Socks, books and Barbie dolls were lying on the red shag carpet. My dresser was made of white wood and had a large mirror. My matching desk and hutch contained all twelve volumes of the *Encyclopedia Britannica,* Judy Blume's *Are You There God? It's Me, Margaret, The Princess Bride* by William Goldman, and *The Giving Tree* by Shel Silverstein.

I had remodeled my small wooden bookcase into Barbie and Ken's house. My favorite poster was on the wall above it. It showed a mountain, a dove and a rainbow over the words "Somewhere over the rainbow, skies are blue, and the dreams that you dare to dream really do come true."

On my desk was a to-do list: spelling, math, call Grandma, bake cookies, polish nails and clean room. All but the last item was checked off.

My dark brown eyes looked back at me from the mirror. My long brown hair needed to be brushed. I was searching for my red rain jacket.

Mom poked her head inside the door. "Are you ready?"

"I can't find my jacket."

"That's because you don't put things in their proper place."

I sighed and rolled my eyes.

"Your jacket is in the living room on the floor. Exactly where you left it."

"Okay," I said, shutting off the radio and walking past her, down the long narrow hallway.

"Tali, I'm talking to you. Don't walk away."

I stopped, turned around, looked up and rolled my eyes again. "I'm going to be late for school."

"And I'm going to be late for work. I don't have time to look out the window and watch you cross the street to school, okay?"

"Okay."

"So, go right to school, okay?"

"Okaaaaaay."

From the kitchen cabinet I got two Pop-Tarts, sealed together in their silver wrapper, and put them in my school bag. I picked my rain jacket up off the living room floor and slipped it on. I grabbed an umbrella out of the hallway closet.

I hollered out to my mom, "Come lock the door."

"How about a kiss goodbye?"

"I gotta go, Ma."

"Go ahead, have a good day."

I stepped onto the crowded elevator. I was the first to exit into the lobby where I heard my mom's voice over the intercom, "Tali?"

Another eye roll. "Yes?"

"Okay, go straight to school."

"I promise. Bye, Mom."

"I love you."

I looked around the lobby. The coast was clear. "I love you, too."

I left the building. The rain was falling hard. I opened my umbrella and headed to my elementary school, directly across the street.

I walked head down, listening to the raindrops hitting the umbrella. I was singing to the rhythm of the falling rain as my new white sneakers splashed the puddles in the street. I didn't realize that someone was calling out to me.

"'SCUSE ME!"

I looked up. There was a white stretch limousine sitting on the right side of the street. The driver's window was halfway down. I stopped walking. I stood completely still in the middle of the street in the pouring rain.

"Can ya tell me where Driza Loop iz?"

"Dreiser Loop? Yes, sir."

I moved closer to the limo. The driver was wearing a black suit; his white dress shirt was unbuttoned. His bow tie was undone. His face was chubby and he needed a shave. The windows were all fogged up, and I couldn't see inside.

"You need to make a right turn onto Baychester Avenue."

"Whatcha name?"

What?

"Come outta da rain." He reached over to open the passenger door.

I have to go to school.

The passenger door swung open and he held up a pen and paper. "'Kay, I'm ready for ya help. I don't wanna see such a pretty young thththing get wet from da rain."

I looked up toward my bedroom window. In my mind I saw Mom looking out and mouthing "Go straight to school."

I walked around to the passenger side. I looked inside and saw that everything was fancy. On the dashboard there was a screen and lots of buttons with lights. When I looked into the back, I saw two rows of empty leather seats with attached cup holders. The carpet looked as soft as fur. When I saw the little refrigerator, I thought the car must belong to a movie star.

I closed my umbrella as I slid into the front seat. I placed the wet umbrella on the floor in front of me, my book bag on my lap.

"Do ya have a name?"

"Tali."

"'Kay, Tal-eee, I make a right onta Baychesta Avenew an thththen what?"

"Then you keep going straight until…"

"Tal-eee," he said smiling, "wouldcha mine closin' thththe door? Just fur a minute."

Okay, just for a minute, said the voice in my head as I closed the door.

Minute, minute, minute.

I heard the doors lock.

"Tal-eee, don't be 'fraid. I just wantcha' ta show me how ta get ta Driza Loop."

I looked out the passenger side window. I saw the ground moving as the car engine revved up. I looked at my book bag – *I have to go to school.* I glanced up once more at my bedroom window and watched it disappear. My heart was beating fast; it was hard to breathe.

I just made a big mistake.

The car continued up the block and then he made a right turn at the light onto Baychester Avenue. The tears welled up. No matter how many times I blinked, it was like looking through frosted glass.

"Iz thththis right, Tal-eee? Right onta Baychesta?"

I said nothing. His stutter made me nervous and I hated the way he dragged out the second syllable of my name. I now sensed he was dangerous. He must have sensed I was scared.

"It's okay, Tal-eee. I ain't gonna do noththththin'."

On Baychester Avenue he passed the little yellow schoolhouse where I had gone to kindergarten. I had danced with my classmates in the basketball court behind that school. A minute later, I raised my trembling hand and pointed for him to make a right turn onto Co-Op City Boulevard.

He turned. "Now where?"

I pointed straight ahead. We passed an apartment building on the right and a vacant lot, a gigantic construction site, on the left. And then, there it was, finally, on the right, 'DREISER LOOP.'

He passed it.

"There! There!"

"What?"

"You passed it. Dreiser Loop."

"Oh," he started to slow down. He turned his head side to side, straining to see through the rain.

"Can I go now?"

"Yup, I'll drive ya back ta school." He didn't look at me.

He made a U-turn. He passed Dreiser Loop and slowed down at the vacant lot before pulling in and stopping.

I felt faint. The window wipers were on high speed. My head began to spin.

Where is everybody? God, are You here? Doesn't anybody see this big white limo? Is there anybody behind these cinder blocks? Please, somebody help me. Mommy!

"Tal-eee?"

I didn't look up. I bit my lower lip.

"Tal-eee, I'm talkin' ta ya." He turned the ignition off.

Tears streamed down. My heart was beating fast and loud.

"I ain't gonna hurtcha…"

He was a liar, but so was I. I had promised Mommy I would go straight to school.

He opened the glove compartment and pulled out a long carving knife. The blade just missed me. I was familiar with knives; my dad was a butcher and I had watched him in the kitchen slice up the steaks he brought home from work.

"…but I'll do it if I hafta."

I wanted to open the door and run but I was too scared to move.

The chorus of *Rainy Days* echoed in my head.

I told myself that I needed to get to school. Miss Levy, my fourth grade teacher, would be collecting our homework assignment on fractions and handing out our new spelling words.

Open the door. Run. Run. Run.

I couldn't.

"Tal-eee?" He took the blade of the knife and traced my inner leg and rested it on the zipper of my pants.

"I wantcha' ta do somethththin' fur me."

Dear God, please hear me. I promise I'll be a good girl. I promise I'll go straight to school. Please God. I won't talk fresh to Mommy. I won't roll my eyes anymore. Ever. Please God, PLEASE!

Was this real? I was back in my bedroom. Maybe I was still in bed in my pajamas. Yes, I was still in bed. This wasn't real. It couldn't be. I was still in bed. Who was the girl in the car with The Man? *She* was no longer *I*.

She felt a hand on her leg. A hard squeeze.

Was that real?

"Tal-eee?" he said softly, "I'm talkin' ta ya." And in a completely different voice, he rasped, "Hafya eva sucked a cock bafur?"

He took the book bag and tossed it into the back seat. Back into the darkness.

She cried out. The tears dripped from her chin onto his hand, the one holding the knife.

"Unzip ya pants."

She was completely paralyzed.

"UNZIP YA FUCKIN' PANTS." He raged. The veins in his neck were about to explode.

He reached over and forcefully yanked the zipper down.

"TAKE 'EM OFF!" he spat out as spittle sprinkled the dashboard like raindrops.

She stared straight ahead. Petrified.

"I ain't gonna tell ya no mo. TAKE OFF YA FUCKIN' PANTS."

She lifted her bottom off the seat and pulled her pants down to her knees. She readjusted her pink panties, the ones that said *Wednesday*.

"OFF… COMPLETELY… NOW!"

She untied her sneakers and slipped one pant leg off at a time. Her pants now sat on top of the wet umbrella.

"Are ya done playin', lil' girl? Are ya ready ta start actin' like a real woman? Are ya ready ta suck ma big cock now?" He reached over and stuck his finger inside her panties.

The raindrops pounding on the car roof drowned out her scream.

He smacked her hard.

He smacked me hard.

Back again, I felt a sting on my face and I saw stars. I tasted blood.

"I neva wanna hear ya scream no mo." He unzipped his pants and pulled out his penis.

"Hangin' around
Nothin' to do but frown
Rainy days and Mondays always get me down."

"Gimme ya hand."

I couldn't move. All I did was cry. I could feel my lip getting bigger.

"I swear ta gawd, I'll cut ya fuckin' throat. Gimme ya fuckin' hand." His sweaty hand grabbed mine, squeezing my little fingers and forcing them around his hard thing.

My eyes were squeezed shut and sealed with tears. My world turned black.

"C'mon, touch it. TOUCH IT!. It ain't gonna bite cha. Aaahhh, yeah... feels good, right? Ya dream of touchin' it, right? RIGHT? Say somethin', GAWD DAMN YA!"

Rainy days and Mondays...Rainy days and Mondays...Rainy days and Mondays.

A hand grabbed my nonexistent breasts.

"Iz thththis whatcha want? Yeah, I betcha want someone ta fuck ya, doncha? Oh yeah... yeah... c'mon, touch me... what da fuck ya doin'?... touch me, c'mon... shit, like thththis... see, look... LOOK! Open ya fuckin' eyes. Watch me, GAWD DAMN YA!"

He smacked me again. Harder.

I opened my eyes. He peered over me and looked really mean. I focused on his mouth. His yellow, crooked teeth. I watched his lips move but all I heard was the sound of the raindrops hitting the roof of the car. I was so scared. I panicked.

Nausea.

"Yeah, ya like thththat? Iz thththat makin' ya hot? Iz ya lil' pussy gettin' all wet? You want me ta put my big throbbin' cock in ya tight lil' pussy? Iz thththat whatcha want, huh? Yeah... yeah... c'mon, kiss it... C'MON... bring ya fuckin' mawf here... NOW!"

He grabbed my head and pushed my face into his lap.

"Open ya mawf." He rubbed his thing across my face. "OPEN YA FUCKIN' MAWF."

PLEASE, God. Where are you?

He pushed his thing into my mouth. I gagged. And again. The third time I vomited in my mouth.

"Ya fuckin' useless. Move outta thththe way." He pushed me away and began to stroke himself, making weird noises.

"Open ya eyes." I didn't. He slapped my face. Harder still. "I SAID, OPEN YA FUCKIN' EYES." He watched me until this stuff shot out of his thing.

"Ya like, huh? Ya wanna taste?" He placed his messy hand behind my head and pushed my face toward his thing.

"NOOOOOO!!!" I screamed.

He slammed my head into the dashboard.

I was woozy and numb. My body trembled.

He took my finger, the one next to my thumb. "I wanna watch ya. C'mon, stick ya finger in ya pussy til ya cum. Let me watch ya do thththat, c'mon, DO IT!"

My face was soaking wet with tears – or was it blood?

With my eyes tightly closed, I felt his hand inside my panties. There was no place for me to move. I was confused; I did not understand what was happening. I couldn't stop crying.

My crying, his shouting and the pounding rain echoed in my brain. He locked his fingers tightly around my throat.

HELP!

I had no voice.

Somebody help me. I can't breathe.

My body was betraying me – it didn't move. My stomach cramped up.

Owwwwwwwwww.

For a second, my eyes opened wide. I saw his sweaty face, matted hair and crooked smile. I gasped for breath. I think I kicked.

Stay awake.

I couldn't.

So much pain.

And then, nothing. That was the last thing I remembered.

I heard heavy breathing and persistent tapping.

Where am I? What's happening?

Lightning struck; I saw The Man. I started to cry again. Thunder fractured my soul.

"Stop ya cryin'. I'll take ya back ta school." His voice seemed to have softened.

I felt something warm and sticky running down my leg. I saw *Wednesday* was bloody. He started the engine. I pulled up my panties and put on my pants. He drove out of the lot and made a right turn onto Co-Op City Boulevard. I put on my sneakers.

He gave me a tissue. "Wipe ya face an blow ya nose." He turned left onto Baychester Avenue. "Stop ya cryin'. Nothththin happened." He turned up the radio volume. I did not realize it was even on. He turned left onto Donizetti Place. "Nothththin happened. Ya hear me?" He stopped the car and reached into the back seat to get my book bag. He dropped it onto my lap. "Ya tell nobody. 'Member, I know where ya live an I know ya famlee. Ya tell and I'll kill ya all. Now, get outta here."

I got out into the rain. The raindrops ran down my face. I was standing in the street, careful not to look up at my bedroom window. The door slammed, the engine roared and the tires screeched. The white limousine got smaller and smaller.

Looking down at my sneakers, now spattered with mud, I walked up the steps of the school, through the front doors, and straight for the girls' bathroom. It was dark but I did not turn on the light. I entered the stall farthest from the door. On the floor, I curled up into a ball. I closed my eyes tight and wished myself back in bed.

My mind drifted. I was in the elevator of my Co-Op City building alone. Just before the door closed a man slipped in. He was dressed all in black with a cloak and a big hat pulled down so I couldn't see his face. He stood in the doorway blocking me from escaping. He opened his hand and sprayed gasoline all over me. Then he threw a match at me; it ignited in midair. I watched myself burn in slow motion, from my feet all the way up to my hair. I saw myself disappear into a pile of ashes on the elevator floor.

Eventually I heard what I believed was my alarm clock. It seemed inordinately loud. Then I realized it was the dismissal bell. I had been in the stall for about three-and-a-half hours.

It was just a bad dream. A horrible dream!

two

What if I had told? What if, instead of hiding in the bathroom stall, I had run into the principal's office? The school surely would have called my mom at work. They would have told her that I didn't go straight to school. They would have called the police. The police would have asked me lots of questions.

What did he look like?

How old was he?

Why didn't you go straight to school?

What color were his eyes?

What did he smell like?

Why didn't you go straight to school?

What was he wearing?

What did his voice sound like?

Why did you lie to your mom?

Why didn't you go straight to school?

Why didn't you go straight to school?

Because I'm stupid.

Why did you talk to a stranger?

Because I'm stupid.

Why did you get into his car?

Because I'm STUPID, STUPID, STUPID!

I'm sorry I lied, Mom. I didn't go straight to school.

I'm sorry I'm bad.

I'm sorry I'm stupid.

I could never tell.

S-E-C-R-E-T.

Se-cret.

Adjective: not known or seen or not meant to be known or seen by others.

Nobody knew I had a secret angst.

Noun: something that is kept or meant to be kept unknown or unseen by others.

I kept this secret for years.

three

It was a sweltering day in July. For my tenth birthday my parents took my two brothers, eleven-year-old Andrew and twelve-year-old Joseph, and me to The Moscow Circus at Madison Square Garden. I had just gotten a new diary with a tiny key for a birthday present and I was excited to have something worth writing down.

And something did happen. The one thing I remember so clearly is how the elephants were bound only by what seemed to be an ordinary rope tied around their front legs. The rope seemed so fragile compared with the massive size and strength of the elephants. I noticed the elephants didn't test the rope; they didn't even try to escape.

At the end of the show my brothers and I ran down to the circus circle.

"Why don't the elephants try to break free?" I asked the trainer.

"When they're babies," he said, "they're bound by these thick heavy chains." As he spoke, he looked down at his feet and lifted up one of the chains. "The young elephants pull on these chains trying to escape, and they fail." He demonstrated the pull with his hand. "They try and they fail again." His hand flung out again and pulled forward. "They continue for days and days. And so, at some point the elephants give up. From that point on, the elephants stop trying, and so heavy chains are no longer needed. An ordinary rope tied around their front leg is enough to keep them from breaking free."

I wrote about the elephants in my diary. It wasn't until I reread the entry years later that I realized how similar we are to the elephants. There are those of us who are bound by limitations, real or imagined, by feelings of inadequacy, by fear, or by some horrible traumatic experience. Struggle as we might, these limitations continue to impede our progress. And after a while, perhaps we just stop trying.

Sometimes though by great luck or good karma we meet someone who helps us to break free and change the path of our journey.

four

My fifth-grade English teacher, Mr. Palumbo, gave us an assignment to write about a dream we had. "First, indicate if your dream was in black and white or color. Then include which senses were involved. Did you hear anything? Did you smell anything? Maybe you felt something? Put in as many details as you can remember."

I couldn't forget the nightmare I had about burning in the elevator. I decided to write about it, hoping Mr. Palumbo could explain it to me. I called it *Ashes*.

The following week my teacher handed back the papers. On the top of my paper he had written, "Please see me after class."

Did I do something wrong?

With my pencil I drew circles around and around and around, *see me*. I slowly approached his desk. I showed him my paper. "You wanted to see me?"

"Yes. Was that a real dream or did you just make it up?"

Should I tell Mr. Palumbo what happened?

"No. It was really real." My jaw clenched involuntarily.

"It's not possible to watch ourselves die in a dream. You must have imagined it."

He was not listening. I became silent. Seconds later, with my pencil now broken in half, I tossed the pieces in the garbage and bolted from the classroom. I was still fragile. No, like the pencil, I was broken.

On Halloween morning, I pretended to be sick because I didn't want to dress up in a costume for school and be around other kids in masks. It was too scary.

Mom put the back of her hand on my forehead and told me, "You don't have a fever. Okay, go back to bed. I'll call you later from work."

I closed my bedroom door, locked the window, crawled into bed, hid under the covers and then curled up with the book *Are You There God, It's Me Margaret*.

When I was hungry, I got out of bed, went into the kitchen and ate a big bowl of ice cream. It made me feel optimistic and carefree for a few minutes. Ice cream became my favorite food.

I had a Thumbelina doll with exquisite aqua eyes, auburn hair, white socks and shoes. Her plastic flesh-colored arms and legs extended from her soft belly and chest. Her body used to wiggle when I pulled the string in the center of her back, but it no longer worked. Andrew pulled the string too hard and broke it.

"I'm broken, too." I told her. "But nobody notices."

When Mom came home from work, I told her that I felt better.

One Saturday night when I was eleven, my parents went out and left my brothers and me home alone. I woke up around midnight, thinking it was morning, made my bed and changed into my favorite sundress. Wide awake, I went into Joseph and Andrew's room. I wondered why *Saturday Night Live* was on television;

Joseph and Andrew usually watched *Davey and Goliath* on Sunday morning.

"It's not morning yet, Tal," Joseph whispered from his bottom bunk bed.

"I'm so confused," I said, laughing at first, and then crying.

"What's the matter with you?" Andrew asked from the top bunk.

Joseph took me back to my room and pulled down my bedspread. "Go back to sleep, Tal. We'll watch *Davey and Goliath* in the morning."

I cried after he left. At first I wondered how it could not be morning. Then I just wondered: Could I have done something different? I should have listened to Mom.

I should have gone straight to school.

My heart was pounding. I curled up into a fetal position under my blanket, but my body still shivered.

Later that night, Andrew came into my room and handed me one of his little green plastic toy soldiers.

"What's this for?"

"For protection," he said as he turned to walk out the door.

"What's his name?"

Andrew shrugged his shoulders up high then dropped them, "Nobody, I guess."

What kind of name is Nobody?

And soon enough it became clear to me. In the days, weeks and months that followed, I shared my secret with Nobody. Nobody knew. I trusted Nobody because Nobody understood.

More than once, Mom poked her head into my room, "Who are you talking to?"

"Nobody."

My once messy room was now immaculate. Every day I vacuumed my carpet and dusted my furniture and everything on it, including Snow White and the seven dwarfs. I cleaned each of the two bathrooms in our apartment.

One day my mom said, "What are you doing?"

"I'm cleaning the bathrooms."

"I clean the bathrooms every morning." She saw the look of disappointment on my face. "You know what, thank you."

When squirting Windex on the shower doors didn't remove all of the grime, I switched to Brillo. I scrubbed and scrubbed and scrubbed. I was satisfied when the beautiful swan and her three cygnets were bright and shiny.

I showered with a Buff-Puff sponge until my skin became raw. No matter how hard I scrubbed, I still felt dirty. My body trembled when the Jean Naté body splash seeped into my open pores and burned like hell, which was appropriate since in my mind I was already there.

I started to do the family's laundry in the basement. I watched the white bubbles rising above the waves while the clothes wrestled beneath the surface. I folded the clothes as soon as they came out of the dryer so they wouldn't get wrinkled. I put everything away before Mom got home. She said thanks and didn't ask any questions.

I could no longer eat meat. My dad, who brought meat home every other day, asked, "Why aren't you eating the meat?"

"I don't like it," I said, as I chipped away at the polish on my fingernails under the table. I couldn't stand the sight of the dripping blood. I imagined the innocent animals living in trapped quarters before being slaughtered.

five

I was always planning my future: *I'll be seventeen when I graduate high school, twenty-five when I marry Alex Kohane, a boy in my class, and twenty-eight when we have our first baby.*

I spent a lot of time saying "I'm sorry" during my freshman year of high school. I'm sorry to the kid who bumped into me by the lockers. I'm sorry to the girl who copied from my test but still failed. I'm sorry I didn't go straight to school.

I started counting how many squares of shredded wheat fell into my cereal bowl. The number was ten. I skipped rope for ten minutes. On the days when I was angry, I skipped rope for sixty minutes, ten times six. I don't know why six – I think it was only because I couldn't skip rope for more than an hour. At that point I was so tired that I couldn't remember what I was enraged about.

When I wanted to control something or someone I played with my dolls. Ken adored Barbie. Unlike me, she was patient and forgiving. But then Ken became angry. Barbie cried. She was submissive and weak. She became uncommunicative. She was not surprised when Ken left. She expected it.

On May 25, 1979, I was clearing off the dinner table when the news came on the television. Six-year-old Etan Patz had left his apartment in lower Manhattan by himself to walk two blocks to catch the school bus. He never made it. Everyone feared he was snatched away. People were still looking for him.

For months I searched every page of the newspaper and watched the news hoping someone would find Etan. Nothing. My nightmares came back. I started to bite my fingernails. When I was alone I cried.

Finally, I stopped watching the news and I stopped searching in the paper. I went right to the comics – *Dagwood* and *Hager the Horrible*. I pretended the world was safe, all people were good, and there was no white limousine.

On Saturday, February 9, 1980. I took the bus, as I did every week, from Co-Op City to Main Street in Flushing. Grandma Devorah lived in the nursing home there because Grandpa could no longer be trusted to take care of her. Her diabetes was out of control. At the nursing home she had twenty-four-hour care.

When I got off the bus I stopped at the candy store to get Grandma some sugarless sucking candy. As I pulled out a quarter from the pocket of my imitation fur jacket, I noticed him sitting on the shelf. His red hair stuck out from under his white hat. He wore a red and white plaid shirt, red bow tie, royal blue knickers, and red and white striped socks.

The salesman asked, "Would you like to hold him?"

"Yes, please," I said eagerly.

He put the three-foot doll into my arms. I touched Raggedy Andy's black button eyes and triangular nose. His red lips were perfectly stitched.

"How much does he cost?" I asked.

"Twenty-three dollars."

I put the doll down. I opened my wallet and pulled out every bill I had. My baby-sitting money didn't add up to that.

"Do you want him?" the salesman asked.

I thought of Grandma. Even if she were willing to sacrifice her sucking candy for Andy, it was still not nearly enough.

I said, "I have fifteen dollars and twenty-five cents."

"Not enough."

"Just the candy, please. It's for my Grandma." I paid for the candy and put it deep into my pocket.

Seconds later, before I was out the door, the salesman called out, "Excuse me!"

The loud voice startled me and I froze in my tracks. I turned around.

"Come here."

I cautiously walked back to the counter.

"Take him for fifteen dollars. It's okay."

"Really?" I said, unable to mask my enthusiasm.

I gave him my fifteen dollars and the candy.

"Keep the candy, sweetheart; it's for your grandma."

I was ashamed when I had to tell him that I needed seventy-five cents for the bus to get back home. He smiled sympathetically and handed me a dollar back and put Andy in a box large enough that I needed two hands to carry it out. I stopped several times to rest during my three-block walk to Grandma's. My watch told me it was one thirty when I finally arrived. I was thirty minutes late.

She sat in the recreation room waiting for me, looking beautiful with her long white hair and flawless complexion.

"Hi, Grandma. This is for you." I kissed her cheek and handed her the candy.

"This is my favorite. Thank you, *Ziskeit* (Sweetie)."

I waited for her to ask what was in the box. She didn't.

"Are you okay, Grandma?" I noticed that she wasn't wearing her glasses.

She nodded her head. It was neither a yes nor a no.

"Grandma?"

"Yes, *Ziskeit*?"

"Are you okay?"

"There is nothing harder than doing nothing."

I was too young to appreciate such a serious thought.

"I brought you a surprise, Grandma." I struggled to get Andy out of the box. "You don't have to be alone anymore."

"Who is this?"

"This is Raggedy Andy. He can keep you company."

"No, *Ziskeit*, he needs to stay with you. I no longer need company."

I didn't know what to say.

"You look tired, Tali. Are you sleeping?" Grandma was very intuitive.

"I'm fine, Grandma." She knew I was lying and I felt awful about it.

"You can tell me. It may help us both to sleep."

"I'm fine."

"Remember you have a first name, Tali, which means dew, like the dew of heaven, and refers to blessings, prosperity and redemption, and a last name, Stark, which means strength." She told me this often.

"Thank you, Grandma."

"Let me teach you a bedtime prayer. It's called *Let Us Lie Down In Peace*."

"Okay." I closed my eyes.

She spoke very slowly, "May it be Your will, Eternal God and God of my mothers and fathers, that I lie down in peace and rise again in peace. Let no disturbing thoughts come to upset me, nor evil dreams, nor evil thoughts. May I know a peaceful rest. And in the morning may You awaken me to the light of a new day."

I said, "Amen."

Before leaving, I brushed her hair. I kissed her. "See you soon, Grandma."

"God willing."

"I love you."

She kissed my hand several times, "I love you more."

Seconds later, with Andy in my arms, I looked back at Grandma. Her eyes closed.

That night she was rushed to the hospital and by morning, she was gone. "Complications of diabetes," my mother told me.

Could I have done more?

I opened my diary and wrote: In memory of Grandma Devorah, born April 13, 1905, died February 10, 1980. I LOVE YOU MORE!

One night my brothers and I pulled out the *Ouija* Board. We sat in a circle on my bedroom floor with our legs crossed, Indian style. The bright border of the closed door lit the darkened room. The *Ouija* Board touched each of our kneecaps. We all rested our fingers lightly on the heart-shaped communication device, called the *planchette*, French for "little plank," which sat in the center of the board.

Andrew threw out a question in an eerie voice, "Is there a ghost trying to connect with us?"

Seconds slipped by. The *planchette* moved to the bottom left hand corner and stopped at YES.

Andrew asked, "Is it a family member?"

The *planchette* didn't move.

"Let me ask a question," I begged.

"Hold on," Andrew convinced me. "Is the ghost a man?" The *planchette* moved to the right side of the board, NO.

"What's the spirit's name?" I quickly proposed to Andrew.

"Okay," Andrew repeated, "What's the ghost's name?"

It took about a minute before the letter 'D' was reached. Waiting seemed like an eternity. Nothing.

I got upset.

Joseph finally said, "Okay, that's enough."

I was desperate to connect with Grandma Devorah.

That night I prayed, "Grandma, I'm sorry. Please forgive me. I didn't tell you my secret because I didn't want to upset you. A stranger, a bad man, touched me where he shouldn't have. Please Grandma, give me a sign to let me know that I'll be okay."

That night I slept well.

During my sophomore year in high school I channeled my hyperactivity into the track team. I didn't tell my mother; I knew she would forbid it. She didn't think girls should play sports. But the more I ran, the less anxiety I felt. My coach taught me the importance of hard work, discipline and visualization.

It was the end of track season and the championship races were at my high school, a short walk from where I lived. On race day I gathered my gear and told Andrew I was heading over to the field. He gave me a wave, but his eyes remained glued to the television screen.

I was running the mile. At the end of the second of four laps, I was in sixth place out of six runners. My tongue moistened my lips. I lengthened my stride and cupped my hands to cut the wind; I was now fifth. Coming around the bend, starting the third lap, I visualized my body doing exactly what I wanted it to do: Run faster! I finished the quarter turn in fourth place.

"You can do this," said a voice in my head. This voice was not familiar. I started the final lap with two girls in front of me. I stayed as close to them as I could. Near the end I heard Andrew's voice rising from the crowd noise.

When did he get here? I thought he was home watching TV.

"GO, TALI!" I couldn't see him until I caught him jumping up and down. "RUN, TALI, RUN."

Andrew's here. For me!

I ran for my life.

I passed Monique Washington, the second runner, and kept running. I ran faster as the crowd stood and the cheers grew louder. I was running neck and neck with Vanessa Something-or-other, the number one runner on the other team. My brother's voice filled my head and my heart as the blood surged throughout my body.

RUN, TALI.

I ran until I passed Vanessa. I ran until I passed the finish line, ripping the yellow tape. I kept on running for another twenty yards. I ran until I cried. I cried until I shook. I shook until I fell. The crowd sounded like a young girl screaming.

What's happening? Are the cheers for me? Did I come in first?

My heart was beating out of my chest and I thought I was going to throw up. I didn't stop crying until Andrew hugged me.

An awards ceremony followed. I received a trophy. It was a generic one with a marble base and a gold figurine of a female runner with an expressionless face. The plate said, "Bronx Championship: One Mile. 1st Place."

Andrew carried my trophy home. I hid it inside Barbie's camper in my closet so Mom wouldn't see it.

After school I made extra money by cleaning Grandpa's new apartment. After Grandma Devorah passed away, my mother moved him to Co-Op City, a ten-minute walk from us. He settled into the tan building across the street from what had been a vacant lot where a white limousine pulled in six years ago. Now there was a four-story building on that site. Grandpa sat in his chair watching television and never said more than "hello" while I cleaned. I avoided looking in his direction because I could see that building from his window.

In my junior year I tried out for the school play, *Guys and Dolls,* based on the Broadway musical. I landed the role of the grandmother, missionary Arvida Abernathy. Two months later,

Mom and Dad sat in the audience while I sang *More I Cannot Wish You* to my granddaughter. I thought of Grandma Devorah. I was so nervous that I forgot part of the second verse. I ad-libbed. Not a single person, not even the director, seemed to have noticed. Though my presence on that stage may not have been significant, I was relieved to be someone else for a little while.

In November of my senior year I began driver's education. Alex Kohane took the class with me. Although I had known him for years, it was this class that brought us closer together. We both passed our road test two months later.

I enjoyed hanging out with Alex whenever I could. I would go to his house where he played Jimmy Buffett songs on the piano. More often he would come to my house, where we played Scrabble and ate the homemade cookies I had baked the night before. One night, in early May, he placed four letters on the Scrabble board. He added the letter 'P' on a triple letter score next to the word ROW and placed his remaining three letters 'R-O-M' under the 'P' to spell PROM.

"Prow?" I asked.

"Sure. It's an SAT word. As a noun, it's the forward part of a ship and as an adjective it means brave."

"Three, six, nine points for the 'P' for each word. Good for you," I said. I added up the rest of his points. "That's twenty-six points."

I knew Alex was looking at me. I knew he liked me. He didn't understand why I wouldn't let him kiss me. I didn't understand either.

"Oh my God," I said. "Look at this!" I placed my 'Q' on the triple word score, used the 'O' that he just placed down and added my 'P' and my 'H' in the double letter score. "That's eight, nine, ten, eleven, twelve plus ten is twenty-two times three is sixty-six points."

"Your math is good, but I'm not sure about your spelling. What's *QOPH*?"

"It's a Hebrew letter," I said.

"What?" Alex laughed. "You're making up words."

"No, seriously."

He reached for the *Official Scrabble Dictionary*. "No offense, Tali, but I'm the one who went to Hebrew school. I would know."

"No offense taken."

"Holy shit, look at that. It *is* a Hebrew letter. How do you know that, Tal?"

"I've looked up words with the letter 'Q' that don't need a 'U'."

He laughed. "Thanks. I won't forget that word."

We caught each other's eyes. I blinked first. Fidgeting with my nails, I looked away. I then started with the pen, clicking it open and closed, over and over again.

"Hey, Tal, listen, can we go back to my word for a minute?"

"Your word?" I laughed. "Which one?"

"Prom" he said smiling. "Will you go with me?"

"Ummm…." I cringed at the thought of our bodies touching as we danced. I lied. "My family will be away that weekend."

Alex left around nine with the rest of the cookies. As I got ready for bed, Mom came into my room. "I heard you turn Alex down." She paused. "Are you gay?"

What?

I didn't know what to say. I wanted to feel something other than uncomfortable in my own skin. I picked at my nails.

"No," I whispered.

After she left my room I tore at my cuticles, first with my fingernails and then with my teeth. I tasted blood. I sat on the edge of my bed, hunched over, sweating. Images flooded my mind. Bits and pieces of an unsolved puzzle incoherently occupied my brain. Was this memory or imagination? I was afraid that I was losing my mind.

Later that week Alex and I were watching television in his parents' living room. He reached over and put his arm around me. I liked the sensation of his fingers on my skin, but I was terrified. I broke free from his embrace.

He said, "What are you afraid of Tal? It's just me, Alex."

I did not say a word, not even goodbye. I ran down the four flights of steps. I saw my reflection in the glass doors as I left the lobby. I did not like what I saw – a girl resigned to move forward.

In June Alex was the valedictorian of our graduating class. I did not attend the graduation ceremony because, aside from Alex, I did not feel connected to my classmates (for reasons I did not fully appreciate until years later). I wanted to run away from my life and fast forward to college so that I could leave my past behind and create a new me with better memories. Little did I know that my past, like a shadow, would follow me.

Alex and I saw less of each other that summer and headed upstate to different colleges. I was heartbroken. From here on, I learned to keep myself so busy that there wasn't enough time to deal with the pain.

six

After a quiet four-hour drive my parents dropped me off at my dormitory. I watched them drive away from my eighth-floor dorm room window. The room was small. I felt confined and claustrophobic. In the cold, Spartan room lit by fluorescent light bulbs, I paced like a prisoner; crying as I unpacked. In the background, Simon and Garfunkel were singing. In a voice, just above a whisper, I sang too:

"Hello darkness, my old friend.
I've come to talk with you again."

My roommate Sheryl arrived two hours later. She was a sweet girl from New Jersey majoring in special education. We didn't share any classes, but we did have dinner together every night. I liked her.

I joined the cross-country track team but quit after one semester because I couldn't do the hard-core training and also keep up with my studies. I jogged on my own and started an aerobics class in my dorm. I told myself I was not an extrovert but if it helped others I took the initiative.

Addictive chemicals were everywhere on campus: alcohol, marijuana, cocaine, amphetamines, painkillers, tobacco, caffeine and sex. I avoided them all. My addiction was "avoidance" – of partying, experimentation and men. I focused all of my attention on my schoolwork.

Sophomore year I moved to a different dorm and became the youngest resident advisor (RA) on campus. Sheryl moved with me but she hated the neediness of the freshmen girls: vomiting from being drunk, overwhelmed by the course load and humiliated from one-night stands. She soon moved back to our old dorm.

Living alone, boxed into my room, I cared for my eighteen freshman girls. My studies were unaffected by their problems, and dealing with their problems distracted me from my own. I learned to study in my room while keeping my door open for them.

One Friday night Linda came into my room, crying.

"What's the matter?"

"I was groped in a bar. I was so mad and nobody cared. They said it was no big deal."

I hugged her. "It *is* a big deal. You were violated. Do you want to report it?"

"There's nothing to report. I didn't even see him. I'm just so mad."

"Maybe reporting it will help."

"What's the point? I didn't see him."

"Okay. Tell me what you need."

"I just needed to tell you."

I understood. "Okay. If you need anything else, I'm here for you."

I took weekend seminars to learn how to handle situations like date rape and discrimination. I learned to screen for depression and suicidal tendencies. Although concerned with the results of my own screening – increased restlessness, self-blaming and weight loss placed me into the "mildly depressed category" – I never discussed it with my supervisor.

One night when I was on duty, David, a senior RA came to visit me in the office. We threw personal and philosophical questions around as if we were playing catch.

"When do you feel that your life is most meaningful?" he asked.

"When I'm helping others. My turn: What's the most important decision you have to make this year?"

"Whether I go on to grad school or medical school. If you could change one day from your past, which day…"

Just as my body tightened, the fire alarm rang. The freshmen boys were at it again. David and I cleared out the building. We started off on the top floor and made our way down to the dungeon, the windowless basement. It was an hour before campus security allowed the students back into the dorm. I went back to the office to lock up for the evening and David went back to his room. I never answered his last question.

I should have gone straight to school.

Later that week David and I shared pizza in my room. That's the night I learned that he had a girlfriend back home. The glow of my schoolgirl crush dissipated in midair. I focused again on my girls and on my studies.

Monday night, October 10, 1983, my girls and I were among the thirty-eight million people watching Adam Walsh's story in the television film called *Adam*. Six-year-old Adam Walsh disappeared from a Sears shopping mall in Hollywood, Florida in July, 1981. His smiling, freckled face under his baseball cap was shown on TV. Two weeks later his severed head was found by two fishermen one hundred and twenty miles away from the mall where he had been abducted. His body was never recovered.

The police lifted bloodstained carpet from a white Cadillac belonging to a man by the name of Ottis Toole. They could not tell if the blood was Adam's because DNA testing was not sufficiently advanced. When the investigators announced that they had lost Toole's impounded car and machete, I stormed out of the room.

How the hell do you lose a car?

Years later, February 7, 1988, Adam's father, John Walsh, began hosting the television program *America's Most Wanted.* He became one of the leading advocates for victims of violent crimes.

I became completely absorbed in my studies. When I was reading I was able to block out everything else in my life. Studying in complete isolation at the library, I daydreamed about writing a book. It would be about a young girl who was abducted. I would make sure it had a happy ending – although the middle was a complete blur.

My professors knew that I worked hard. My peers thought I was really smart. Neither group saw the real me: lost in the fears of my past, struggling not to drown in murky water and trying to stay afloat by convincing myself that I truly was who others thought I was.

I signed up for an after-school theater group where I was always greeted by name. On stage I was no longer invisible and I couldn't be silent. I was always on time for rehearsals. In fact, I was always early. I was soon asked if I was interested in trying out for the school play, *The Wizard of Oz.* I landed the role of the Cowardly Lion.

Off stage I was terrified to feel deeply, afraid to experience any emotion and scared to lose control. On stage I owned my emotions, gave voice to them and became empowered by them. Off stage I was afraid of conflict. On stage I embraced it. Off stage I tried to forget The Man. On stage I had to remember my lines. I found bits of truths while journeying down the Yellow Brick Road to Emerald City.

The Cowardly Lion ultimately received what he desired the most, courage, only to realize that he had it all along.

The Wizard told me, "You're a victim of disorganized thinking. You are under the unfortunate delusion that simply because you run away from danger you have no courage. You're confusing courage with wisdom." He hands me a medal.

But I didn't run away from danger.

My childhood trauma exploded out of my voice on stage. "Read what my medal says: COURAGE. Ain't it the truth? Ain't it the truth?"

The audience stood up. The applause sounded like a symphony. By the final performance, I was sleeping better and I felt calmer and more focused. I was much happier.

The following year, my old roommate Sheryl invited me to move off campus with her. I thought I was ready for the responsibility and I wanted a different experience. I resigned as an RA, but I gave three of my freshman girls my new phone number so they could reach me if they needed anything.

In my advanced nutrition class I studied the role of vitamins and minerals in health and various disease states. I was impressed by the work of one nutrition scientist, Dr. Daniel Benson, a pioneer in vitamin B_{12} and HIV (human immuno-deficiency virus) and AIDS (acquired immunodeficiency syndrome) research. In the field of modern medicine, he was a hero – a superstar.

I wanted to learn more. I wanted to make a difference in the world. I had already looked into the graduate program in nutrition at New York University (NYU), but it was so expensive. I had to find a job when I got home.

That August my grandfather passed away. He was buried next to Grandma Devorah. I knelt down onto the ground, my bare knees touching the earth, and whispered to Grandma.

"Thank you for watching over me." My fingers touched her footstone, caressing the word, Grandmother. "I felt you on stage with me. I felt your love and I heard your voice. I am strong." My voice cracked and I could no longer speak.

You're not alone anymore, Grandma. Grandpa is here to keep you company. I miss you so much. I love you.

In my last semester, I volunteered as a phone operator at the student crisis hotline. I dealt with rape victims, girls who had eating disorders and girls who were pregnant and didn't know what to do.

One call caused me to have a major setback:

"Student crisis hotline. This is Tali. How may I help you?"

"I was just raped," said a hysterical voice.

Oh my God.

"I'm so sorry. What's your name?"

"Caryn."

"Caryn, I'm going to send someone to bring you to the hospital. Where are you?"

"I'm scared." She was still crying.

"I know, Caryn. Tell me where you are so that I can send someone to help you."

No answer.

"We're here for you, Caryn. Please tell me where you are."

No answer.

"Caryn?" My heart raced. Beads of sweat started to accumulate on my forehead.

Dial tone.

"CARYN!" I yelled. As the knot in my stomach twisted, I gagged. I could taste the vomit in my mouth.

I froze.

What do I do?

I couldn't call her back – neither *69 nor caller-ID existed at that time. I called my supervisor and together we called Campus security.

It was impossible to fall asleep that night. I couldn't stop thinking about Caryn. I also thought about The Man in the white limousine. How many more lives had he destroyed? I wondered how my life would be different if I had had the resources and the courage to ask for help. I told myself for the umpteenth time that I should have gone straight to school.

At the end of my last semester I was emotionally exhausted.

seven

When I got home for Thanksgiving break, Mom told me that Alex had called. I still knew his number by heart even though we hadn't spoken in four years. We got together at my parent's apartment. He had graduated in June as a pre-med student and was now enrolled in NYU medical school. I hoped to go to NYU too, but I needed a job to pay for it.

He said, "I just finished interning at the Bronx Veterans Hospital doing research on vitamin B_{12} and folic acid."

"Really? I just studied Dr. Daniel Benson's work on vitamin B_{12} and folic acid. What did you do there?"

"I was *in* Dr. Benson's lab working with one of his colleagues."

"What?" I couldn't believe it.

"I'll give you the number to the lab. Maybe they need another assistant."

"Oh my God, that would be amazing."

"Hello?" A man answered the phone.

"Dr. Benson, please."

"Speaking."

I was caught off guard; I wasn't expecting him to answer the phone himself. "Hi, my name is Tali Stark. Alex Kohane gave me your number. I'm an undergraduate student majoring in dietetics and graduating next month. I was wondering if I can come in to meet with you. I have so many questions about nutrition."

"Sure. Do you want to come in today?"

"I'd love to, but I can't. I'm going back to school today." In that moment I realized my mistake on calling him so impulsively.

"Okay, call me when you get back. Good luck with your exams."

Although I was busy with class assignments and finals, I still made the time to study Dr. Benson's work. I read about his 1961 self-experiment that was written up in the Sunday Magazine section of the *New York Times*. Dr. Benson had given himself megaloblastic (large red blood cell) anemia to demonstrate that a deficiency in folic acid can be caused by a poor diet. This was an important discovery because it led to the fortification of folic acid in many foods and reduced the incidence of neural tube defects in newborns.

I graduated that December with honors. Although I had made more connections than in high school, I had no intention of heading back in June for graduation. I just wanted to get on with my life.

Right after the New Year, I called to schedule an appointment with Dr. Benson. That week I walked past the Bronx Veterans Hospital toward the gray-brick research building next door. The hematology laboratory took up almost half of the third floor. I entered his office as a twenty-two-year-old college graduate looking for a job in nutrition research. His secretary told me to have a seat.

Dr. Benson came out of his office. He was about five ten with a medium build and appeared to be in his fifties. He wore a dark blue suit and a white shirt with the top two buttons undone. His eyes were a piercing emerald green. His salt and pepper hair was thinning and his trim beard and mustache showed a touch of gray.

He greeted me with a warm smile and a firm handshake, "Daniel Benson. Nice to meet you, Tali."

I stood up, "Nice to meet you too, Dr. Benson."

He took me on a tour of his laboratory. Two of the rooms contained cabinets, drawers, work benches, sinks and desks. The last room was a storage room for two big centrifuge machines and four freezers storing test tubes of patients' blood. It doubled as a staff lounge and held a long rectangular table where he invited me to sit down.

"How did you find out there was a job opening here?"

"I didn't know there was one. Alex Kohane told me he was working here and that I could call you. I loved reading about your work."

"Oh, Alex, yes, he's a very bright young man. He has a great future."

I smiled.

Dr. Benson suggested a game of chess. He wanted to play right then and there.

How interesting.

He talked while we played: top grossing films of the past year (*Top Gun*, *Crocodile Dundee* and *Platoon*), quackery (fraudulent mail order nutrition diplomas, laetrile and hair analysis), AIDS (over 16,000 known deaths worldwide).

The room was not quiet; Aside from listening to Dr. Benson, I found myself competing with the clamor of the centrifuges. He won in nine moves, but he was a gracious winner.

"Have you ever worked in a lab before?"

"No."

"We run radioassays on both vitamin B_{12} and folic acid. We just started a new research study with Mount Sinai Hospital. It's big. Are you interested in research?"

"Yes. Yes, I am."

"How'd you do last semester?"

"Four As and a B."

"What was the B?"

"Music."

"Son of a bitch."

I laughed nervously.

"What do you know about HIV and AIDS?"

"Not much, but I think I'm a fast learner."

His secretary called him from the front office.

"Wait here, I'll be right back."

He returned with a copy of his 1985 book, *Vitamin Supplements: Trick or Treat?* I opened it up. He had written the following inscription: "1/7/87, To Tali, Welcome to the lab. It's good to have you on the team. Dr. Daniel Benson."

I couldn't believe it.

Two weeks later Dr. Benson told his team, "Liberace was hospitalized, reportedly for anemia, but it sounds to me like it's pneumonia related to AIDS." Hundreds of fans kept a vigil outside his Palm Springs, California, home until his death on February 4, 1987. An autopsy confirmed the sixty-seven-year-old entertainer had AIDS.

During my first year in the lab, Dr. Benson shared his ideas about nutrition, genetics and disease with me.

"Your genetic blueprint plays a role in your susceptibility to disease. Diseases like heart disease, hypertension, diabetes, cancer, obesity, even alcoholism."

I took notes. Unlike Dr. Benson, I didn't have a photographic memory.

"There's a link between health and genetics. If we can teach people, actually show them, how to plot their family medical history, then they can learn to eat better and avoid the diseases they're most susceptible to."

He always used "we." He was a team player.

"It's very important to remember that genetic predisposition, alone, does not determine fate. Our environment and our free will also play a major role in determining our destiny."

On another day, "Tali, I need you to visit a new patient on Ward 4C. His name is David Whitney. He has AIDS. We need a vitamin B_{12} level."

"No problem, I'm on my way."

"Be careful. Wear protective gear." This meant covering my clothes and wearing gloves and a mask.

We all knew that AIDS was a death sentence.

By this time, thousands of people diagnosed with Kaposi's sarcoma, *Pneumocystis carinii* pneumonia (PCP) and a host of other illnesses related to AIDS and HIV had been treated. There were also more and more reports of HIV infections in healthcare workers exposed through accidental transmission. Everyone's anxiety had increased; precautions had to be taken.

Mr. Whitney was a forty-year-old African-American. His chart said that he was six two and one hundred and forty pounds. He had lost sixty pounds since his diagnosis eight months ago.

"Hi, Mr. Whitney."

Frail, with skin lesions all over his body, he breathed oxygen through a tube in his nostrils. On his lunch tray lay his uneaten meal of pureed foods. He watched me put down Latex gloves, alcohol swabs, tourniquet, butterfly needle, three vacutainers (blood specimen tubes) and tape. I labeled the tubes. He didn't say a word.

"How are you feeling today?"

No answer.

Working in the hospital, I had learned that victims of trauma, like victims of stroke, could not put their thoughts and feelings into words because a part of their brain controlling speech was affected. Their pent-up disturbing images would most likely be expressed in the form of nightmares and flashbacks. Veterans could discuss

43

their stomach aches and chest pains but never their trauma. I understood. Nobody wants to revisit a war zone.

I followed his subtle shifts in body position.

"Would you like me to feed you some chocolate pudding?"

I waited for a change in his facial expression. There wasn't any.

"I'm sorry I have to draw blood. Do you prefer right arm or left arm?"

His eyes gazed at me as he raised his left arm and formed a fist.

"Thank you."

I held his arm, palm up, spotted a median cubital vein that hadn't collapsed yet, and sterilized the inner part of his forearm with an alcohol swab.

"I'll make this as fast as I can."

I tied the tourniquet around his upper arm – tight enough to make the vein bulge. I patted the vein gently, swabbed the area clean again, and, at an angle, inserted the needle with a smooth but fast motion. Keeping the needle steady, I pushed the vacutainer into the holder. It filled automatically with blood. I replaced the first specimen tube with the second and then the third. I placed the three tubes into a secure holder. I pulled the needle out of his arm and disposed it into a hazardous safety container. I elevated his arm and applied pressure to the gauze bandage I placed on his wound. Finally, I taped the bandage.

"I hope I didn't hurt you, Mr. Whitney."

"That was my dad's name. Call me Davey, my kid name."

"Okay, Davey. You can call me Tal, my kid name."

"Are you scared to die, Tal?"

"I don't know. Why do you ask?"

"I'm scared."

Scared. Scarred. We are all scared and scarred from something.

"Do you want to speak with a pastor?"

"No. He can't make the pain go away."

I moved a chair over to his bedside and sat down. I took off my mask and gloves and placed my hands on top of his. I couldn't help it, no matter what Dr. Benson said. I knew Davey needed more than professional care. He needed human contact.

"Oh, Davey, I'm sorry, I'm so sorry. Do you want the doctor? He can increase your pain meds." I tried to stand up.

"No." He held onto my hands.

He started to sob like a little boy.

"It's okay, Davey." I put my hands on his shoulders. "You're going to be okay," I said, holding him. "You are brave, Davey. You are so brave."

Minutes later, as I was leaving, he said, "You're da bomb."

No, just scared and scarred.

Dr. Benson was standing outside Davey's room. He looked at me, shaking his head. "First of all, what you did was very dangerous, but it was also very compassionate. We're not going to save him, but you gave him a moment of peace. Atta girl."

A week later when I went to pay Davey a visit, I walked into an empty room with the bed stripped. The nurse told me that Davey had just passed away. I prayed that he wasn't scared.

I took my work seriously; I was more interested in completing experiments than in going home. Late one summer night, when Dr. Benson was out of town and everyone had left, Alex showed up at the lab. I hadn't seen him since Christmas break. He was carrying a take-out bag and a boom box.

"How'd you know I was here?"

"Your mom told me you were working late. I thought you might be hungry."

How sweet.

I was in the middle of doing an assay. I set the timer for forty-five minutes before we sat down in the staff lounge. Alex pulled out Dr. Benson's big leather chair at the head of the table for me. The sounds of the refrigerators and centrifuges played in the background. He lit a Bunsen burner and placed it in the center of the table.

After we ate he plugged in the boom box and pushed the table and chairs back against the centrifuges. He hit the play button.

I began to fidget with a pen, clicking the point open and closed. I wanted to get back to work.

In his deep voice Barry White spoke the lyrics to the song, "I'll Always Love You."

At the same time, Alex whispered the same words: *"There's that look again. You know what I'm talking about. That insecure, that unsure that, that wondering look. It's all in your eyes baby."*

I wanted to die.

"You're sitting there and you're wondering; does he really love me as much as he says he does?"

Alex took my hand and pulled me up. He placed his other hand around my waist. He swayed me to the music as he improvised in this small space.

"Does he really need me and want me as much as he says he does? Baby, I can't sit around you twenty-four hours a day telling you baby I love you and I need you and I want you."

I tried to focus on how his fingers caressed mine; how his hand gently rubbed the small of my back; how his eyes looked into mine as he continued to whisper Barry White's lyrics. I smelled his cool peppermint Certs candy. For just a minute, I stood up taller.

"But I feel like right now at this moment I should try to make you feel reassured about me. Women are sensitive. Very sensitive. Just as hard as a woman can love a man, a man can love his woman. And, baby believe me, I do love you."

I looked at the refrigerator. I wondered how many vials of blood were stored in it.

He held me tighter.

I thought about the test tubes incubating at thirty-seven degrees Celsius for forty-five minutes.

Please, let the timer go off.

"Everything I have is you. And I don't like to see you look this way."

I was wearing no makeup. My hair was flat, oily and pulled back in a ponytail. I was wearing jeans and a tee shirt.

"I don't like to see you feel this way. I don't."

The sounds of the centrifuges continued to echo around the white walls. I took a deep breath. I knew it was just a song; why was I feeling so uncomfortable?

"I want you to be together and know and feel and be sure at all times."

Oh, please, shut up, both of you, just shut up.

I tried to move away. Alex tried to kiss me. I turned my head away. He tried again.

"What's the matter?"

"I just want to do my work."

"I'm sorry." He silenced Barry White, turned off the Bunsen burner, put the table and chairs back, and began to leaf through the medical journals. I went back to finish my assay. Two hours later he drove us home to Co-Op City. It was mostly quiet. Finally he said, "Is there something going on between you and Dr. Benson?"

I looked at him, then out the car window and shook my head.

When we arrived at my building he said, "I think you're making a big mistake."

I twisted my unbound hair before pushing it behind my ear.

"Goodbye, Tal. Good luck."

"Bye, Alex."

I was a full-time graduate student at NYU. Between work and school, I was learning exponentially fast. At the lab, I had begun an experiment to test the vitamin B_{12} levels in vegans. Dr. Benson had asked me to "stop eating everything that swims, walks or flies" for the duration of the experiment. He wanted to see how long it took for me to become vitamin B_{12}-deficient. He guessed it would be four to six months. I saved all my urine for twenty-four hours to test it for vitamin B_{12} levels.

One night after class I was walking the thirty blocks from NYU to Penn Station. I was holding my black bag in my right hand and one of the lab's sixty-four ounce plastic containers with some of my urine in my left hand. Sensing that someone was following me, my eyes darted back and forth. My heart was pounding. By the time I decided to look behind me, his hand was across my mouth.

"Shut up and don't scream," he demanded belligerently, dragging me toward a darkened bowling alley-like side street that led to a dead end.

NOOOOOO!

Like a hypervigilant fish trapped on a hook, I recoiled. My rage erupted. I dropped my bag and hit him with the container of urine. He groped at my pants zipper. My right hand fought to free my mouth.

"I have AIDS," I screamed.

"What? What'd you say?"

"I have AIDS. This is my urine. The doctors say I'll be dead in a month."

"No shit. Hey, sorry, okay, sorry." He turned and ran.

Although I was scared I didn't cry. My mind screamed, *That's right, motherfucker, run away.* I was hyperventilating, but I picked up my bag and ran on to Penn Station. When the adrenaline rush dissipated, I felt exhausted but strong. I had conserved my energy for the fight-or-flight response. Freezing was no longer an option.

Working with Dr. Benson is bringing out the tough girl in me.

During my second year Dr. Benson began to share his feelings with me. "People tell me I'm too abrupt. Working with you brings out the softer side in me."

"I see only a soft side," I said.

"I've fought in four wars. That can harden anyone."

He had served voluntarily in the Army in World War II, Korea, Vietnam, and the Persian Gulf, eventually retiring as a Green Beret Lieutenant Colonel.

"Having you around makes me less critical of others. I listen more."

"Thank you."

"You restore my trust in people. I like who I am when I'm with you."

Ditto. I hadn't liked myself in over a decade.

"We're a good team, Sweetie."

Did he just call me sweetie?

Dr. Benson's charisma and energy made him popular in the media. Everyone wanted to hear his exposures of health frauds. Television reporters came from all over to interview him. Television producers sent limousines to his lab to bring him to their studios.

He was often asked to give lectures on nutrition, cancer, AIDS and vitamin supplements. One evening he was asked to speak at Mount Sinai School of Medicine in New York City, about a thirty-minute car ride from the lab.

"Why don't you come along, Tali? This may be a good learning experience."

"I'd love to. What do I need to do?"

"*Shema,*" he told me. "Listen."

We left the office late and there was traffic heading into the city. He drove calmly. I was constantly looking at my watch. While he sang along with George Jones on the radio, there was no mention or discussion of the upcoming lecture.

He must really be prepared.

We arrived just minutes before the lecture was supposed to start. Dr. Benson was introduced and walked up to the podium. He whispered to the Chairman, "What's the topic I'm addressing?" With hundreds of seminars filed away in his brain, he pulled out the relevant mental file and began. He recited references from decades earlier and described metabolic pathways verbatim. He had a passion for engaging both colleagues and students. He used a classroom as a stage but he also got his audience to participate. He wowed them.

eight

I was twenty-four years old, working full time in Dr. Benson's lab while completing my final semester at NYU. One evening after everyone had left, Dr. Benson was in his office with the door open. Music played from *LITE FM*. I poked my head into the door.

"Dr. Benson?"

"Yes?"

"I just wanted to say good night."

"I didn't know you were still here."

"I wanted to finish up."

"Thanks. You did a yeoman's job today!"

"Thank you."

"Do you have someone picking you up?"

"No, I take the bus home."

"Would you accept a ride to the bus stop?"

"No thank you, I don't want to keep you from your family."

"You won't. I'm divorced and my girls are grown."

I'm sorry you're divorced. How many girls do you have?

What came out of my mouth was, "Thank you anyway. I don't mind walking. I actually prefer it."

"Okay, but before you leave," he said, and continued in a monologue: "There's a chap at a bench in a park and there are way too many annoying pigeons. The chap tells the pigeons, 'Fuck off, ya pigeons!' A little old lady hears him over and over again telling the birds to fuck off. 'Excuse me,' says the old lady, 'We don't use that kind of language around here. We speak respectfully to the pigeons. We roll up our newspapers and tell the birds to 'shoo, shoo'… then they fuck off'."

I laughed and said, "Did you hear the one about the centipede?"

"No, tell me."

"This lonely guy decides life would be more fun if he had a pet. So he goes to the pet store and tells the clerk that he wants to buy something unusual. The clerk recommends a centipede. He takes the centipede home, puts him into a little box and places it on the table. Later that night, the guy decides to take his new pet to the bar for a drink. So he asks the centipede, 'Would you like to go to the bar with me and have a beer?' There's no answer. He waits a few minutes and then asks again, 'How about going to the bar and having a beer?' But again there's no answer. He waits a few more minutes. He puts his face up against the little box and shouts, 'HEY, YOU IN THERE! DO YOU WANT TO GO TO THE BAR AND HAVE A DRINK?' A little voice says, 'I heard you the first time! I'm putting on my freaking shoes.'"

Dr. Benson smiled. "The centipede should say, 'I'm putting on my fucking shoes.' Where'd you get that one?"

"My brother. And yes, the original joke said, well…" I blushed.

"Older or younger brother?"

"Older. I have two older brothers."

Dr. Benson started to cough.

"Are you okay?"

"Yes," he said, still coughing. "I have asthma." He took an inhaler out of his jacket pocket and took a deep inhalation. "How old are your brothers?"

"Joseph's twenty-seven and Andrew's twenty-six. Do you have any siblings?"

"I had an older brother, Larry, who died a few years ago."

"I'm sorry."

"Our parents died when we were young. My brother and I moved around to many foster homes but we always stayed together. He was older and bigger than me, but I always looked after him. I think he had Asperger Syndrome but he was never diagnosed. He was a brilliant Scrabble player. He traveled all over the world winning Scrabble tournaments. And it all ended when he was hit by a car. He was riding his bike." He started to cough again. He looked at me and quickly turned his head away. He was crying.

"It's okay, Dr. Benson. I'm so sorry." Now I was crying.

"Call me Daniel."

"Oh, no, I can't."

"How about Dan?"

I shook my head no.

"Okay, call me Doc? Try that."

Uncomfortably, I repeated, "Doc."

"Good night, Tali."

"Good night, Doc."

In the following days and weeks, he continued to offer to drive me to the bus stop. One Monday evening in April, it was raining so hard that I knew my umbrella wouldn't protect me. He offered again and I said yes. We got into his four-door sedan. It was a Nissan. He asked for my address.

"The bus stop is fine."

"It's okay. I prefer to get you home safely."

My hands were folded neatly in my lap, and my eyes were focused on my shoes. I told him where I lived. We talked the entire thirty minutes it took to get me home.

He said, "How about we share a rose and a thorn story?"

"What's that?"

"One thing we are grateful for and one thing we could do without."

"I'm so grateful to have you as my mentor."

"I'm grateful to have you on the team, Tali. What's your thorn?"

"I don't have any thorns for today. What about you?"

"My thorn for today was dealing with bureaucratic bullshit. I've got too much on my plate."

"I'm sorry."

"It's not your fault, Sweetie."

I nodded and resumed the study of my shoes.

I was the first one to arrive in the morning and the last one to leave at night, usually with Dr. Benson. He asked me to write a nutrition chapter for his next book.

"I can't do that."

"Why would I ask you to do something that I didn't think you could do?"

"I've never published anything before."

"And now you will."

He made everything seem so simple.

The two of us saw Peter, Paul and Mary's *Holiday Celebration* at Lehman College, a short drive from the lab. They sang "If I Had a Hammer" and "Puff the Magic Dragon." We laughed at their rendition of "There Was an Old Lady Who Swallowed a Fly." We sang that one together as he drove me back home.

One evening, in June, as Dr. Benson was driving me home, he asked me to call him Daniel. I agreed.

"Have you ever been to New Orleans?"

"No."

He invited me to attend a nutrition conference where he would be the guest speaker.

My parents asked about the sleeping arrangements. I told them I would have my own room. That's what I believed. Reluctantly they approved and I packed my bags.

We arrived at the Bourbon Orleans Hotel, and since we were running late, Dr. Benson decided to check in later. The hotel arranged to deliver our bags to our rooms. Daniel was led directly to the ballroom where his lecture was about to begin. As he walked in, he made sure that I was by his side.

The elegant New Orleans Ballroom had an extraordinary chandelier in the center of the room. Red velvet chairs were lined up in rows of fifteen chairs each. Every chair was occupied.

Daniel received a standing ovation after his ninety-minute lecture on vitamin B_{12} depletion in HIV and AIDS patients. The audience bombarded him with questions: "How does the HIV medication interact with vitamin B_{12}?" "Is it dangerous for a person living with AIDS to be a vegetarian?" "Can vitamin B_{12} supplements be sufficient for an AIDS patient with vitamin B_{12} deficiency?"

After questions and answers, the Chairman brought the conference to a close and escorted Daniel and me to dinner.

Daniel asked me, "How did you like your first conference?"

"It was absolutely amazing. I loved it. You're like a walking encyclopedia."

It was then that I knew that I wanted to teach college-level nutrition in addition to consulting with patients.

We dined with the host and a few of his colleagues at Commander's Palace in the heart of the New Orleans Garden District. We were surrounded by wine, an assortment of artisanal cheeses and a rich selection of soups and salads. I tried their classic turtle soup and sampled each of the salads. By the time the main course arrived, I was exhausted but Daniel was still going strong.

He lifted up his glass. Everyone, including me, followed.

"*Salud, Dinero, y Amor...y tiempo para gastarlos.* Health, Money and Love...and time to enjoy them. It's a Castilian toast from Spain."

It was close to eleven when we finally got back to the hotel and checked in. There was only one room. I stared at the king-size bed. He sensed my discomfort and called the front desk for a cot. He told me to make myself comfortable in the bed and he would take the cot. I felt a great sense of relief. I got into the bed and realized that I wanted to share it with him. I invited him in. He accepted.

Nothing happened. We talked. I learned that he loved Broadway shows. *Man of La Mancha* was his favorite. Don Quixote was his hero because they both fought against impossible odds.

"Have you seen *Man of La Mancha* on Broadway?"

"No."

"Have you seen the movie version starring Peter O'Toole and Sophia Loren?"

"No."

"Oh, you've got to see it."

"What's it about?"

"Peter O'Toole plays Alonso Quijana, an old retired man from La Mancha who loses his mind from reading too many books about chivalry. He becomes delusional and believes that he is a knight named Don Quixote."

"Where does Sophia Loren's character come in?"

"She plays the beautiful Aldonza Lorenzo, a barmaid who prostitutes herself at night. Quixote defends her as his perfect Lady Dulcinea."

"What does doll-sa-nay-a mean?"

"Dulcinea means sweetness. It's a made-up name that he gives her. There is so much to the story but I don't want to give it away. You've got to see it."

"I promise I will, but please tell me, when does he sing 'The Impossible Dream'?"

"At the end, he sings it to Dulcinea." Daniel sings:
"To dream, the impossible dream
To right, the unrightable wrong
To love, pure and chaste from afar
To try, when your arms are too weary
To reach the unreachable star."

"I love it; you have a great voice. Does she fall in love with him?"

"Yes, but not at first."

"Do they marry?"

"No. He collapses after she rejects him."

"She rejects him? He collapses?"

"See, I've told you too much."

"Tell me."

"He comes to realize who he really is, Alonso Quijana, and barely remembers Don Quixote. But Aldonza wants to go on living as Dulcinea and begs him to remember. He dies in her arms."

I started to cry.

"Don't cry, Sweetie. Don Quixote stays alive in Aldonza's heart. She insists that her name remain Dulcinea. To this day, a reference to someone as one's Dulcinea implies hopeless devotion and love."

"What does Don Quixote represent to Dulcinea?"

"He restored her trust in people, especially men. Her belief in Don Quixote's quest made her believe in herself. In the beginning she has no self-worth. It's because Quixote believes she's nothing less than a Princess – he calls her 'my queen and my lady' – that she begins to believe in herself. You must see the movie."

He kissed my forehead, said "Good night, Sweetie," turned to the other side and fell right to sleep. At that moment, I knew I loved him.

In the morning we headed to Brennan's Restaurant in the heart of the French Quarter. Daniel ordered for both of us. He wanted me to have the full breakfast dining experience: southern baked apple with cream on the side, eggs *hussarde* and hot French bread topped off with their famous dessert, Bananas Foster. He bought me an apron with the Bananas Foster recipe so that I could re-create it at home. With just minutes to spare we placed our bags in the trunk of the taxi and headed to the airport.

I thought of Daniel constantly. When he traveled, I wondered if he was eating well and taking care of himself. I missed him on weekends.

One Saturday morning he called me at my parent's house.

"Did you eat breakfast yet?"

"No, not yet."

"Good, I'm picking you up and we're going to City Island."

An hour later, while I ate my French toast, Daniel shared a history lesson. City Island was originally known as Great Minnefords Island before the Revolutionary War. During the two World Wars it became a busy shipbuilding center, and after that, island yacht yards Nevins and Minneford produced several America's Cup yacht race winners: Courageous won twice, in 1974 and 1977, and Freedom won in 1980.

In July, for my birthday, Daniel gave me a music box and a card. The card said, "A forever perfect flower for a forever perfect flower." Inside he had written a story:

Once upon a time, there was a king who owned the most perfect ruby. It was his prize possession. When he wasn't looking at it, he kept it wrapped up in velvet, under lock and key in his vault. One day, he was not being mindful and he dropped his precious stone. To his horror, his carelessness caused a deep scratch in his ruby rock. Artisans from all over the world attempted to mend the stone. All failed. Then one day, an ordinary stonecutter offered his help. With nothing to lose, the king agreed. When the stonecutter returned, the king gasped with appreciation. The injury had been replaced with a delicate stem that now held a perfect rose. The stonecutter had transformed the wound into something even more beautiful.

Tali, you are that perfect rose. May you wear this flower and be reminded that you, too, are transforming into something even more beautiful.

The music box was only two-by-three inches, but it was decorated with twenty-two karat gold bands and delicate gold beading. I lifted up the lid and saw a ruby carved into the most beautiful rose. I turned the knob: It played "Wind Beneath My Wings."

"I love it. It's so delicate," I said.

"Happy birthday, Sweetie." He kissed my forehead.

"I also love the story. Did you make it up?"

"No. It's from the 1700s *Maggid of Dubno*." He saw the blank look on my face. "A *maggid* is a preacher or teller of parables. His name was Jacob ben Wolf Kranz. The parable is known as *The Scratched Diamond* or *The Blemish on the Diamond*. I just changed it to a ruby, your birthstone."

One night, in September, while driving me home from work he took my hand.

I started to tremble.

He immediately let go of my hand and pulled the car over.

"You're okay, Sweetie."

You're okay.

I needed to hear that. Emotions collected in my heart.

"I will never let anything happen to you." Distress gathered between his brows.

I believed him. I wanted to cry in his arms, tell him that I was scared and full of shame, but instead I slipped my hand into his. His eyes lowered to our holding hands and then sauntered back up to my eyes. Like a blind man reading braille, he slowly traced my face with his fingertips.

Trust. Faith. Courage.

I looked into his green eyes and I kissed him. I kissed him on the lips. He held my face with his hands. He kissed my lips. Because of who *he* was, I felt special. His tongue embraced mine.

I was intimidated. I admired Dr. Benson, I mean, Daniel. I was infatuated with him.

What does he want? Where will this go? Can I make him happy?

He kissed me again. I took a deep breath. My body was tingling. Goose bumps appeared on my arms and legs. I wanted to stay there, in that moment, forever.

We spent the next month working together, reviewing data, attending seminars and writing articles. I traveled with him more frequently. He was so involved in the world of ideas and theories that he paid little attention to his physical needs. On most mornings I brought him fresh fruit and yogurt for breakfast. Once a month for lunch, I brought in his favorite, pastrami on rye. He often took me out for dinner.

Some evenings he ate dinner with my family. My parents invited him over to show appreciation for his contribution to my education. They appeared to like him and never asked what was going on with us.

We played chess and Scrabble, and shared conversations, movies, meals and walks. He took me to *Man of La Mancha* – the play, not the movie. Raul Julia played Quixote and Sheena Easton played Dulcinea. At the end, the entire cast sang "The Impossible Dream." I was awed by the energy that flooded the stage. When the stage went black and the lights of the theater went on, I saw that Daniel was crying.

After the show, I bought Daniel a miniature Don Quixote paperweight. He kept it on his desk. I also drew a Don Quixote caricature on a tee shirt for him. I felt so lucky. How did I get the golden ticket inside the Wonka Bar?

In November, after a romantic dinner at La Cirque, he invited me to his Upper East Side apartment. I was curious to see where he lived and how he lived.

His apartment was spacious. There were too many books to count on his mahogany bookcase that ran the length of the living room. A vast window allowed plenty of light to flow through the apartment. The crochet throw pillows on his chocolate leather sofa added a feminine touch. Photographs of his kids hung on the walls. A plush gray carpet lined the hallway; bleached wood covered the kitchen floor.

He invited me out onto the terrace overlooking the East River. "Can I get you a drink?"

"No, thank you. I'm okay." I nervously moistened my lips with cherry lip balm.

He pointed out all of the bridges that we could see from his terrace – Brooklyn, Queensboro, Manhattan, Williamsburg, Hells Gate and Triborough. After giving me the history lesson of the 9.4-mile FDR Drive, he said, "May I have this dance?"

I beamed, "Absolutely."

He placed one hand in mine, the other on the small of my back and swayed with me from side to side. Even without soft music competing with the booming sounds of the city below, it was peaceful. He stroked my hair and gently kissed my lips.

"Come with me."

He led me back inside to his bedroom. It was tidy, with a mirrored wall closet that made the room appear larger than it actually was. He closed the vertical blinds, dimmed the Tiffany lamp and turned down the elegant duvet. I liked his eclectic taste.

I didn't say anything as he undressed me, placed me onto his bed and covered me with a blanket. I closed my eyes while he got undressed. I wasn't ready to see him naked. I opened my eyes when I felt his hairy legs and chest against me. My eyes filled with tears.

Why am I crying?

I was overwhelmed with emotion. For the first time I was allowing myself to feel vulnerable. And I was scared.

Daniel was looking into my eyes. "Sweetie, nothing is going to happen until you want it to. Okay?"

I nodded. I was still a virgin at twenty-four. Again, I was scared. But I trusted him. As each tear fell he caught it with a gentle kiss. He kissed my lips once. Twice. He waited.

"Please hold me," I said.

"Anything you need."

He held me until I reached for one of his hands and placed it on my breast. He traced my excited nipples with his fingers. "Are you okay?"

"Yes."

"Are you sure?"

"Yes."

"Are you sure you're sure?"

I smiled, "I've never been more sure."

Daniel began kissing my nipples and then my navel. When his fingers entered my body I was shaking. My right hand kept jerking like I was air-drying my nails after they were polished.

When he kissed my vagina, I went wild. I felt his body weight on top of me. He slowly moved inside me. My entire body trembled. My legs wrapped tightly around his lower back as I clung onto his neck. I pulled him closer and closer as we rocked back and forth. We kissed even deeper.

"I love you so much, Tali."

"I love you too." I was crying again.

This is love. This is what I was waiting for. Thank you, God.

What happened next was incredible. As I looked at Daniel, I felt embraced by a magnificent white light. I experienced rhythmic contractions as I felt his body tense. Our breathing was suspended for several glorious seconds. I felt a sensational release of energy as he quivered inside me. There are no words to describe how I felt except for maybe the Hebrew word *echad,* meaning oneness – as if our souls had united as one.

Daniel said, "I've had many experiences, but none like this. I love you, Tal."

All I could say was, "I love you, too."

At that moment, the beauty of my relationship with Daniel erased the ugliness of my encounter with The Man in the white limousine.

For Chanukah, he gave me another music box that played "Love Story." Inside was a necklace with a gold six-pointed Jewish star. He put it on me.

"You have the neck of a swan," he said. "Just beautiful."

"Thank you so much." I caressed the star. "I love everything: You, the song, the box and the necklace."

"I love you more."

That was what Grandma Devorah used to say.

I felt completely connected and safe. "Daniel, I need to tell you something."

"What is it, Sweetie?"

I told him what had happened years ago.

"You are courageous. I wish I had been there to protect you."

I told him I still felt the shame and anger.

"Tell me what you need – I want to help you."

"I just needed to tell you."

He invited my parents to join us for dinner and a Broadway show, *Les Miserables.* Although my parents were more quiet than usual, I know they had a good time.

A few days after that, Daniel and I were having dinner at Josephine's Restaurant, across from Lincoln Center where we had just seen *Madame Butterfly*.

"I've made a lot of mistakes in my life, Tal, but loving you is not one of them." His voice was gentle but his eyes were sad. "I'll always love you and there's a place in my life that only you can fill. But I'm being selfish, and that's a mistake."

What's a mistake? What's going on?

"I only want what's best for you. You need to find a younger man who can give you children. You'll be a great mother."

You're best for me. Where is this coming from? What did I do wrong?

"Are you still friends with Alex Kohane? I know he is so fond of you."

Why did he bring up Alex? Why couldn't he just break it off?

There was no graceful escape hatch. I was caught up in a hurricane of emotions. I wasn't angry at Daniel; he could do no wrong; I was angry at myself. I wanted to argue with him, fight with him – fight for him – but I couldn't. I didn't understand what had just happened.

I didn't find out until years later.

nine

I had analyzed our breakup to death. I tormented myself. *Why was I not good enough? Did he feel I was too damaged?*

I still had no answers. I became depressed and lonely. I understood that, but another buried emotion returned and scared me because I had never learned how to express it.

Rage.

Planted in my heart years ago, it started to grow again like a poisonous vine. It encircled and choked arteries, veins and capillaries. My throat tightened; I could no longer speak.

I chose to write him a letter. The words were written with pent-up rage.

To The Man with the soulless devil eyes and the heart and compassion of a rock:

You are a worthless piece of shit; no, worse than that, because even shit has a purpose - manure to nourish the earth. You have no worth, no value. You are a nothing. A no thing!

Only a no thing preys on a vulnerable child who is unable to defend herself.

Only a no thing baits a child as if she is the catch of the day.

Only a no thing terrorizes a child in slow motion.

Only a no thing strikes a child with her small eyes shut and her young body trembling.

Only a no thing violates that young body and stunts the growth of her mind.

Only a no thing performs acts of hell that teach my brain to dissociate from that moment and from many moments in the future.

Only a no thing refuses to see the correlation between HIS despicable actions and MY undeserved consequences.

Only a no thing is oblivious to the fact that karma is all around us. What you did to me (and most likely to others) will one day come back to you.

I still hear ya fuckin' voice an' I pray thththat an angry an' starvin' pit bull corners ya in a dark alley an' tears at an' slowly shreds ya fuckin' cock ta pieces. I pray thththat he makes ya his six-course meal, with ya semen an' ya blood actin' as thththe gravy on ya fuckin' meatballs.

You murdered my precious spirit. You extinguished the light within me. You taught me to dissociate and to distrust. Because of you, I'm afraid to close my eyes at night, and I pray they don't open in the morning.

You, yes, YOU, NO THING, are responsible.

my middle

"We don't receive wisdom;
we must discover it for ourselves
after a long journey
that no one can take for us
or spare us."

Marcel Proust

ten

I tried to convince myself that marriage to Daniel would not have worked anyway. I just wasn't good enough for him. We stopped socializing after hours. I was heartbroken and I missed him. I missed making his lunches and sharing dinners; I missed his jokes, his touches, and his beautiful green eyes; I especially missed his intellectual stimulation and spiritual bonding. I missed everything about him.

Surgeon General C. Everett Koop's *Understanding AIDS* was mailed to over one hundred million people in the United States. The number of deaths in 1988 was 4,855. The death toll was rising fast. There was still no effective treatment and no hope of a cure.

Months passed. Ready or not, I was twenty-four years old and I had to start dating.

My family still lived on the eighth floor of our building in Co-Op City; my mother's friend Sandy lived on the twenty-second floor.

All twenty-six floors shared the same laundry room. One day, Mom and Sandy were in the basement folding clothes. Sandy asked about me and mentioned her single nephew, Stuart. Two incorrigible matchmakers did their thing.

Stuart called me. We had many long phone conversations. He was twenty-seven years old, born and raised in Brooklyn, and living in Manhattan. He had graduated from Tufts University School of Dental Medicine in Boston and was working with a dental group in the city. He loved it. He was Jewish, but neither religious nor spiritual. He came from a big family, with two brothers, two sisters, two dogs and a cat.

We met on St. Patrick's Day. He took me out to dinner. I dressed conservatively, wearing my green silk top with knee-length black skirt and boots. My wavy hair was blown out straight and looked two inches longer.

Stuart was soft-spoken and handsome, with distinctive cobalt eyes. He reminded me of a young Bruce Willis. We started seeing each other once a week for dinner or a movie or both. I liked him, but I needed to take things slowly. He never brought up having sex and I loved that.

Four months later we celebrated my twenty-fifth birthday with a romantic dinner at the elegant Bouley Restaurant in Tribeca, near Stuart's apartment in Manhattan. We mostly hung out at my parent's apartment in Co-Op City, but that night I agreed to go to his place.

His studio apartment was compact but immaculate. Strategically placed in an alcove were a glass bistro table and two stools that Stuart built. I assumed that the living room, complete with a trendy sofa bed and matching breakfront, was his bedroom. Twenty-five roses and a new red *caliente* Schwinn bike adorned with a big red bow were waiting for me.

"Happy birthday, Tal."

I kissed him "thank you" and the next thing I knew we were in a lip-lock. He started to undress me. I panicked. I excused myself to the bathroom. I cried. I felt that I was being disloyal to Daniel, but I knew that didn't make any sense. I still loved Daniel and I couldn't let him go. Stuart was a good man and I wanted it to work. Although I felt love for him, I was not in love.

When I came out of the bathroom, Stuart was in the dining area freeing a queen-size Murphy bed from the wall. I was amazed at the space efficiency.

Stuart said, "Are you all right?"

I nodded yes.

When we sat down on the bed he stroked my thighs.

I am back in the white limousine.

"Tal?"

I feel the blade of the knife on my inner leg.

"TALI?"

Move on. Let it go.

"Can you hear me?"

I can't. I am unable to let go of The Man.

"What's going on?"

"What? I'm sorry."

"Are you okay?"

"I'm sorry. Please don't take this personally but I need to go home."

"Okay, no problem."

I told myself that Stuart was a man I could grow to love. He was as genuine as they came.

One day in September Stuart picked me up after work. I was tired and I looked forward to getting home. He missed the exit to Co-Op City. Despite the sun beginning its calm descent, I was irritated and I gave him a look.

"I'll turn around, no big deal," he said. But he missed the next exit also.

71

"Where are you going?" I asked.

"I thought we can watch the sunset at Orchard Beach."

How romantic.

"But, the sun is setting. We'll never make it in time."

"You're right." He pulled off the road onto the grassy divide. He got out of the car, came over to my side and opened the door. He reached for my hand. He got down on one knee.

The sun was still low in the sky, glowing yellow and orange. I had to squint to see him.

"What are you doing?"

"We've known each other for only six months, but I've fallen in love with you. Please tell me that you love me too and that you'll marry me."

Now white, the sun aligned between the trees.

I laughed. I cried. I kissed him. I said, "Yes."

Then I panicked.

Can I make you happy? Can I be happy with a man who doesn't know what I've been through? I am not who you think I am.

I said, "Yes" again.

The sun disappeared below the horizon.

A special engagement dinner awaited us when we arrived at my parent's apartment. Stuart had already asked my Dad for my hand and received an enthusiastic yes. Mom, not knowing what my answer would be, knocked on wood and made brisket, the family's favorite. She had forgotten that I didn't eat meat.

I wanted my mom's size twelve wedding dress taken in to fit me, but that would have required sacrificing most of the pearls. I was thrilled when Stuart's mom asked if I wanted to wear her wedding dress. I hoped that wearing her dress would bring Stuart and me luck. It meant more to me than buying a brand new, expensive dress that would only be worn once. She let me alter her thirty-eight-year-old dress any way I wished. I changed the high button-up lace neck into a more modern sweetheart neckline.

My cousins, who were my bridesmaids, were disappointed that I wanted to escape the rite of passage of flipping through bridal magazines, imagining which gorgeous dress I would walk down the aisle in, and spending months traveling from the Bronx to Queens and maybe even to Brooklyn searching for the dress of my dreams.

We made love twice before we were married. I cried both times.

"Are you okay?"

"Yes."

"Am I hurting you?"

"No."

"Why are you crying?"

"I don't know."

I really didn't know.

My period was always on time. I counted thirty-six days from my last period, eight days late. My breasts were tender, my belly was bloated, and my emotions were boiling over like a screaming teapot. I knew I had conceived the second time we made love; we were unprotected.

Stuart asked, "What do you want to do?"

"I don't know."

"I don't think we're ready."

I hugged my belly and cried.

He said, "At least we know we can have children when we want to."

A week before the abortion I could not zip up the dress I wore to my brother Andrew and Hera's wedding. Without anyone knowing, I paid extra to let the seams out of my bridesmaid's dress.

Their bridal party piled into a white limousine. Instantly I felt my fight-or-flight response kick in. Everything in my body increased: blood pressure, heart rate, and breathing. I swear I even felt the increase of blood flow to my muscles. I was going to vomit. The beads of perspiration started to accumulate on my forehead. My fingers were swollen and my hands were clammy.

I refused to get in.

I asked Stuart if I could ride with him instead.

He said, "Of course," and didn't ask why.

After the abortion, I was empty, numb and overwhelmed with shame. We promised to keep our secret to ourselves. I now had two secrets.

I graduated with a Master's Degree in Nutrition from NYU in December, 1989.

Daniel said, "I want you to apply to medical school. You get the applications for Downstate, NYU and Mount Sinai and I'll help you fill them out. And if you get accepted I'll pay your tuition."

I got the applications and looked them over. It was too much. I told Daniel, "I can't do this. I don't believe I can be both a good wife and a full-time medical student."

"Of course you can."

"No, I can't. I'm not like you. I can't do ten things at once."

"Okay, I understand, but I don't agree."

I could see how disappointed he was.

Stuart and I married in April, 1990. Mom said, "It's your wedding day. Let's ride in a white limousine."

"Absolutely not. I want to ride in the Buick with you and Dad."

"What's the matter with you?"

If you only knew.

The rabbi walked down the aisle first. Stuart and his parents followed, then the groomsmen with the bridesmaids. Stuart's precious two-year-old nephew was the ring bearer. From behind the curtain I heard Melissa Manchester's "Looking Through the Eyes of Love" begin to play.

Mom kissed me. She smiled but didn't say anything.

I saw my reflection in her eyeglasses. I looked so serious. So sad.

I glanced over Mom's shoulder. "Hi, Daddy."

Dad kissed me, "I love you."

"I love you too."

The curtain lifted and there I stood with my parents by my side. Everyone stood up and faced the back of the room. The three of us walked down the aisle together.

As I inched forward with an exaggerated slowness, I searched for a face that might know of any reason that Stuart and I should not be joined in holy matrimony. Everyone was smiling at me. Nobody could see my emotional scars. "So beautiful," I heard a stranger say. They were all strangers – even Stuart. Nobody knew of my secret except Daniel, but he wasn't there.

Speak now or forever hold your peace.

I should have gone straight to school.

Shut up.

For the sake of my marriage, I held my peace.

Our wedding ceremony took place under the *chuppah*, a white canopy resting on four poles, decorated with flowers. It symbolized the bride and groom creating a home together that would always be open to guests. The Bible says that Abraham and Sara were the first couple to be married under a *chuppah*.

We also followed the tradition of the bride circling the groom seven times. This came from the Biblical story of Joshua leading the Israelites into the Promised Land. First, however, he needed to conquer the city of Jericho, which was protected by a great wall. God commanded the Israelites to walk around that wall seven times. After they did, the wall came tumbling down. Like the city of Jericho, every man has a wall built around his heart that prevents his true self from being seen. A bride circles her groom seven times, surrounding him with her love and protection with the hope that he will feel safe enough to allow the wall of his heart to come tumbling down.

It should have been Stuart who circled around me seven times.

The ceremony began with the rabbi reciting a blessing over a cup of wine that the two of us drank from.

Stuart and I exchanged vows and the rabbi told Stuart to slip the wedding band onto my left ring finger. I slipped a gold band onto his.

The rabbi read the *ketubah*, a Jewish wedding contract, in Hebrew. It took about three minutes. All I understood were our names and the date.

The rabbi continued, "I was going to say something very deep and profound, but the kids have the rest of their lives to be serious and they preferred something funny. So, I'm going to share a joke.

"A young girl brings her fiancé home for the first time to meet her parents. After dinner the mother tells her husband to take the young man into the study to learn more about him.

"In the study, the father asks the young man, 'What kind of living will you be making?'

"'I'm a Torah scholar.'

"'A Torah scholar is admirable, but how will you afford an engagement ring and the wedding?'

"'I will study and God will provide for us.'

"'How will you provide a nice home for my daughter to live in?'

"'I will concentrate on my studies. God will provide for us.'

"'And children? How will you support your children?'

"'God will provide.'

"After thirty minutes of 'God will provide,' the father walks back into the kitchen. 'How did it go?' asked his wife.

"'Well, there's good news and bad news. The bad news is, he has no job or plans for the future, but the good news is, he thinks I'm God.'"

Laughter – what a wonderful way to begin a marriage.

The rabbi then said, "Here's to love, laughter and happily ever after."

Everyone said, "Amen."

Stuart and I drank from a second cup of wine.

At the conclusion of the ceremony, Stuart broke a glass with his right foot to symbolize that our marriage would last as long as the glass was broken – forever.

Two hundred guests shouted, "*Mazel tov* (Good luck)."

I moved out of my parent's apartment in the Bronx and into Stuart's apartment in New York City. It took me hours to pack. I took my clothes from the closet and folded them into boxes. Sitting in the corner of the closet was Barbie's camper. Before I put it into the donation pile, I took out my *One Mile, 1st Place* trophy. I eventually gave it to a client, a young girl, who was overweight but who finally succeeded in running a mile for the first time.

I emptied my desk drawers. Inside a manila envelope, the kind with the antiquated string, not the aluminum clasp, I found a red envelope, a handful of letters and three photos. I scanned the photos: Alex and me sitting in the back seat during a drivers ed class; Alex standing in front of his new red car; and Alex, me and Daniel in the lab.

Wow.

I opened the red envelope – a Valentine's Day card from Alex.

I wonder how he's doing.

One by one I opened the letters, all signed, "Love, Alex."

Sorry, Alex.

I slipped everything back into the manila envelope and safely tucked it between two sweaters.

In another drawer, beneath my childhood books, I found my diary, the one with the tiny key, now missing. I opened it up to a random page:

At the end of the show, I ran down to the stage with Andrew and Joseph and asked the trainer how the big elephant was trained to not break away from the rope. He said something about her being chained up when she was a baby and then how she'd pull on the chain over and over again trying to escape but couldn't.

I think she was too little, too weak and too stupid.

The trainer said once the elephant gave up, an ordinary rope tied around her foot was enough to keep her from breaking free.

I kissed the book and placed it under a layer of clothes in the box. I used my pillow case to dry my eyes.

By the end of 1990, the number of known deaths from AIDS in the U.S. had climbed to 18,447. They included fashion designer Halston, artist Keith Haring, and teenage hemophiliac Ryan White from Kokomo, Indiana, who became a national poster child for HIV/AIDS after he was expelled from middle school because of sheer panic.

eleven

By the summer of 1992, Stuart and I settled into a cozy, three-bedroom high ranch on a quiet cul-de-sac on Long Island. The previous owner had planted a baby Japanese maple that now, twenty years later, sprawled out over the entire front lawn. It was magnificent.

While building my nutrition practice at home, I continued to work with Daniel twice a week at the lab. One night, after everyone had left, I went into Daniel's office to say good night. He was standing by his desk looking at a photo. Without saying a word, he passed it to me. It was a photo of a black sedan banged up against a tree. The hood was crushed up to the windshield like an accordion.

"Oh my God. What is this?"

"A photo of an accident."

"Whose accident?"

"Mine."

"Yours? When?"

"On your wedding day."

My questions rose above the lump in my throat. "On my wedding day? What happened? Were you hurt?"

He nodded his head, "I was fine."

"How do you let two years pass? Why didn't you tell me?"

It took a long moment for him to answer. "What could I have said? That I was still in love with you and I didn't want you to marry Stuart?"

"Yes!"

"I couldn't."

"Why?"

"I was doing what was best for you."

"It wasn't best for me. I was in love with you."

"Please trust me. I have to believe I did the right thing."

I was not easy to live with. Stuart never got a warning when my smile or laughter was replaced by melancholy or anger. He still knew nothing of my childhood trauma.

I could not control my thoughts or emotions. I told myself, "I shouldn't be crying anymore," "I have to start a family," "I need Stuart to say he loves me." After two years of marriage, I no longer had the energy to pretend that everything was okay.

And then the day came when Stuart and I saw the movie *Good Will Hunting*. Matt Damon's character, Will Hunting, is in the office of his psychiatrist, played by Robin Williams. The doctor and Will are discussing Will's childhood physical abuse by his father. The doctor holds up Will's file: "This is not your fault." Will nonchalantly responds, "Oh, I know." The doctor repeats, "It's not your fault." Will says, "I know." The doctor says it two more times and Will starts to cry. The doctor takes Will in his arms and holds him like a child. After a moment, Will hugs him back. The doctor hugs Will even tighter.

Applause, applause, applause!

I was crying. Stuart reached for my hand but said nothing. After the movie ended, he asked if I wanted ice cream. He knew ice cream was my drug of choice. I told him that I'd rather go to Oyster Bay, by the water.

When we arrived, I stared out into the bay. I finally told Stuart my *secret*. Until that moment, Daniel was the only one I had ever told.

Stuart looked scared. He held me but he didn't say anything. I wanted him to encourage me to tell him more. He did not. I wanted him to recognize that I was out of control and to tell me that I was normal. He did not. I wanted him to tell me that I no longer needed to be a silent screamer. He did not. I needed him to help me grieve for the fearless and trusting woman that I felt I would never become. He could not.

That night as I was curled up in a fetal position, a little girl in a woman's body, Stuart said, "What are you doing?"

I answered, "Resting."

Silently I screamed, *Dying.*

Years passed; the friction in our marriage remained. We both worked long hours. Every once in a while Stuart asked, "Do you want to have a baby?"

"I'm not ready."

I would never be ready. I never felt the same connection with Stuart that I had felt with Daniel. I wondered if staying married to him was a mistake.

One day, with trembling hands, I went into the kitchen, took everything out of the refrigerator – the food, the trays, the shelves – and I scrubbed and scrubbed and scrubbed the inside and the outside until it looked brand new. Then I cleaned the glass shower doors; washed, dried and folded three loads of laundry; vacuumed the entire house; and ran five miles around the neighborhood. By the time I got back home, I was depleted.

Stuart asked if there was something I wasn't telling him. I nodded. I felt exposed, ashamed and too guilty to talk about it. Instead I handed him a photocopy of a page from my journal. My eyes watered and my hands began to wrestle. I felt the shame bubble in my blood and rise to my face. I whispered, "I'm sorry."

1. Loneliness: I have associated loneliness with the sad feelings of my past. Daniel had taken away my loneliness in the past; I assumed he could take it away even now that I was married.

2. Insecurity: My insecurity has led to unfair demands on Stuart. I need to hear him say, "I love you and I feel lucky to have you in my life." That's what Daniel says.

3. Intimacy: I had found both emotional and physical comfort with Daniel in the past. Our innocent "good morning" hugs at the lab have gradually developed into longer hugs and passionate kisses.

I honestly don't remember when all of this started. I have a history of blocking out information. I don't want to acknowledge negative things about myself. I accept full responsibility for my actions. I can't blame Stuart or Daniel. I wish things could be different.

Stuart said nothing. I saw neither love nor forgiveness in his eyes. He stormed out of the house and didn't return for hours. When he did, I promised him that Daniel and I would never be intimate again. I still hoped that Stuart and I could be together for the rest of our lives, even though I knew an essential connection was missing. I was too emotional for him and he was too logical for me. He didn't get me and I didn't get him.

I escaped my feelings through work. I thought that as long as I felt productive in the daytime, I could avoid despair at night. That worked for a while.

One night while having dinner with Stuart's parents, his mom said to me, "What's the matter? I can see that you're not happy."

I just cried.

"You're my child as much as Stuart is. You've got to do whatever you need to do to be happy."

I hugged her. I wondered if I could ever be like her. She was on such a high spiritual level.

I called Daniel and asked him if he could recommend a therapist. He gave me the name of Dr. Rose Gottlieb.

twelve

In 1995, the World Health Organization reported over ten million people had HIV worldwide. More than a million were in the U.S. The number of deaths in the U.S. in that year alone was 32,330. We had lost rock singer Freddie Mercury, actor Robert Reed, tennis legend Arthur Ashe, ballet superstar Rudolf Nureyev and actor Paul Michael Glaser's wife, Elizabeth. AIDS did not discriminate.

I was on the Long Island Railroad heading into New York City's Penn Station. I stared at the posters of Magic Johnson and Greg Louganis telling the world they were HIV-positive.

I turned to my book. In *Leaving the Saints*, Martha Beck recalled her own childhood trauma:

"After I experienced the trauma memories, I studied a range of research materials about how the brain records and remembers images. I learned that lost memory is very common after traumas such as car accidents, wartime violence, criminal assault, or

sexual abuse. Scientists report that young children are especially likely to repress memories of such incidents. I've come to understand that the mind can protect you until you're ready to cope with the fallout of remembering."

I was "ready to cope with the fallout of remembering." I sought the ability to confront change, anxiety and dissociation. I sought not only knowledge, understanding and wisdom, but also responsibility, acceptance and trust. If I couldn't save my marriage, then I sought the courage to leave and start anew.

I walked the three miles from Penn Station to Dr. Gottlieb's Upper East Side office. I arrived twenty minutes early for my two o'clock appointment, signed in at the front desk and sat down in the waiting room where there were too many magazines to count. I picked up the one closest to me, *Prevention*. I flipped through the pages.

Prevention. Prevention. Prevention.

My mind concocted a list.

Abduction. Sexual abuse. Secret. Shame. Anger. Fear.

I had so many issues I could have been a magazine stand.

"Tali?" She was nearly six feet tall, with long brown hair and dark brown eyes. She wore her glasses on top of her head. "Rose Gottlieb, nice to meet you."

I stood up. "Nice to meet you too."

She led me to her office where we began our first fifty-minute session.

I told her about my childhood trauma, my relationship with Daniel, my marriage with Stuart and all of my shame.

"There is a test of what is constructive versus destructive shame," she said as she lowered her eyeglasses to her nose.

I nodded.

"Ask yourself two questions. Number One, is the shame due to your mistake or due to someone else's?"

I thought to myself, *Both.*

"And Number Two?" I asked.

"And Number Two, what effect does it have on you? Are you allowing it to demoralize you or to motivate you? If the answers are that it is not your fault and it's demoralizing, then we have to work on that because it's not a healthy shame. And this destructive force will prevent you from moving forward."

"What if I *am* responsible and the shame *is* appropriate?"

"If you are truly responsible, you can learn to fix it and move forward. Moving forward is always the goal."

I nodded.

"It takes courage to live bound by shame."

Courage?

"And it takes courage plus strength to break free from it."

I half-smiled.

That's the empowering message I needed to hear.

We agreed to make a follow-up appointment. It wasn't until I left her office that I realized it was almost three thirty. She paid no attention to the time.

One week later I told Dr. Gottlieb, "I feel broken."

"What does that mean?"

I looked at the framed wedding photo of Dr. Gottlieb and her husband. I thought about my own wedding day, standing under the *chuppah* when Stuart stepped on the glass. "Like a thousand pieces of shattered glass. There's no way to connect the pieces back together."

"Can you consider this brokenness an opportunity to transform yourself? Shattered glass can be recycled into something new."

That's true. I thought of Daniel and *The Scratched Diamond.*

"Being broken is painful, but transforming into *unbroken* can bring greater strength. If you had a broken leg, after setting the bone, you would go for physical therapy to train your muscles to become stronger. Right now your spirit is broken and you are here, in talk therapy, to strengthen your mind. Only you can decide if your brokenness will transform you for the better."

I want to be stronger.

"You've been using your energy to run from your past. It'll take time to learn the techniques of calming your mind. This mindfulness will help you to understand the relationship between your childhood trauma and your present thoughts, feelings and actions."

"Okay," I whispered. I had been running from my past all my life, but I had finally had enough. I didn't want to run anymore.

"Brain scans of trauma patients show a change in brain chemistry. There's increased activity of the amygdala, the fear center, and decreased activity of the prefrontal cortex, the decision-making center of your brain."

I don't want to be afraid anymore. I want to make better decisions.

"You can change your brain chemistry, Tali. I'll help you."

The following week Dr. Gottlieb said, "According to the statistics, child sexual abuse is one of the most underreported crimes. One in five adults reports being sexually abused as children but nearly ninety percent of survivors never report the crime. Do you know why the number of unreported cases is so high?"

I nodded. I knew exactly why.

"Because children are afraid and ashamed to tell anyone. The long-term emotional and psychological damage of sexual abuse can be devastating to the child."

I told her that I was one of the unreported cases. "Is it too late to help me?"

"No, it's never too late, but it's not easy. You've blocked out the distressing thoughts and feelings for a long time."

While she talked, I stared at the *Footprints in the Sand* plaque on the wall behind her. I read the last three lines of the popular poem about having faith in God:

"...during your trials and testings,
When you saw only one set of footprints,

It was then that I carried you."

"Tali?" I returned to her voice. "Many children who have been sexually abused have serious problems when they reach adulthood."

I nodded. I wanted her to know that I was listening.

"Growing up, did you have unusual interest in sex?"

"I avoided it."

"Total avoidance?"

"I was twenty-four when I lost my virginity."

"How was the experience?"

"It was beautiful. I felt safe. I was in love."

"Are you talking about Daniel?"

"Yes."

"What about other men?"

"The only other person was with my husband."

"Do you think the two of you have a healthy sex life?"

"No. But it's not him, it's *me*."

"What do you mean by that?"

"I don't know."

Demoralized? Disheartened? Destroyed?

"Tali, we are all fallible."

But we are not all broken into. Yes, that's the word – vandalized. The Man broke into my body and tore apart my spirit. He broke me.

I wish I could have said that.

"Are you okay, Tali?"

I nodded. I just nodded.

"Are you okay to continue?"

I nodded.

"What about sleep problems or nightmares?"

"I remember one nightmare. I was trapped in an elevator with a man dressed all in black. I couldn't see his face. He sprayed gasoline on me and then threw a match. I burst into flames and watched myself burn to death."

"That's a horrible dream. Was it after your abduction?"

I nodded. "It was right after."

"What do you think it means?"

"I felt trapped. I was in trouble and nobody was there to help me. I watched myself disappear. A part of me died that day."

"Anything else?"

"Nobody saw me get into the limousine? It was morning rush hour. How could nobody see me?" I was crying.

She passed me a tissue. After a moment of silence, "It's okay, Tali."

"I became so withdrawn. I spent a lot of time alone. I didn't feel like I fit in anywhere."

"Do you feel like you fit in now?"

"Now I really don't care if I fit in or not. It's more important for me to have a sense of purpose."

"What gives you that sense of purpose?"

"Helping people."

"How do you feel when you're not helping people?"

"I'm not sure."

"That's okay."

I nodded.

"Did you miss a lot of school?"

"No, I loved school!"

"What about drugs or alcohol?"

"No. Many kids experimented with them, but I didn't."

"When did you first tell someone what had happened to you?"

"The first person I told was Daniel. I was twenty-four. I eventually told my husband."

My mind flashed back to that day at Oyster Bay with Stuart.

Oh my God, are we done yet?

Dr. Gottlieb asked me something but I didn't hear her.

"Tali?"

I heard her call my name.

"Tali, look at me."

I did.

"Where did you go?"

I didn't answer.

"What were you thinking of while I was talking?"

I shrugged my shoulders.

"Do you know what dissociation is?"

I nodded.

"It's an instinct that most people have to help them survive an overwhelming and terrible event. It's the ability to separate your mind from your body."

Been there, done that.

"We'll take a proactive approach. Do you know what that means?"

"I need medication?"

"Although medication can help with curiosity, clarity, confidence, creativity and connectedness, also known as the five Cs, and all relevant for treating trauma, it cannot *cure* trauma. Instead, we'll start with you learning a new inner dialogue. People with dissociative disorders are often intelligent and creative. You used your intelligence and creativity to escape your childhood trauma the only way you knew how. You're not crazy. I'll teach you to identify your triggers before the symptoms appear – symptoms like negative thoughts and self-destructive behaviors."

She said I'm not crazy.

I'm not crazy.

"Enough time has gone by for you to accept what's happened. Eventually you *will* reach a place of forgiveness. Forgiving the man who hurt you, and most important, forgiving yourself. There may come a time when you will be able to revisit that day in your mind without any traumatic symptoms and you can empower and free the little girl who is still trapped inside of you."

I nodded.

She asked when I would like to come in again. I purposely asked for a different day and time. It made me feel like I was in control. As if controlling my appointment could turn back time.

She agreed. She did not have to be in control.

The following week Dr. Gottlieb allowed me to rant without interruption. "I'm scared I won't move on. I can't move on. I'm scared to trust people, even myself. I can't stand myself. I'm so angry. I'm afraid of exploding, of hurting someone, physically, mentally, I don't know. Who knows why people do what they do? He was sick. Maybe he was molested. He needed help. Nobody helped him. Oh my God, what if you can't help me?" I started to cry.

"Healing is a choice. You can and will overcome this trauma. We'll do it together. We'll begin with regaining a sense of self-esteem and coping with guilt feelings."

I believed her. I liked that she said *we*. She recommended reading *Stolen Tomorrows: Understanding and Treating Women's Childhood Sexual Abuse* by Steven Levenkron and *The Courage to Heal* by Ellen Bass and Laura Davis.

In the following months I learned from Dr. Gottlieb that my anger was not my primary feeling.

"First there is an activating event, let's say, the abduction, which stirs up an uncomfortable feeling and creates a consequence, let's say, anger. Anger is the drug dealer, standing on the corner of your mind, yanking your chain every time you give in to your habitual negative thoughts."

And I am the loyal customer with a serious habit. I know I have to change.

"You can break this chain with your free will. You can choose to meet anger with sympathy. You can choose to meet contempt with compassion. When you're no longer buying the negative thoughts, they'll be no more dealing."

Dr. Gottlieb handed me a pamphlet, *Rational Emotive Behavioral Therapy* (REBT), written by Dr. Albert Ellis. "It's not the activating events that cause your anger, but rather your irrational beliefs. You can learn to think more rationally. I'll teach you to be less demanding of yourself. I'll teach you to change the irrational thoughts like – should, shouldn't, have to, need and must – into the more rational thought – prefer."

In another session she said, "Don't rush to end your marriage. You'll know when the time is right."

"How will I know?"

"Trust me, you'll know."

Dr. Gottlieb told me that she was moving out of state in a month and gave me the name and phone number of a colleague on Long Island.

I hated the thought of starting over with someone new. I took a deep breath, imagined myself crawling out of my former self and leaving it behind, much like a caterpillar molting.

Please, God, help me to accept the things I cannot change.

"She specializes in childhood sexual abuse. You'll love working with her. Her name is Dr. Miriam Remsay."

thirteen

Before I went to a new therapist, I wanted to connect with my Jewish roots. Not having gone to Hebrew school, I felt that I was missing out on Torah knowledge. I had only read the first two books, Genesis and Exodus. I wanted to see if Judaism could satisfy my twin longings for self-discovery and spirituality. And I was intrigued by the mysteries of *Kabbalah*, meaning "to receive."

When I was seventeen years old, I read Marilyn vos Savant's column in the *Newsday Parade* magazine. Every week people would send in questions and she would select two or three to answer. One day a woman asked, "What is the best way to grow as a person?" Marilyn's answer: "Travel to a foreign country by yourself."

I had thought to myself, *By yourself? Why would anybody want to do that?*

At thirty-five years old, her answer felt right. I told Stuart that I wanted to go to Israel by myself. I needed some time and space.

"I won't stop you."

I signed up for the "Eight Day Israel Tour."

My Mom was upset, "I don't want you to go. It sounds dangerous." When she finally realized that I was not asking for her permission she said, "*Gay gezunta hait, kim ahame gezunta hait* (Go in good health and come home in good health)."

When I arrived in Tel Aviv, it was quiet, but there was a policeman standing on every corner with his hand firmly holding a rifle.

The first thing I purchased was a gold ring for myself. It said *DEVORAH* in Hebrew. In the land of my fathers it felt good to have Grandma with me. I also bought diamond stud earrings and wore them out of the store. In Safed I purchased a beautiful candle composed of blue, green and yellow waxes braided together. It was my first *havdalah* candle. *Havdalah* means separation and it's used at the end of *Shabbat* (Sabbath) as a gesture for its light to linger for the week.

In Jerusalem, a pretty young girl with knotty hair, dirty clothes and no shoes held up a spool of red yarn. "Would you like to buy a bracelet for protection?"

"Of course. How much?"

She looked at an older woman, six feet away, who sat on the ground holding a baby. She held up her index finger.

"One dollar."

I put out my right wrist.

"No, the other one." She wrapped the red string around my left wrist, tied a few knots and cut it with a pair of scissors.

"Thank you so much." I handed her a five dollar bill and waved goodbye.

The most meaningful part of the trip for me was my visit to the *Kibbutz Beit Yisrael* where there was a lecture on *Kabbalah*, the mystical teachings of Judaism. The lecturer was Rabbi Solomon.

He opened with a question, "What sorts of things would you like to receive in life?"

Peace of mind, a sense of purpose, love. Am I asking for too much?

A man in the audience called out, "Money." From the back of the room I heard a woman say, "A nice house." A young man in his twenties called out, "Cars. Fast cars." "Beautiful clothes and jewelry," from a woman who was dressed in beautiful clothes and jewelry. An older woman in the front row said, "Health."

"Why do we want the money?" the rabbi asked.

"To buy us all the things we want," said the young man who wanted fast cars.

"And when you buy these things, how will you feel?"

"Happy," he answered.

"When you're happy, you'll also feel what?" The rabbi pointed to an older man for an answer.

"At peace and more secure?"

"So, it's not really the money or the material things that we want, but it's the feeling of peace and security that we get from them, yes?"

Twenty heads nodded in agreement.

"The things we really want in life boil down to an energy that we cannot see. It presents itself in the physical world, the one percent realm, as happiness, peace and contentment.

"Understand that our five senses – sight, hearing, smell, taste and touch – fool us. We don't have the ability to perceive all things the way they actually are. How many of you have ever made a decision that you thought was right but turned out to be wrong? Raise your hands."

Everyone raised their hand.

I got into the white limousine. I raised my hand.

"Don't ignore your five senses, but learn to rely more on the other ninety-nine percent of unseen energy. What's that called?"

The room was quiet. I thought, *Sixth sense.*

"Your sixth sense, your intuition, your inner voice. Whatever you want to call it. It's the ninety-nine percent realm."

He went on to explain that in the ninety-nine percent realm there is harmony. Things do not happen suddenly because we can perceive the relationship between cause and effect. It's only in the one percent realm, the physical universe where we live, that things happen suddenly.

I had always wanted to understand that traumatic day in my past, but I first needed to see the cause and effect.

The rabbi reached for the water bottle on the podium, unscrewed the cap, lifted the bottle to his lips, took a sip and set the bottle back down.

The Man in the white limousine asks for help.

I want to help.

The Man opens the door.

I should go straight to school. But I really want to help.

The Man locks the door.

I know I made a mistake.

The Man drives away.

I was already gone. In the time it took to take a sip of water, I was already gone.

The rabbi cleared his throat.

I was back.

Rabbi Solomon continued, "The ninety-nine percent realm – the realm beyond our five senses – contains *spiritual* energy. *Kabbalists* call it *"Or"* – Hebrew for *Light* – because Light is all-giving. It's endless. The nature of Light is to share its energy. It lacks only one thing. Anyone know what that is?"

No one answered.

He said, "A recipient, a Vessel. *Us.* We live in the one percent realm."

He drew on the board.

LIGHT   →   VESSEL
99%   1%

Someone asked, "So in the one percent realm, the physical realm, you have the five senses. So what does the 100 percent realm represent? That is, Light is 99 percent of what?"

"A very good question, but please understand that the 100 percent realm equals the spiritual realm, the Light, plus the physical realm, the Vessel."

We must have looked confused.

"Please," he asked, "turn around and take a look at the coffee maker in the back of the room."

We all turned around. It looked like an ordinary coffee maker.

"The coffee in the pot is unseen," he said. "It's there, but we don't see it. In order for the coffee to be revealed, we place a cup, a recipient, underneath it." He walked toward the back of the room, placed a clear glass under the machine and pushed a button. Coffee poured into the cup. "As this cup receives the coffee, it also reveals it." He walked back to the front of the room with his cup of coffee. "So it is with the Light. The Light is received by the Vessel and is also revealed by the Vessel."

He takes a sip of coffee. "We become the recipient of the Light after we desire something good and work hard to accomplish it."

I desired to help The Man. That was something good. But The Man was darkness.

I should have gone straight to school.

I should have gone straight to school.

The recurring thought brought burning tears to my eyes.

The rabbi looked at me, "Are you okay?"

Yes, I nodded.

He smiled, "You're really taking this all in, aren't you?"

I gave my best pretend smile.

If you only knew.

The rabbi wrote on the board, "The Bread of Shame."

"This means receiving something that was not earned. The Vessel keeps receiving from the Light with no means of giving

97

back to the Light. The Vessel wants to *be* like the Light in a similar way that a student wants to be like the mentor."

I wish Daniel were here.

"The Vessel now wants to share. The student now wants to teach. But it can't share with the Light because its nature is to receive from the Light. The Vessel will always have a desire to receive from the Light. The student will always have the desire to receive from the mentor. That is the nature of our soul. Understand?"

I did.

"So the Vessel has this Bread of Shame. If the Light doesn't allow the Vessel to share in return, the Vessel will no longer want to receive from the Light. So the only thing the Vessel can do to remove The Bread of Shame is to reject the Light."

He drew a big 'X' across the arrow.

"Now, the Vessel restricts the Light. The Light still shares. It's only from the Vessel's point of view that it does not receive. Now what does the Vessel experience?"

The older woman said, "Darkness."

"Yes, what else?"

"Emptiness?" said Beautiful Clothes and Jewelry.

A hand went up.

"Yes, please, you have a question?"

"How does *giving* equate to *energy* and the 99 percent realm?"

"So, although we cannot be the Light, there will be times when we act like the Light, giving, like the mentor, teaching, and other times when we act like the Vessel, receiving, like the student, learning. The key is balance. We should avoid both giving and receiving The Bread of Shame.

"Finally, when we, as Vessels, act like the Light and we remove our Bread of Shame, we get more Light. The Light is endless whether or not we choose to receive it. We are responsible for the amount of Light we receive and reveal in our lives.

"I have one final comment. An important Kabbalistic ideology is: Never – and that means never – blame others for your negative thoughts and actions. If God, the Creator, is in everything, then we must embrace that everything that happens *to* us happens *for* us. Look for the opportunity to grow and you will never feel like a victim. Thank you for coming. God bless you."

Wow. That's going to take some time to process.

"Thank you, Rabbi. I understand cause and effect in a way different than before."

There is no shame in wanting to help people. We intuitively help people because this is how we act like the Light.

"*L'shana Haba B'Yerushalayim.* Next year in Jerusalem."

"I've heard that before. What does it mean?"

"Jerusalem means 'city of peace.' The goal is to attain internal peace of mind, body and soul and external peace for the world. Every time we say this one-line prayer, we hope that everyone and everything can be at peace, living in a place of balance between giving and receiving."

"Yes," I said, "Next year in Jerusalem."

fourteen

I returned home from Israel feeling revived. I was inspired to move forward. I listened for the small voice within me – the one I hoped had followed me home.

To receive more guidance, I went for the first time to my local temple, introduced myself to Rabbi Levine and enrolled in his weekly Judaism class. To return the Light, I spent time food shopping with the rabbi's wife and helped her modify her meals to make them healthier for her family.

By this time, Stuart and I were living separate lives under the same roof. This was not okay with me. I wanted our relationship to have meaning.

After another month of crying, I knew what I had to do. Dr. Gottlieb had said I would. I had to leave my marriage and start over. I told Stuart.

He gave me a resigned look and said, "I love you too much to see you so unhappy." He recognized that we had come to the end of the road. Within a week I moved out of our house and into my aunt and uncle's house two miles away. I went back to our house only to see my clients. I stopped crying; the anxiety about what to do was gone.

Aunt Kim and Uncle Lloyd were in their early fifties and more than accommodating in allowing me to use one of their empty bedrooms. My stay with them was bittersweet. For the first time, I saw their close intimacy, mutual comfort and playful banter, which I missed in my own relationship.

Will I ever have that?

I believe that everything happens for a reason. I had to marry Stuart to learn that there are good men out there. My marriage may have failed but it began my transformation. Life was not what I imagined the day I stood under the *chuppah* and told Stuart that I would love him forever.

It wasn't until several weeks after I moved out that I began to learn how to care for myself in normal physical ways. I wrapped myself up in a blanket as if I had my very own cocoon. I made myself hot tea, restarted my exercise routine and attended self-awareness classes. I learned to do whatever was comforting. I learned to do it without guilt.

I was sad but not depressed. I was filled with hope that I would find my new "self" and fulfill my sense of purpose.

If there were such a thing as a cordial divorce, Stuart and I had one. We remained more considerate of each other than our attorneys did. We should have gotten a mediator instead. My attorney wanted me to fight for Stuart's pension, his apartment in the city and his new Harley Davidson.

Two years earlier Stuart had brought me into a Harley dealer. It was right after we looked at refrigerators, dishwashers and ovens at P.C. Richards.

The first thing I saw when I walked into the showroom was this sparkling red motorcycle. "That's gorgeous," I said. "I love the side bags."

"Those are called saddlebags," Stuart said, as he caressed the passenger seat. "It's the Electra Glide Sport."

"I love the color."

"Victory Red. The motor's 1340 cc."

That meant nothing to me.

"I was hoping you'd like it," he said in a whisper.

"You're riding out of here on our new kitchen, aren't you?"

I was happy for Stuart when he bought the bike. He never asked for anything for himself. I knew that I never made him that happy.

"No, no, no," I told my attorney.

His attorney wanted him to fight for half of my business.

He had built my home office with his own two hands. Every night after work, he had knocked down walls, put up sheet rock, plastered and painted. Stuart did this for me – for us.

"No," he told his attorney.

We both fought for our respect for one another. We won.

Despite the chrysanthemums in full bloom, on October 29, 1999, Stuart and I walked into the Courthouse of Nassau County to fill out the paperwork for our divorce. On the third of November, at nine-fifty-three in the morning, the paperwork was approved and we were granted our Judgment of Divorce from the County Clerk.

I took off my wedding band and put it into the safe deposit box at the bank. I thought that removing it would increase the flow of blood to my heart. I had learned in anatomy class that only the ring finger has a vein connecting it directly to the heart. But instead I felt as if the finger had been severed.

Too much pain; too little freedom.

In the news, South African Judge Edwin Cameron announced he was HIV-positive. For the first time ever there were more women living with HIV disease in Africa than men. The number of known deaths in the U.S. in 1999 was 18,491.

By December, I bought out Stuart's share of the house and he moved back into his Manhattan apartment. It was less stressful living and working in the same space again.

I found one big box of letters that Stuart had sent me through the years. I was told by close friends, "throwing everything out makes it easier." But it wasn't easy; I couldn't throw out ten years of my life.

I also found a videotape. I put it into the VCR and pressed play. The color bars appeared on the screen, then the countdown, and then finally the title, *Tali and Stuart's Wedding*.

I listened to the song "Sunrise, Sunset" play as photos of me from infancy to adulthood came and went. I knew that I was the only one who caught the photo where the innocent little girl disappeared and the terror-stricken child appeared.

Childhood trauma isn't something that just goes away. I still haven't grown out of it.

The song "Forever Young" followed while I watched Stuart grow up. "Endless Love" captured photos of us together in the short year we had known each other. The final photo was at my parents' house, the night we got engaged.

My college roommate Sheryl was visiting. She told me that she had just called off her January wedding. I wasn't surprised; I knew he drank too much. We sat in my dining room healing our hearts, a bottle of red wine for her and a pint of frozen yogurt for me.

"What am I going to do with my dream honeymoon?"

"Can you cancel it?" I didn't know what else to say.

"It's nonrefundable."

"Is there someone else you can go with?"

"I'd only want to go with someone fun."

After a moment of hesitation, "Am I fun?"

"*Ohmygawd*, you're so much fun."

I went downstairs to my office to get my new appointment book for 2000. I opened it to January. The moment I inked in "African Safari," a new and spontaneous Tali was born.

fifteen

Sheryl and I took off from JFK airport. We landed on time in Johannesburg, South Africa, picked up our rental car and drove nearly five hours to Botswana. It was a perfect drive on the wrong side of the road.

Savior, our safari leader, took us in a cable car across the Limpopo River. We then drove forty minutes to The Mashatu Animal Safari Park while learning about Botswana. It is a very wealthy country with a population of only 250,000 people. Its wealth is from the De Beers' diamond mines. The government pays for everyone's schooling even if citizens choose to study abroad. Citizens work for the government for one year before the government finds them a job in their chosen field. Although citizens pay for the cost of their homes, the government gives them the land.

During one afternoon safari, Savior told us everything we wanted to know about the elephants. They are the largest land mammals and have a life expectancy of about sixty years. They communicate over huge distances by low-frequency sounds that we cannot hear. They have a highly developed social system with supportive, matriarchal family units that travel in herds, and they eat about six hundred pounds of food every day. It takes twenty-two months for the calf to be born, weighing, on average, two hundred and sixty pounds. Delivery lasts thirty seconds and other females guide the newborn to the mama's nipple for its first suckle. The calf sucks with its mouth, not with its trunk. Within two hours of birth, the baby is walking alongside its mama.

Savior pointed to a dead baby elephant with its face eaten away. Its leg had been accidently bound and cut by a wire from a fence put up by the park. Elephant dung around the body proved that the little elephant had been mourned by his family.

In my mind the baby elephant struggled to break free from the wire. He tried again and again. I cried thinking about how many attempts he must have made before giving up.

sixteen

After my return home from safari, I found myself thinking about death. I missed Grandma Devorah and drove to the cemetery in New Jersey to visit with her and my grandfather.

DEVORAH BENDIT
BELOVED AND DEVOTED
WIFE, MOTHER AND GRANDMOTHER
APRIL 13, 1905 – FEBRUARY 10, 1980

I visited Grandma first. I knelt down onto the ground wet from snow, took off my *Devorah* ring and placed it on her footstone next to the word "Grandmother."

Where are you, Grandma? This can't be the end.

I thought of the beautiful *23rd Psalm* of David, "Surely your goodness and love will follow me all the days of my life, and I will dwell in the house of the Lord forever."

I whispered, "I miss you so much. You taught me that every minute can make a difference in the spirit of another human being. This difference can never be lost."

But, I'm lost, Grandma. I've been lost since I was nine years old. How can I find myself if I don't even know where to look?

I was crying. "Grandma, tell me again what my name means." I caressed the word "Grandmother" with my fingertips. "Tell me I'm blessed. Tell me I'm strong." With the back of my hand I wiped my nose.

I slipped my ring back onto my finger and put a stone in its place. A small stone on a Jewish grave inspires the living to visit their loved ones. When passersby see the stones, they're happy that the deceased had visitors. A stone signifies a permanent memory that will never fade.

"I love you, Grandma." I kissed my fingers and placed them on the word "Grandmother." I closed my eyes and sang the *Shema* prayer: *"Shema Yisroel, Adonai Eloheinu Adonai Echad* (Hear O Israel, Lord is our God, Lord is One)."

I moved over to Grandpa's gravesite two feet away and placed a rock on his footstone.

HYMAN BENDIT
BELOVED HUSBAND,
FATHER AND GRANDFATHER
JANUARY 12, 1903 – AUGUST 27, 1986

I'm sorry that we weren't closer.

I recited the *Shema*.

I sat in my car, stared out at the hundreds of unknown burial plots and wondered how many of the deceased, including Grandma and Grandpa, had given any thought to their life purpose. Were they happy with how their lives turned out? Did they settle for less than they had dreamed of in their jobs or with their spouses? Did they really love their children? Had they learned to rise above adversity?

Leaving the cemetery, I drove past a funeral service where the collective mourners were most likely reflecting on the life of their loved one. A young girl, holding a bouquet of flowers, was crying. Tears, once again, welled up in my eyes as I tried to imagine how many secrets were also buried here.

seventeen

Judaism teaches that we are obligated to acknowledge our misdeeds to those we have hurt. Through my studies, I was learning to ask for forgiveness and make restitution. Rabbi Levine told me to search within my soul to find out what caused me to transgress in the first place. This would help me not to repeat the same mistake. This is called *teshuvah* (repentance).

It was now seven months since our divorce. Stuart and I remained friends. We spoke about once a month.

I asked, "How are you?"

"Okay. How are you?"

"I'd like to ask a favor." There must have been sadness in my voice.

"What's the matter, Tal?"

"Would you agree to a *get?*"

"A what?"

I wasn't sure if he didn't understand what I said because I was crying or because he didn't know what it meant. "A *get*. It's a Jewish spiritual divorce. I need to do this to move on."

"Of course, Tal. Whatever you need."

"I'm so sorry, Stu. For everything."

"Me too."

The civil decree was not enough for me to let go. Let go of what? I didn't know. I hoped a spiritual divorce would give me a real sense of closure.

I Googled "Jewish divorce." *Wikipedia* said that, according to the Torah, a Jewish marriage ends when the husband gives his wife a *get*. This document is written in Hebrew and given to the wife in the presence of qualified witnesses. As described in Deuteronomy 24:1: "A man takes a wife and possesses her. If she fails to please him because he finds something obnoxious about her, he writes her a bill of divorcement, hands it to her, and sends her away from his house."

This sounded like a joke.

I thought asking Stuart for a *get* would empower me, but instead it reminded me of the trauma, my flaws and my failed marriage.

On Friday, June 16, 2000, we met the *mesader gittin'* (a rabbi with special training in divorce law) in a private office in the Orthodox Rabbinical Court on Long Island. Rabbi Moshe Silverman explained what was about to take place.

He nodded to the five men in the room, all of whom were wearing suits, ties and *yarmulkes* on their heads, with *tzitzit* showing from underneath their shirts. He spoke each word distinctly, "These witnesses will thoroughly examine the *get*. This man," he touched the arm of the tallest man in the room, "the *scribe,* wrote the *get.* "

He looked at us both. "Understand?"

We nodded our heads. Stuart looked calm. I was nauseated.

Rabbi Silverman brought both of his hands to his chest. "After I, the supervising rabbi, ascertain that the *get* has been properly prepared and that all the parties to this transaction have been properly identified, and that both the husband" – he looked into

Stuart's eyes – "and the wife" – he looked into my eyes – "are acting out of free will and without coercion, and that no one has made any statements which might contradict the terms of the *get,* we will begin."

When the rabbi was satisfied with our answers, he told me, "Remove all jewelry from your hands."

I wasn't sure if I was allowed to speak. I raised my hands to show that I wasn't wearing any jewelry.

He nodded his head. "Hold your hands together with open palms upward in a position to receive the *get.*"

I did what I was told.

The scribe folded the *get* and gave it to Rabbi Silverman.

The rabbi gave the *get* to Stuart and told him to hold it in both hands and drop it into my open palms and repeat: "This is your *get* and with it you are divorced from me from this time forth so that you may become the wife of any man."

I received the *get* in my cupped palms. Rabbi Silverman told me to walk five steps away, return, and give the *get* back to him.

Rabbi Silverman read the *get* out loud in Hebrew. I didn't know what he was saying. He asked the scribe and the five witnesses to identify it and the signatures. He cut the four corners of the *get* so that the document could never be used again. He placed the pieces into an envelope and then into his folder. He gave the *p'tur,* divorce papers, to Stuart and me to certify that our marriage was now dissolved according to Jewish law.

He told me, "Should you choose to remarry, it is *your* responsibility to make sure your future husband is not a *Kohayn.*

"I'm sorry. A what?" I asked.

"A *Kohayn.* A descendant of the Priestly lineage. A *Kohayn* cannot marry a divorcée for he must remain holy. Your divorce now renders you desecrated."

Desecrated? Now I'm desecrated? I'm afraid someone has beaten you to the punch.

The rabbi told me that I would receive my certificate of proof in the mail.

On July 7, 2000, I received an envelope from Orthodox Rabbinical Court. Rabbi Silverman's note said, "Ms. Stark: Enclosed please find your original certificate of *get* from Stuart Sachs. Please keep it secure! Best wishes to you for the future. Rabbi Moshe Silverman."

All six lines were written in Hebrew. I went to Rabbi Levine for a translation:

> *"I hereby release you and send you away and put you aside so that you may be free and have control over yourself and may marry any one you desire, and no one can hinder you from doing so in my name from this day forward forever, And this will be to you a bill of letting go, a document of release and a letter of freedom, according to the law of Moses and Israel."*

"Freedom?" I told myself I should feel happy; I had gotten what I wished for. Freedom. But I was not running toward it. I felt dismissed and humiliated, unloved and unlovable.

December 31, 2000. I was standing in a huge living room in Andrew and Hera's house in Westchester. In one corner, champagne was sweating in a black ice bucket; in the other, were photos of my family. The living room was stuffed with people: my brothers, their wives, their young children and a dozen of their friends. I was alone. I had left my smile at home, but I wore my new watch, a divorce gift to myself. This Movado reminded me that I can take care of myself.

The television was on; the volume was *loud.* With my arms crossed against my chest and my legs crossed at the ankles, I waited.

The countdown began, "TEN…"

I looked around the room, filled with balloons.

"NINE…"

Women held onto their men, getting ready to lock lips.

"EIGHT…"

Men held onto their half-empty green bottles. Heineken.

"SEVEN…"

The snowflakes accumulated on the window's ledge.

"SIX…"

Laughter. High-pitched annoying laughter.

"FIVE…"

The partygoers blew the paper streamers out to full erection. I was a party pooper. I had no streamer. The final seconds of 2000 ticked away.

Goodbye and good riddance.

"FOUR…"

Dick Clark's sweet voice.

"THREE…"

Voices already sang off key.

"TWO…"

Auld Lang Syne (Times Gone By).

"ONE…"

The clock struck midnight.

"HAPPY NEW YEAR!"

Kiss, kiss, kiss. Everyone kissed to the popular Scottish poem written by Robert Burns in 1788.

I could not kiss. Nothing or nobody could enter my padlocked heart – not the champagne or laughter, not Dick Clark, not even my brothers.

eighteen

Creating a new life for myself was harder than I thought. I didn't know the rules and I didn't know where I fit in. Was I even supposed to be married? Maybe I was supposed to be alone. I rationalized that there was nothing to figure out; my being alone was *bershert*, meant to be. Instead of going back to therapy, I spent two hundred dollars for a KitchenAid mixer. Kneading bread was therapeutic. After giving away dozens of cookies, challahs and pretzels, I felt better.

I continued to work long hours; it was safer there. I waited for my intuition, my inner voice, to whisper, *Go back out there. Look for the relationship you deserve.*

For my thirty-seventh birthday I bought myself a three-month membership to an Internet dating site. I searched through too many men to count. I was not finding him. I went out on a few dates and I got scared. The men came on so strong and seemed dishonest. One man told me that he was five nine. When we met I was not in heels and, at five six, I was taller than he was. If they lied about their height, weight and age – the things I could see – what else were they lying about?

I could *never* date a man who resembled The Man. For a long time I recoiled from an aggressive touch or wet kiss. I knew my reactions scared some men away and I didn't wonder why they never called again.

It was eight in the evening on Saturday, July 14, 2001. I finished having tea with another first, and last, date. As I walked to my car, parked right in front of the restaurant, I thought about what I needed to do when I got home.

I got into my car, put the key into the ignition and reached for my seatbelt. In a flash I saw headlights in the rearview mirror and heard honking, slamming brakes and then *BAM*!

When I opened my eyes I saw a lot of people and heard sirens.

A police officer tapped on the window of my car. "Can you unlock the door?"

I shook my head no.

I couldn't move. My driver's door was smashed in, my body was pushed to the center of the front seat and my legs were trapped under the steering wheel. It hurt to breathe.

He said, "Keep your head down and close your eyes. We're going to break the back window."

What happened?

I heard the back window shatter. "We'll get you out of here. What's your name?"

I was in a lot of pain. It felt like someone was stabbing me in the lower back.

"Miss? Can you hear me? What's your name?"

"Tali," was all I could say. My mind was racing.

Who should I call? Oh my God, I feel so alone.

"Okay, Tali, we'll have you out of here in a jiff. Can you move?"

"I can move my hands and arms, but my back…"

"Tali, be calm, you're going to be okay. We've got an ambulance here already."

The next time I opened my eyes I was alone in the emergency room with curtains drawn around my bed. I was calm and not in pain.

Aunt Kim and Uncle Lloyd arrived around ten. Aunt Kim told me, "Witnesses said that a car coming out of the parking lot collided with a minibus and the minibus hit you."

I was diagnosed with a mild concussion, four herniated discs in my lumbar spine and severe muscle spasms of my cervical spine. It could have been much worse because my car was totaled. I was given a cortisone shot and told to rest. It was almost two in the morning when my aunt and uncle drove me home. They each took hold of one arm and escorted me up the steps into my bedroom, where I spent the next six weeks.

Sequestered in my room, I slipped into a depression deeper than I had ever known. Disgusted by the inability to do anything, I asked Aunt Kim to bring up some journals from my office downstairs. I hoped to catch up on some professional reading.

From one journal I read: "With depletion, iron stores are low but there is no dysfunction." It didn't register. I tried again: "With depletion, iron stores are low but there is no dysfunction."

What the hell does this mean?

"With depletion, iron stores are low but there is no dysfunction."

I threw the journal across the room.

I loathed the uninterrupted days that gave me too much time to obsess over my situation. I hadn't a clue of what I needed to do. I tried to read a book on *Kabbalah*, but nothing, not a single word, sank in. I recalled my trip to Israel and meditated on the Light, aware that I had to desire it in order to receive it. But with my mind scattered, my heart vacant and my spirit disconnected, I attracted only darkness. I told myself that I was being punished. I needed to keep busy to have some sense of control in my life. But no degree of control would enable me to turn back time.

Uncle Lloyd moved my computer from my office to my bedroom. "Now you're not alone; you have access to the Internet," he said, as if that were a good thing.

Bored and angry, I turned to the Internet and Googled "child abduction." The official site of *The National Center for Missing and Exploited Children* came up. It featured the images of too many precious little faces.

I clicked on a familiar face and date. May 25, 1979. Six-year-old Etan Patz, left his Soho apartment in lower Manhattan by himself, for the very first time, to walk two blocks to catch the school bus. He never made it. I remembered reading about this little boy when I was fifteen years old.

That would make him twenty-eight years old today.

My bedroom became my library and university. Tapping away at the keyboard of my laptop computer, I searched for more stories about children who had been abducted. I took notes on loose papers, sticky notes and napkins.

Six-year-old Adam Walsh from Hollywood, Florida.

I had watched his story on TV and I can still see his smiling, freckled face and baseball cap.

Eleven-year-old Jaycee Lee Dugard from South Lake Tahoe, California. Seven-year-old Megan Kanka from Hamilton Township, New Jersey. Nine-year-old Amber Hagerman from Arlington, Texas. Nine-year-old Michaela Joy Garecht from Hayward, California. Eleven-year-old Jacob Erwin Wetterling from St. Joseph, Minnesota. Twelve-year-old Polly Klaas, from Petaluma, California. Ten-year old Katie Beers from Bay Shore, Long Island.

Wow. Not far from where I live.

Reading about these children, these little lost children, murdered or still missing, I cried. I read that some of the abductors, rapists and killers had been caught, found guilty and sentenced to life in prison or even death. I shuffled these notes into a timeline. I needed some order in my life.

nineteen

By September I was seeing clients again and I was thrilled to start teaching nutrition classes at a local university. Still recuperating, I was not interested in dating and determined to learn more about childhood abduction and sexual abuse. I told Aunt Kim what I was doing.

"That topic is so upsetting. Why not choose something else?"

"Because..." And then I told her what had happened to me twenty-eight years ago. She looked at me but said nothing. "You're the only family member who knows."

"That's horrible." Aunt Kim paused. "And all these years you told no one? I wish we all had known." She reached for my hands and then she hugged me.

"That's why I want to talk to other victims. I want to encourage them to talk about what happened to them. I've read that trauma from childhood sexual abuse was most correlated to the time spent in secrecy – more than anything else – frequency, age and even violence."

The next day Aunt Kim bought me a notebook and suggested that I transfer all of my notes into this one book. "You're methodical, Tali. You'll figure out a way to organize it all."

I made a chart with the date the child was abducted, name, age, hometown and status. I hoped to update the MISSING to FOUND ALIVE.

DATE	NAME	AGE	HOMETOWN	STATUS
May 25, 1979	Etan Patz	6	Soho, New York City	MISSING. Jose Antonio Ramos, a convicted pedophile serving time in prison was a suspect, but there had never been enough evidence to prosecute him.
June 27, 1981	Adam Walsh	6	Hollywood, Florida	Murdered by Ottis Toole, who died in 1996, while serving multiple life sentences for at least 6 murders.
Nov 19, 1988	Michaela Joy Garecht	9	Hayward, California	MISSING.
Oct 22, 1989	Jacob Erwin Wetterling	11	St. Joseph, Minnesota	MISSING. (Jacob Wetterling Act)
June 10, 1991	Jaycee Lee Dugard	11	South Lake Tahoe, California	MISSING.
Dec 28, 1992	Katie Beers	10	Bay Shore, New York	FOUND ALIVE 2 weeks later. Family friend, John Esposito, was found guilty of kidnapping and sexual assault. He was sentenced to 15 years in prison.
Oct 1, 1993	Polly Klaas	12	Petaluma, California	Murdered by Richard Allen Davis, who was later sentenced to death.
July 29, 1994	Megan Kanka	7	Hamilton Township, New Jersey	Raped and murdered by a neighbor, Jesse Timmendequas. He received the death sentence. Her murder attracted national attention and led to the passage of "Megan's Law."
Jan 13, 1996	Amber Hagerman	9	Arlington, Texas	Murdered. Unsolved case. (AMBER ALERT)

A few days later I showed Aunt Kim the first few pages. "These are only the high-profile cases of non-family abductions. There are hundreds, thousands, more."

"What's the Jacob Wetterling Act?" she asked.

"It was the first law to require states to form registries of sex offenders. It also requires states to verify the addresses of sex offenders for at least ten years. Sexually violent predators must verify their addresses quarterly for life."

"And what's Megan's Law?"

"It requires that the public be informed of sex offenders living in their area. Nobody knew that Megan's neighbor had two previous convictions for sexually assaulting young girls."

"I've heard of the Amber Alert, but what is it?"

"It's an agreement between law enforcement, transportation and newscasters to immediately alert the public when a child goes missing."

"What happened to Amber?"

"She was abducted while riding her bike near her grandparents' home in Arlington, Texas. Her body was found four miles away four days later."

"Did they catch the guy?"

"No. There were no witnesses."

"Who are these sick people?"

I typed "Registered Sex Offenders" **in** the search engine of my computer. A collage of many faces appeared: men and women, young and old, black and white, average and good-looking.

I didn't see The Man.

"Look," I said. "I can't believe how many of these sick people are in our area."

"Some of them look normal."

"Lots of them *look* normal. Lots of them *act* normal. Some get jobs where they're near children, like coaches, counselors, clergymen and teachers."

"Oh my God."

"It says here, 'The FBI says that only one to ten percent of child sexual abuse cases are ever reported.' That means the majority of sex offenders are *not* on the registry."

"Unbelievable. That's a very scary thought."

"'Ten percent of sex offenders do not know their victims.'"

That's my offender.

"'This small group of sex offenders is the most dangerous. They usually have committed prior crimes of violence and they deny or minimize their crimes. In most cases they have a personality disorder. They are most likely the ones to abduct and physically harm a child.'"

I am lucky The Man brought me back to school.

"'The top three places an abductor imprisons a child are the abductor's car, the abductor's home and the abductor's apartment building. Most abductions are carried out within a quarter mile of the child's home.'"

"Tali, this is so upsetting. Do you think obsessing about this is the way to heal yourself?"

"Absolutely," I said with conviction.

I had a vision: Perhaps one day our children will carry an alert system just like elderly people do. It's easier to push a button than to dial a phone number. There may even come a day when we microchip our kids as well as our pets.

After Aunt Kim left, I Googled "Etan Patz." The six-year-old boy left his Soho apartment in lower Manhattan by himself, for the very first time, to walk two blocks, *two blocks*, to catch the school bus. He never made it. He's *still* missing. We will probably never know what happened to him.

I read about advances in the search for missing children since Etan's disappearance. His picture on the milk cartons was only the beginning. Unfortunately, it took hundreds of thousands of abductions for Congress to pass legislation creating The National

Center for Missing and Exploited Children. The Center monitors the FBI's database of missing children and collaborates with local law enforcement to get the word out as quickly as possible.

Since 1979, the year Etan disappeared, many laws have been passed to protect children. May 25, the day Etan disappeared, is National Missing Children's Day, proclaimed by President Reagan in 1983 in honor of the missing boy.

That night I couldn't sleep. I kept thinking about another predator – the *online* predator. In the past, we felt safe when the doors and windows were locked. Not anymore; now they can't be locked out.

The following day I called my brothers. "If the kids are going to have a computer in their room, you should monitor their use of the Internet and the websites they visit. And please use the parental controls."

They had the same response, "Since when are you so wary?"

This was the day they learned about my childhood trauma and the day that they set the security controls on their home computers.

I soon added another name to my list:

DATE	NAME	AGE	HOMETOWN	STATUS
Feb 2, 2002	Danielle Van Dam	7	San Diego, California	Murdered by neighbor, David Alan Westerfield, who had no prior criminal record.

twenty

My mom, suffering from "matchmakeritis," had created a profile for me on a dating website without my knowledge. She emailed me a note along with the profile of a man she thought I'd like.

"I wrote a letter to Richard. He matched you 50%. I told him to write back. We'll see if he answers. Take a look at his profile. His name is Big Dick."

I called her. "Really Mom? What were you thinking?"

"I don't understand. Why are you so upset?"

"How could you not understand?"

"Tali, he's six three. He's a big guy and his nickname is Dick. You think too much. What's the matter with you? Just relax. You need to get out more."

"You write to a strange man using my name, without my knowledge or my permission and you're telling me to *relax*?"

"He looks like he can take care of you."

NEWS FLASH: Tali Stark can take care of herself.

Lots of thoughts went through my mind – none of them nice.

"Bye, Mom."

"I love you. *Zie gezunt,* be healthy."

"I love you too. *Zie gezunt.*" I hung up.

I got this email from Richard, answering the email my mom had sent him: Hi, Tali: Thanks for the nice note. You are obviously smart, creative and sweet, and many of your interests align with mine. Could I have a picture so I can see who I'm "talking" with? Thanks, Richard

Do I really want to reply? Well, OK, here goes.

Hi Richard: I guess this is as good a time as any to tell you the "story." For the past several months I've been recovering from a car accident. It was my mom (bless her big heart) who found your profile. She wrote to you and asked you to write to me (without your knowledge that she was not me). I have no idea what she wrote. I know she wouldn't lie (ha). That's a conversation that I'll have with her (on Mother's Day). Tali

Richard responded after he got my photo: Dear Tali: Your smile is radiant. That's a great story about your mom. And you tell it well, especially the parenthetical "on Mother's Day." Intending only to express concern and not to pry, are you okay? Welcome back to the world of socializing.

My response: Thank you. I'll explain the accident at another time. If you would like to talk, please email me your phone number.

He sent three phone numbers: home, work and cell. I called his cell phone. He picked up after the first ring. He told me he was forty-seven, never married, no kids and worked as an international investment banker. I enjoyed talking with him. We made plans to meet in the city for lunch. But, forty-seven and never married?

I don't know.

He forwarded me Zagat's write-up for the restaurant he had chosen, Cheese Haven, in mid-Manhattan. I didn't tell him that I was lactose intolerant and was not a cheese lover. I figured I could find something on the menu.

He was tall, handsome and smiling. He kissed my right cheek, then my left. We were led to a cozy table by the fireplace. I liked that he asked me what I wanted to eat and then ordered for me.

We spoke of family, friends, work and relationships. By the end of the meal our legs touched under the table. We left holding hands. He kissed me on the cheek with little pecks. I usually didn't like that type of attention, but I didn't mind.

"Enjoy the rest of the day." I said.

I loved his reply. "It's all downhill from here."

My Mom sent me an email: This is what Richard just sent me. I didn't want to answer his email because you told me not to.

Gee, Tali, I haven't heard from you in HOURS. I hope you haven't: become overwhelmed with work; forgotten me; changed your mind; run off with another man; decided you prefer women. Xoxo Richard

He had accidentally sent the email to my mom. Months later I would regret not making any of the choices above, but at the time I enjoyed getting to know him. He seemed so capable of handling the world.

I, on the other hand, could barely handle a conversation with my mother.

In mid-March, three weeks after my lunch date with Richard, I was going through my mail when the phone rang. I picked it up on the third ring.

"Hello?" I cradled the phone to my ear with my shoulder.

Junk mail. Junk mail.

"Where were you?"

"When?"

Bill. Junk mail. Bill.

"Just now?"

"Mom, this is not a recording. It's me live. I'm home." I tossed the junk mail in the garbage.

"What took you so long to answer the phone?"

I opened up a bill.

Electric. Two hundred and eighty-eight dollars?

"Tali?"

"Yes?"

Why so much?

"How's it going?"

I opened up the phone bill.

"How's what going?"

I was pacing the kitchen for my checkbook, address labels and stamps.

"Tali, what are you doing? I'm trying to have a conversation with you."

"Ma, I'm sorry that I can't give you my undivided attention. I'm trying to pay my bills. If I don't, then Ma Bell will disconnect my phone and you won't be able to call me anymore." My voice cracked with irritation.

"Don't be upset."

"I'm not upset."

"How are things with Richard?"

"Okay I guess." I wrote out a check to the phone company.

"You've got to give him a chance. I'm sure he's a nice man."

"I'm sure he is."

"You didn't make him dinner yet, did you?"

"No." I was writing out the second check.

"Good. You should let him take you out a few times…"

Why is the electric bill so damn high?

"Did you hear me?"

"Yes. I'll give him a chance."

"I said, I hope you didn't sleep with him yet."

Lightning flashed in my eyes.

She still doesn't know me.

She said in a honeyed voice, "Don't be mad. I'm just trying to help."

"I'm not mad." I spoke through clenched teeth.

The bills were done and so was the phone call.

At the time I didn't remember that it was never the external event or person that triggered my anger. The problem was internal. A boat doesn't sink because it's surrounded by water. It sinks because it takes on water. I was taking on water. My low frustration tolerance was causing me to sink.

I added two more names to my book:

DATE	NAME	AGE	HOMETOWN	STATUS
June 5, 2002	Elizabeth Smart	14	Salt Lake City, Utah	MISSING.
July 15, 2002	Samantha Runnion	5	Stanton, California	Murdered by Alejandro Avila, acquitted of molesting two other young girls.

I grew closer to Richard and told him about my childhood trauma. I thought I was coming out of my shell and he thought I was still too inhibited. He was certain our problem all related to my past.

Ugh. Why did I even tell him?

He told me I would be fine, with his help. I ignored my sixth sense when it spelled out C-O-N-T-R-O-L-L-I-N-G.

One evening, at my house, Richard said, "I'd like you to do me a favor."

"Of course. What do you need?"

"Shave your pussy," he said with a mirthless grin. "Shave it completely bare."

I considered it for a moment. "Why?" I thought it was an odd request - I kept myself neatly trimmed.

"Why can't you just do what I ask you to do?" He looked grim.

My voice shook, "Wouldn't that make you feel like you were having sex with a child?"

His eyes turned arctic. "I don't need this aggravation."

A wild energy raced through my body. With my hands in my hip pockets, I picked at the lining, tearing apart the double-stitched seam like I was picking at an old scab.

His parting words had something to do with my missing his dick.

If I were younger, I would have cried. Instead, knowing that I did not want him in my life any longer, I looked away. I took a deep breath and stood with my arms crossed. I watched his back until it disappeared through my front door. I double-locked the door behind him. A strange, calm urgency came over me.

twenty-one

Although Daniel and I no longer worked together, I spoke with him often on the phone. This time his voice sounded different. I sensed something was wrong. I told him that I wanted to see him.

I met him at his apartment. He opened the door wearing baggy jeans and a Polo shirt. He was clean-shaven but looked thin and tired. He promised me that everything was all right. I promised him the same, but he didn't believe me either.

When he prodded me for more information, I told him about the list of child abductions that I had been keeping. "The list keeps getting longer. I just added five-year-old Samantha Runnion from California."

"What happened?"

"She had been sexually abused and strangled. Her body was found fifty miles away in Cleveland National Forest. They matched the DNA found on her body to a man who had been acquitted of molesting his ex-girlfriend's daughter and niece who lived in the same housing complex as Samantha. How do people keep getting away with this?"

"Life isn't always fair, Sweetie. You know that. Keep on updating the list. You'll know what to do with it when the time is right. I think this will be very healing for you."

He pulled out the chess board and asked if I wanted to play. About twenty minutes into the game, with most of my good men captured, I went into the kitchen. I saw an open box of Entenmann's Ultimate Crumb Cake on the counter. I returned to the living room carrying a tray with a mug of coffee for Daniel, tea for me, two forks and two plates with sliced crumb cake.

We talked about his youngest daughter, who had just returned from France where she was studying poetry.

I said, "Lara must get that talent from you."

"Maybe, but I don't write that much poetry anymore. What about you?"

"I write best when I'm melancholy."

"Most great writers are depressed. I, on the other hand, write better when I feel well." He placed a piece of cake in his mouth. "I'm on antidepressants."

"Oh, Daniel, why?"

"Let's just say, I'm not as strong as I used to be." He lifted up his mug.

I lifted up mine.

"*Salud, Dinero, y Amor… y tiempo para gastarlos,*" he toasted.

"I remember: Health, Money and Love… and time to enjoy them."

"Atta girl."

I clicked his mug.

"It's your turn, Sweetie."

I moved my pawn from E4 to D5, capturing his pawn.

He said, "The bishop is the elephant in this game. You may think it's slow but the truth is these elephants are just as fast as the rook, but in a different way." He then moved his bishop diagonally from C8 to G4. "Check."

I moved my king from D1 to its original spot on E1.

Daniel moved his queen from D8 to E7. "Check."

I moved my king to F1.

He moved his knight from H5 to G3. "Check."

I could only move my king from F1 to F2.

Daniel moved one last time, sliding his queen down from E7 to E2. "Checkmate."

I was happy he won but sad the game was over.

He said. "We keep ourselves busy to keep our sense of control." He stopped and touched my hand. "Then something happens and we're shown that we don't have as much control as we thought."

I need to have control.

"Unless you're the queen!" I held up the piece before putting it into the box.

"Even if you're the queen, you're held to the laws of the game."

"What are you saying?"

"Thomas Huxley said, 'The chessboard is the world, the pieces are the phenomena of the universe, the rules of the game are what we call the laws of nature and the player on the other side is hidden from us.' You see, you need to learn the rules but you don't have to follow them all the time."

I sensed he was trying to tell me something but I didn't know what he was talking about.

"Some people think freedom is being able to do whatever they want, but true freedom occurs when you are unaffected by external circumstances. No matter what's going on around you, fight to remain loyal to your purpose and do your best."

With a lump in my throat I said, "Is there an external circumstance that you want to talk about?"

"No, Sweetie."

He insisted on driving me home to Long Island. I agreed that he could take me to Penn Station. On this clear August night lots of people were walking the streets at eight o'clock. The smell of barbecued chicken and roasted potatoes lingered when we passed an elegant restaurant.

Daniel drove and I sat in the passenger seat. We were traveling west on Forty-third Street. I saw miscalculations in his eye-hand-foot coordination as he darted back and forth between the yellow cabs. Suddenly Daniel stepped on the gas instead of the brake. We hit the cab in front of us.

Daniel cradled his head in his hands, tilted his head back and shook it in disbelief. I saw a look of suffering in his eyes. I knew something was *very* wrong but I was afraid to ask what it was. Fortunately, no one was hurt.

A few days later Daniel called and left a message: "Hi, Sweetie. I'm here at Sloan Kettering. I was wondering if you would be able to drop by to say hello. I don't need anything. Just your smile."

Sloan Kettering is a cancer hospital.

I made plans to go into the city first thing in the morning.

That night I dreamed, I was alone walking very slowly up a big mountain covered with snow. The ground beneath me shook as the snow cascaded down. The trees fell like dominoes. Buried beneath this avalanche, I couldn't tell which way was up. Frantically, I dug through the snow. I told myself that I was getting closer to the Light, but I was actually digging myself further down into the darkness.

I visited Daniel in the hospital. He asked how my project on abducted children was going, but I changed the subject. I asked what was going on with him. He avoided the question. I fed him ice cream and held his hand until he fell asleep.

I wanted to call his family to get the truth, but I didn't. I was certain that I couldn't handle it.

twenty-two

The following week Daniel was discharged home. I traveled into Manhattan as often as possible to see him. At each visit I brought six homemade peanut butter cups, one for him, one for me, one for his nurse and three extras. When Daniel no longer ate his serving, I ate mine and his to hide the evidence – from myself – that he was not getting better.

September 10, 2002. My first home visit with Daniel. I arrived early afternoon and introduced myself to his nurse, Peter. He was a big man, over six feet, about two hundred twenty pounds. He was around fifty, fair-skinned and had a clean- shaven face.

I asked Peter, "What's going on?"

"He doesn't want you to know," was all he said.

"What do you mean?"

"I'm sorry. Those are my instructions from Dr. Benson."

"I don't understand."

"All he said was that he didn't want you to know."

Books, papers and Ensure Plus surrounded Daniel in his home hospital bed. The room smelled of rubbing alcohol. The blinds were half open to allow some light to enter. On his nightstand sat the Don Quixote paperweight that I had given him years ago. The empty video holder of *Man of La Mancha* sat on top of the TV set. Peter O'Toole sang in the background:

"... This is my quest,
to follow that star –
no matter how hopeless,
no matter how far..."

Above the bed, displayed on the wall, was a copy of Gustav Klimt's most popular painting, *The Kiss*. Love and passion are very much alive as two lovers embrace, their bodies interweaved in gold and vibrant-colored robes.

Daniel's skin was pale. His wire-framed glasses magnified his bloodshot green eyes.

Peter O'Toole continued:

"...To fight for the right
without question or pause,
to be willing to march into
hell for a heavenly cause.
And I know if I'll only be true
to this glorious quest..."

I sat in the chair by Daniel's bedside and held his hand, lacing my fingers in his until our two hands made one fist.

"...that my heart will be peaceful
and calm when I'm laid to my rest.
And the world will be better for this..."

We stared at the television, but we were not watching it, only listening to the words.

"...that one man scorned and covered with scars
still strove with his last ounce of courage.
To reach the unreachable stars."

Daniel's eyes closed.

September 12. Daniel kept saying that by the end of the month he would be back to his normal self. I believed him even though he was very short of breath.

"How are you, Sweetheart?" I asked.

"Fine, Sweetie."

September 19. Daniel sat in his chair for an hour trying to pay his bills. He couldn't focus. His three daughters were visiting. Lara, in her late twenties, Alison, in her early thirties, and Katie, in her early forties.

Katie said to me, "Dad really appreciates you being here. We all do."

September 21. "I remember the first day I met you," I said to Daniel, thinking back to that happy day.

"I remember as well, Sweetie. What do *you* remember?"

"Aside from your gorgeous green eyes," I smiled, "I remember looking at the *New York Times* plaque about your 'Self-Experiment in Medicine.'"

"Was that before or after our chess game?"

I laughed. "That was after I lost the game."

"But you still got the job, Sweetie. Remember, it's not if you win or lose, it's how you play the game. You played a good game."

"And you know what else I remember?" I asked. "Your self-experiment proved that folic acid deficiency can result from a poor diet. Because of you, cereals are now enriched with folic acid and pregnant woman have healthier babies. I'm so proud of you."

"Please bring my briefcase over to me. It's by the desk."

I placed the black leather bag on the bed and unzipped it."

"Thank you." He took an envelope out and handed it to me. I recognized the "D.B." in my handwriting. I opened it up. It was dated January 8, 1994. He passed me another one. It was a birthday card from me, dated the same year. And another card tucked into a blue envelope, this one marked "Daniel."

"Look," he pointed to dozens of notes and cards. "I saved them all, Sweetie. It is me who is so proud of you."

I had also saved everything he had given me, but I was too choked up to tell him: every card, letter and even notes written on napkins from restaurants:

• From Albert Einstein: I must be willing to give up what I am in order to become what I will be.

• From *Song of Songs:* You have stolen my heart with one glance of your eyes.

September 28. I sat and held his hand while I listened to whatever he wanted to say. I did not have any comforting words for him. I prayed that he was not in pain, that there was some miracle that could reverse whatever was going on. I still didn't know what was going on and I still didn't want to know.

October 2. I woke up a little past four in the morning. I felt better after skipping rope for an hour. I hadn't felt this anxious in a long time. Daniel slept most of the day.

October 4. I went with Peter and Daniel for his appointment with the neurologist. The doctor confirmed that he had lost all movement in his left leg. While Peter ran errands, I pushed Daniel in his wheelchair to the Sloan Kettering cafeteria for lunch. Daniel ordered fried clams and fries – a dietitian's nightmare – and dipped it in salsa. He ate less than half of it. While we waited for Peter to return, Daniel rested his head in my hands. The people around us smiled sympathetically. They probably thought he was my dad. I wish I had been brave enough to tell them that he was not my dad, but the love of my life.

Daniel asked, "What have you been working on?"

"I'm still teaching nutrition at the university."

"I'm sure you're a great teacher."

"I had a great role model."

He smiled. "And the missing children?"

"I'm still keeping track."

"You can question the past, Tal, that's fine. But you've got to break away from the past in order to live in the present."

"I will."

"Don't wait too long."

"I won't."

"You promise?"

"Yes. Soon. I promise."

October 5. Daniel asked me to read to him. I read Rabbi Moshe Chaim Luzzatto's *Derekh Hashem* (*The Way of God*), written around 1740:

> *"The soul only improves through struggles. It gets perfected after being challenged. The physical world consists of urges and desires versus the spiritual world where there is harmony through delayed gratification. We mourn the loss of human beings. The soul goes back to heaven. How reconnected they get to God depends on their ability to produce mitzvot in the physical world. This is the only place to 'produce' (to earn our paycheck). We are here to have the struggles. Our purpose is to overcome them so that we become closer to God."*

"I love you, Tal."

"I love you, Sweetheart."

"Take the book home. Finish reading it."

Daniel was still teaching me. For the first time in months I felt resilient.

As I walked down Third Avenue from Daniel's apartment to Penn Station, a scruffy homeless man walking toward me said, "I'm hungry."

I kept walking.

"I have AIDS and I'm hungry."

Here's my chance to do a mitzvah.

"C'mon, I'll get you something to eat."

"Can I have pizza?"

"Anything you want."

"Can I have two slices?"

"As many as you'd like."

"Can I have a root beer?"

"Of course."

"Can I get two Sicilian slices and a root beer?"

"Absolutely."

I paid the seven dollars and change. "You take care of yourself, okay?"

"Yeah, thanks. I really appreciate this."

Everyone carries a spark of the Creator. This could have been me. The scared meets the scarred again. Thank You, God.

October 10. It was hard to concentrate. I tried to read for fifteen minutes straight – I couldn't. I lay down in bed with *The Way of God.* I prayed. I cried, but now my tears were from joy. I felt fortunate to have experienced this kind of love.

October 11. I visited Daniel with my homemade matzo ball soup and peanut butter cups. I was glad I brought extra because Daniel's former wife, Mandy, was visiting with their youngest daughter, Lara, who had just gotten engaged.

Lara said to her dad, "You're walking me down the aisle next October, right?"

"Of course I will."

He won't make it.

Before I left, Daniel said to me, "Just like in the game of chess, each move you make should bring you closer to checkmate.

What's happening in the news isn't just *news*. Your actions can affect it. You can help change the headlines. Keep doing what you're doing. One day your actions will help someone." He gave me a newspaper clipping. "This is for your notebook."

I added another name:

DATE	NAME	AGE	HOMETOWN	STATUS
Oct 6, 2002	Shawn Hornbeck	11	Richwoods, Missouri	MISSING.

October 12. "He hasn't eaten all day," Peter said as soon as he let me in.

Daniel looked busy sitting behind his desk in the living room.

I said, "Daniel, would you like to join me for a snack?"

"After I post these important messages." He wanted the sticky notes up on the wall.

"Would you like me to do that for you?"

"Okay, but first I want to read them to you."

"Okay."

"First, Katie's boy, my grandson, is celebrating his birthday in March. He's turning two years old." He paused to take a breath. "Second, Lara is getting married next October. Will you make these into posters for me?"

"Of course."

How precious.

His priorities had changed from deadline dates and speaking engagements around the world to a baby's birthday party and a wedding.

Daniel asked to be moved back to bed. Peter called for me after he had settled Daniel in.

"You will be granted fifteen hundred years of no pain," Daniel said to me. "It's guaranteed."

"Starting when?"

"Next month."

Next month?

Daniel was not making sense. A deep pain touched my heart. He said something about his soul. I was listening, but I couldn't hear.

"I love you because you have a beautiful soul," I said.

"Thank you, Sweetie. I'm so tired. Can you stay until I fall asleep?"

Don't cry.

I held his hand and brushed back his hair. "Would you like for me to sing to you?"

He nodded yes.

"I'm going to sing you a prayer."

"Perfect," he whispered.

I started to sing, "*Shema.*"

Daniel then sang, with renewed energy, "*Yisroel.*"

And then together we sang the rest of the prayer, "*Adonai Eloheinu Adonai Echad.*"

"We're still a great team, Sweetie."

"Yes, we'll always be a great team."

Then he said very clearly, "Much have I learned from my teachers, more from my colleagues, and most of all from my students."

"From the Talmud!"

"Atta girl!"

Atta girl. Those two little words embraced me; like a little prayer, they comforted me.

I kissed his forehead. "Sweet dreams. I'll see you again in a few days."

This was a good visit. Thank You, God!

October 17. Daniel was in a lot of pain, but he masked it.

"Break out the music!"

"What do you want to hear?" I asked.

Silence.

140

"Do you want to sing?"

"Yes, that's the music I want. Let's sing together."

"Okay, you start."

"Okay!"

Silence.

"How does it start?"

I began, "*Shema*."

"WOW," he moaned, shuddering in pain. When he moaned a second time I called Peter, who asked me to leave while he gave Daniel his injection.

I returned moments later with the *Les Miserables* videotape marked, "$9.99." I knew Daniel loved talking about bargains.

"Daniel, you paid nine-ninety-nine for this classic?"

"Yes, I did."

"It's got to be worth four times as much now."

"More. I bought it fifteen years ago."

"Do you remember seeing the show with my parents?"

"Of course I do." He closed his eyes for a moment before continuing. "I also remember asking your father if I could marry you."

"What?" My eyes widened.

Is that true?

"Your father sat me down and told me I should let you find someone your own age."

"I didn't know that. What else did he say?"

"He told me I was out of my fucking mind." He laughed.

I didn't.

Now I understand.

Before sunset, I lit the *Shabbat* candles in Daniel's room. We prayed and sang the *Shema* together.

That night I called my Dad. He confirmed the conversation with Daniel took place.

"Please don't be mad at me," he said. "I'm sorry he's sick. I know how important he is to you."

"It's okay, Dad. It's all going to be okay."

The conversation ended after we both said, "I love you."

So that's what happened. Daniel wanted to marry me. Dad made the decision for me. I had no voice. Please, God, let everything be okay.

I stabbed at some food without appetite before I cried myself to sleep.

October 24. Daniel grew smaller in his bed. He wanted to watch *One Day in September*, the 1999 Oscar winner for Best Documentary. It was about the eleven Israeli athletes murdered by Arab gunmen at the 1972 Munich Olympics.

We watched silently. At four thirty in the morning on September 5, 1972, eight terrorists carried duffel bags loaded with AKM assault rifles, Tokarev pistols and grenades. They climbed over a fence into the Olympic Village. Twenty-five minutes later they knocked on the door of Israeli wrestling Coach Moshe Weinberg. He and weightlifter Yossef Romano were shot dead.

We watched mesmerized for the first hour, but then it became too depressing. Daniel asked for the posters that I had agreed to make a week ago, the ones announcing his grandson's birthday and his daughter's wedding. I had made them as cheerful as possible. He loved them.

We never watched the end of the film. Although he didn't eat his lunch or dinner, he did ask for my peanut butter cups. I massaged his shoulders and caressed his face.

When I got home I Googled "1972 Munich Olympics Terrorist Attack." I learned that after Weinberg and Romano were murdered in cold blood, the terrorists held the remaining nine Israeli athletes hostage. The terrorists demanded the release and safe passage to Egypt of two hundred thirty-four Palestinians in exchange for the hostages. By midnight, the terrorist leader realized he wouldn't get what he wanted. He shot and killed all of the hostages. The police opened fire on the terrorists. Three of the terrorists survived; all of the hostages and one German police officer were killed. Fifty-three days later, on October 29, 1972, two Palestinian hijackers of a Lufthansa passenger jet demanded the release of the three surviving terrorists. After the German government released them, they were flown to Libya where they received a triumphant welcome from Colonel Muammar Gaddafi.

I took a deep breath and exhaled slowly. I refused to allow more hatred into my heart.

October 25. It had been fifty-two hours since I slept and I was not even tired. I was manic and very productive in the kitchen: I made more peanut butter cups, matzo ball soup and challah for Daniel. My house smelled delicious.

October 28. As Daniel was resting, I asked, "Do you ever remember your dreams?"

"Sometimes."

"Do you dream in black and white or color?"

"Both, and sepia."

"Sepia?"

"Look it up." He pointed toward his desk.

On his desk I saw dictionaries in six different languages. I took an English dictionary back to Daniel's bedside and flipped through the pages until I got to "S."

I read out loud, "Sepia, noun. A brown pigment obtained from the ink-like secretion of various cuttlefish and used with brush or pen in drawing."

I closed the dictionary. Daniel once told me that I didn't need to know all the answers, I only needed to know where to find them.

"Tal?"

"Yes"

"I love you."

I smiled with such deep yearning, "I love you."

"Please write about a student and her mentor."

"A poem?"

"I trust you."

I told him I would and then I sang the *Shema* to him.

November 1. I arrived at Daniel's apartment at one in the afternoon. Peter told me that he had just gone back to bed. He had asked to be seated at his desk expecting me to arrive by noon, but by twelve thirty he was exhausted.

"Hi, Sweetheart," I said, "How are you feeling today?"

"Better, now. I expect to be back at work by the end of the month."

I wanted to believe him, but I knew he was still trying to protect me.

"Thank you. I'd rather visit you at work. I made you some more matzo ball soup."

"Good. And my chocolates?"

"Making your chocolates is easy. Writing something about a mentor and a student is much harder. But I'm working on it."

"We'll do it together."

"Do you want me to read what I wrote so far?"

"Please."

I sat on a chair next to the bed and I started to read, "*A Mentor and a Student.*"

"No," he said, "*A Student and Her Mentor.*"

"Okay," I smiled, "*A Student and Her Mentor*. Like the sun, the mentor is a brilliant resource who nourishes and sustains our society. After a rain, the sun bestows upon us the gift of a rainbow; the mentor bestows upon us the gift of his knowledge. The student is like a rainbow. She depends on the mentor for Light just as the rainbow depends on the sun."

"That is beautiful."

I sensed he was too tired to hear any more. "One day I'll read you the rest."

"Yes." He was dozing off.

"Rest. I'll be back in a little while."

Another conversation was going on in the kitchen between Katie and Peter.

"Do you think it's time to look into hospice care?"

"Yes, I do," said Peter.

"Hospice care?" I asked.

They looked at each other and then at me.

Katie asked, "Do you know what's going on?"

"No."

"He's terminal. He was diagnosed with melanocytoma."

"Cancer?"

I was obviously in denial.

"Yes. It's a rare neurological cancer. It's in his brain and spine."

I whispered, "Prognosis?"

Peter said, "We're only guessing."

"I understand."

"One to three months."

Katie added, "He knows."

I started to cry.

"I already spoke with Dad. He wants to be buried at Arlington National Cemetery. There's a long waiting list. There's no guarantee that he will be buried by Jewish law."

"What does that mean?" I asked.

"It means that when he passes, Arlington may bury him a month later rather than within twenty-four hours."

"Is that okay with him?"

"It's what he wants."

Good for him. He fought for his country in four wars. He deserves it.

Peter said, "He doesn't want you to know."

"Why?"

"You remind him of everything positive."

Daniel called me from the bedroom.

145

"I'm coming," I called back as I quickly pulled myself together.

Daniel said, "We're still a great team, Sweetie."

"Of course we are."

"Will you turn the story into a screenplay?"

"A screenplay? I can try."

"I want Russell Crowe to play me." He was absolutely serious.

"Not Sean Connery?"

"Russell Crowe."

"Okay."

"Promise?"

He knows I take my promises seriously.

"I promise, I'll try my best."

I had no idea what this project entailed, but my promise to complete it gave me strength. Nothing was impossible.

I kissed his forehead.

How am I ever going to write this screenplay?

"One more thing."

"Anything."

"I want us to watch *Love Story*."

"Do you have it here?"

"I don't know."

"I'll look. If you don't have it, I'll get it. I'll see you in a couple of days."

He reached for my hand: "I love you."

"I love you, more."

When I got home, I Googled "melanocytoma." When the screen appeared, I hit the *escape* button. It was too much to handle.

November 4. When I arrived, Daniel was in bed wearing a bright red plaid shirt. It made me smile, a real smile.

"Hi, Tal."

"Hi," I said. "You look great in red."

"I want to kiss you."

With undiluted love, I leaned over and gently kissed his lips.

"Again."

I did.

"Can we be partners again?"

"Partners?"

"Like last week."

I wondered if he wanted to sing the *Shema* or read *A Student and Her Mentor*.

"Sure we can."

"Now?"

"Sure, anything you like. Do you want to sing?"

"No."

"Would you like for me to take notes?"

"Whatever you prefer." Then he said, "Tal, I'm sorry."

"What are you sorry about?"

"I'm about to fall asleep."

"Would you like for me to come back later?"

"Yes, in a little while."

"Okay. No problem." I kissed his forehead. "Sweet dreams."

Peter filled me in on Daniel's improved blood sugars. We said – only half-joking – that it must have been from the peanut butter cups. Peter then turned serious. He said that Daniel had screamed at him to take down the posters.

Is Daniel accepting the inevitable – that he won't be around to celebrate his grandson's birthday and his daughter's wedding?

An hour later he was awake.

"Do you remember what movie you said you wanted to watch?" I hoped he didn't.

"Love Story."

Crap.

"Yes, *Love Story*. I ordered it. I'll have it soon."

"Good."

"Would you like to sleep?"

"Yes."

"Okay." I gave him more kisses and then I left the room.

Peter told me to say goodbye. "Otherwise he will ask for you when he wakes up."

"Is that what happened last week?"

"Yes. He was very upset."

I went back in, kissed Daniel and told him that I was leaving for the day. I started to walk out but then I stopped. "Daniel, I forgot to show you. Look!" I leaned over to show him my earrings. They were the classic blue and white earrings that he had brought back for me from China.

"They're beautiful."

"Do you remember them?"

"Yes."

I left his apartment and did not cry. Now I had a sense of purpose: to remind Daniel of as many wonderful memories as possible.

November 7. At the university, I taught a nutrition class and had a great time. In the classroom, I was able to avoid my negative thoughts. I focused on the lesson. I felt happy to be teaching and it was well received by my students.

I met with Rabbi Levine. I needed help to prepare for the inevitable.

He said, "God hears your prayers. Tears may turn up the volume a bit, but if you're looking to bond with God, the doors are open in a joyous state. Depression shuts the doors and therefore any opportunity to elevate the self."

He taught me the prayer for the healing of others: "O God, who blessed our ancestors, Abraham and Sarah, Isaac and Rebekah, Jacob and Leah and Rachel; send Your blessing to Daniel Benson. Have mercy on him, and graciously restore his health and strength. Grant him a *refuah shelayma*, complete recovery, a healing of body and a healing of spirit, along with all others who are stricken. May healing come speedily. Amen."

November 15. I remember the exact time that Peter called me at home: It was 7:07 A.M. "Daniel has taken a turn for the worse. You should be prepared."

I skipped rope for thirty minutes while watching the news. I wore the ruby rose that Daniel had given me years ago. I caught the nine-fifteen train into the city and gave a nutrition bar to a homeless man I encountered en route to Daniel's apartment.

I said hello to the doorman; he was used to seeing me by now. Peter had left the front door unlocked. He was talking to someone on the phone about hospice care. He waved to me to wait.

"It isn't good. Daniel hasn't been eating much. He has cleansed himself with episodes of diarrhea. These are the signs. I think Daniel has less than one week."

I listened.

"The family needs to agree on which hospice agency is going to take over. His wish is to pass at home."

"Peter, may I ask a selfish question?"

"Sure."

"You were here when Daniel asked to watch *Love Story*. I finally have it with me. Do you think…?" I got choked up.

"Yes, of course. But he won't be able to watch the whole thing."

We walked into Daniel's room. He was curled up and sleeping.

"Daniel, Tali's here."

I hated to wake him. I held his hand, stroked his hair and kissed his cheek.

Every visit there was less and less of him.

I can't bear to be here.

I can't bear not to be here.

"Hi, Sweetheart," I said. And then I saw his familiar tee shirt. I rolled the blanket down. "Daniel, you're wearing the Don Quixote tee shirt I made you sixteen years ago! You just made my day."

"A forever perfect flower for a forever perfect flower," he said.

"Oh my God, yes, you remember," I touched the rose pinned to my blouse. "That's amazing. You're amazing. You remember."

Daniel went back to sleep and I waited in the living room.

An hour later I returned. "I finally got *Love Story*."

"Great. Let's watch it."

Peter put the movie on.

The scene opened with Ryan O'Neil's character, Harvard Law School student, Oliver Barrett IV, sitting by the Charles River talking about how he lost the love of his life, twenty-five-year-old school teacher, Jennifer Cavilleri, played by Ali MacGraw.

For the next thirty minutes I watched Daniel while he watched the movie. He appeared to be watching closely, but said nothing and showed no emotion. When Daniel fell asleep, Peter shut the tape off. I kissed Daniel's forehead and told him that I would see him tomorrow.

Peter walked me to the door. "Daniel is lucky to have you in his life. Your visits are exactly what he needs."

Thank You, God, for letting me be here when he needs me.

November 16. Daniel's apartment now had two opposing smells: in one corner, the precious aroma of baby lotion, in the other, the more powerful odor of decay. I followed the latter to Daniel's room.

Katie arrived. "Do you see a difference in Dad?"

"Yes."

"Even *you* see it."

"Yes, I'm so sorry."

Peter brought Daniel into the living room. We sat together, the three of us, Daniel, Katie and me. I wanted to give them some privacy, but Katie was too emotional and instead she left the room for a few moments.

"Daniel?"

He looked into my eyes. I sandwiched his two hands in mine. It was impossible to know who was drawing reassurance from whom.

"You smell good – like a fresh bagel."

He laughed.

Oh, thank You, God, for his laughter.

"I thought you might want to know the FDA approved the first Rapid HIV test kit."

He nodded and sighed with satisfaction.

"Do you remember the koala bear you brought back for me from Australia?"

He nodded yes.

"Would you like to have it?"

He smiled.

"Okay, I'll bring him on Monday. What about the green alligator from Florida?"

He nodded yes.

"Do you want the koala bear or the alligator?"

"Both," he whispered.

I was happy to hear his voice. Until then he hadn't said a word.

twenty-three

The promise I had made to Daniel weighed heavily on my mind. With thoughts of Daniel, this chapter is in screenplay format:

FADE IN:

INT. DANIEL'S BEDROOM - MORNING

The clock reads 11:19 A.M. PETER takes the needle out of DANIEL'S arm. TALI holds his hand. A stuffed koala bear and alligator lie on the dresser, next to a Quixote paperweight.

                                        CUT TO:

INT. DANIEL'S BEDROOM - LATER

The clock reads 2:22 P.M. Daniel is sleeping. Tali sits by his bedside with her eyes closed. Her fingertips are touching his.

INT. DANIEL'S BEDROOM - LATER
The clock reads 6:50 P.M.

             TALI
        Daniel? Sweetheart? I'm
        going to need to leave
        soon.

Tali holds his hand, strokes his hair and caresses his face.

             DANIEL
          (Barely audible)
        We're still a great team,
        Sweetie.

             TALI
        Yes, of course we are.
        We'll always be a great
        team.

Tali cradles Daniel's hands in hers.

             DANIEL
        I love you so much.

Daniel moves his fingers inside her hand. Tali grabs a tissue from the nightstand and wipes her eyes.

             TALI
        Please let me know when
        you get home. Look for
        your brother, Larry. He
        misses you.

Tali caresses Daniel's face.

             DANIEL
        I promise.

Tali looks over at the dresser and sees the Quixote paperweight.

                    TALI
               (quoting Dulcinea from
               Man of LaMancha)
          God, this is crazy. I've
          got to let you sleep… my
          Don Quixote.

                    DANIEL
               (faint)
          Don Quixote? Ooh. You
          must forgive me. I have
          been ill. I'm confused
          by shadows. I do not
          remember.

                    TALI (V.O.)
          He remembered the lines
          from Man of LaMancha. I
          continued to play along
          as Dulcinea.

                    TALI
          Please! Try to remember!

                    DANIEL
               (Faintly)
          Is it so important?

                    TALI
               (trying to find the words)
          Yes. Everything. My whole
          life. You spoke to me and
          everything was… different.

                    DANIEL
               (Very softly)
          I spoke to you?

                    TALI
You spoke of a dream. And
about the quest!

                  DANIEL
          (Softly)
Quest?

                    TALI
How you must fight. How
it doesn't matter whether
you win or lose. If only
you follow the quest.

                  DANIEL
          (Softly)
The words. Tell me the
words.

                    TALI
To dream the impossible
dream. But they're your
own words. To fight the
unbeatable foe. Don't you
remember? To bear with
unbearable sorrow. You must
remember. To run where the
brave dare not go!

                  DANIEL
          (A bit louder)
To right the unrightable
wrong?

                    TALI
Yes.

                  DANIEL
To love, pure and chaste,
from afar.

                    TALI
          Yes.

                    DANIEL
                (Making an effort)
          To try, when your arms
          are too weary, to reach
          the UNREACHABLE STAR!

                    TALI
                (Cries)
          Oh, thank you! Daniel,
          Sweetheart. Thank you!

Tali kisses Daniel on the forehead and then on
the lips. She glances up at his face. A single
tear escapes from his left eye. She laughs and
cries at the same time.

Peter enters the bedroom.

                    PETER
          Is everything okay?

Tali nods her head yes. Daniel smiles dimly.

                    TALI
                (Kisses Daniel's forehead)
          Rest. I'll be right back.

Tali gestures to Peter to follow.

                                        CUT TO:

EXT. DANIEL'S TERRACE - DUSK.

The sky is clear. A cold wind blows. Peter
follows Tali out onto the terrace.

                    PETER
          I need some fresh air,
          too.

                    TALI
          I don't know how you do
          it.

                    PETER
          I can say the same thing
          about you.

                    TALI
               (Teary)
          May I ask a favor?

                    PETER
          Anything.

                    TALI
          I brought over two animal
          puppets. Tonight… can you
          make sure that…

Tali can't speak. Tears well up in her eyes.

                    TALI (CONT'D)
          Tuck them in with him
          tonight.

                    PETER
          Count on it.

                                        CUT TO:

INT. DANIEL'S BEDROOM - NIGHT

The clock reads 7:07 P.M. Daniel, lying on his
back, breathes with difficulty. His eyes follow
Tali as she walks across the room and sits in the
chair beside his bed. She holds his hand.

                    TALI
          I have two guests for
          you tonight.

Tali lets go of Daniel's hand. She puts her hand into the koala bear puppet and walks it up Daniel's leg.

> TALI (CONT'D)
> (as the koala bear)
> What's up, Doc? Remember me?

Tali puts the koala bear down and picks up the alligator.

> TALI (CONT'D)
> Oh, wait, there's someone else.
> (as the alligator)
> You remember me, don'tcha? Okay, later-gator!

Tali tucks both puppets into the bed next to Daniel.

> TALI (CONT'D)
> They're going to keep you company tonight.

> DANIEL
> (softly)
> Please hold me.

Tali leans over the bed rail and gently hugs Daniel.

> DANIEL (CONT'D)
> No. Lie down with me.

> TALI
> Anything you need.

Tali tries to lower the bed rail. She can't. She kicks off her shoes, pulls a chair over, steps onto it and over the rail. Carefully, she lies down with Daniel and hugs him.

>   TALI
>   Oh, Sweetheart, you touched
>   my soul. I feel so lucky to
>   have you in my life. Thank
>   you for everything.

Seconds pass. Peter enters the bedroom and sees Tali in Daniel's bed. His initial look of worry turns into a smile.

>   PETER
>   Tali, I'd never want to
>   send you away, but it's
>   getting late. I've got to
>   get him ready for bed.

>   TALI
>   Okay, two more minutes?
>   Please.

>   PETER
>   Sure, I'll be right back.

>   TALI
>   Okay, Sweetheart, one more
>   time.
>   (sings alone)
>   Shema Yisroel Adonai
>   Eloheinu Adonai Echad.

>   DANIEL
>   (voice fading)
>   Don't miss the dance.

Tali leans in closer.

>   TALI
>   I'm sorry, Sweetheart,
>   I didn't hear you.

Daniel's eyes close.

                         TALI
          Daniel?

                         TALI V.O.
          His hand reached upward,
          past me, reaching for
          something, perhaps reaching
          for his own impossible dream.

                                        DISSOLVE TO:

INT. TALI'S BEDROOM - NIGHT

It is a turbulent night. Tali is in bed asleep.
The clock reads 1:56 A.M. She tosses and turns.

                                        CUT TO:

INT. TALI'S BEDROOM - NIGHT

1:57. Tali cries out in her sleep.

                                        CUT TO:

INT. TALI'S BEDROOM - NIGHT

Tali wakes up, 1:58. She is sweating.

                                        CUT TO:

INT. TALI'S BEDROOM - NIGHT

Tali looks at the clock, 1:59.

                                        CUT TO:

INT. TALI'S BEDROOM - NIGHT

2:00 A.M. Tali is overwhelmed with grief.

                         TALI
                    (hysterical)
          Oh, God! Daniel!

                                        CUT TO:

INT. TALI'S BEDROOM - MORNING

The clock reads 7:07 A.M. The phone rings. Tali wakes up and reaches for the phone. She gets it by the second ring.

SUPERIMPOSE VOICE OVER ACTION...

                    TALI V.O.
          It was Peter. He told me
          that Daniel had passed
          at 2:00 A.M. The puppets
          were by his side.

Tali hangs up the phone and allows herself to fall apart.

                                        FADE OUT:

FADE IN:

EXT. CEMETERY - DAY

TITLE CARD: ARLINGTON NATIONAL CEMETERY.

Dr. Daniel Benson's funeral. It's a bitter cold but sunny winter afternoon. Cars are parked in single file. MOURNERS walk from their cars down a narrow gravel path toward the gravesite.

Leading the crowd is a horse-drawn carriage holding Daniel's coffin with the American flag draped over it.

THIRTY SOLDIERS march in unison across the grass. CIVILIANS follow behind on foot.

Daniel's FAMILY walk slightly ahead of FRIENDS. Daniel's two-year-old GRANDSON is being carried by his MOM.

Everyone reaches the gravesite. The coffin is lowered off the carriage. SIX SOLDIERS carry it to the gravesite. All soldiers stand at attention. The bugles PLAY the Jewish song Ein Kellohaynu (*There is none like unto our God*). One soldier stands alone and BLOWS his horn once.

The RABBI recites the prayers.

A soldier folds a flag twelve times in the Flag Folding Ceremony and presents it to Daniel's oldest daughter, Katie.

Seven soldiers fire their guns three times (21-gun salute).

Thirty uniformed soldiers stand at attention while six soldiers PLAY *Taps* on their bugles, the final good night to the departed soldier.

One by one family and friends use a shovel to cover the coffin with earth.

People start to depart.

Tali visits the grave for one final farewell.

> TALI
> (whispers)
> Sweetheart, this is for
> You. *A Student and Her*
> *Mentor.*
>
> A mentor is like the sun,
> a brilliant source of Light
> energy that nourishes and
> sustains our society.
>
> And as we all know, after a
> good rain, the sun bestows
> upon us a marvelous gift –
> the rainbow.
> (MORE)

                    TALI (CONT'D)
                (whispers)
It's as if the sun, in all
of its wisdom, understands
that through the rainbow we
can appreciate some of the
wondrous talents the sun
possesses.

The mentor, through wisdom,
knowledge, research and
teaching nourishes the
student.

He feeds her curiosity and
prepares her for the
challenges ahead.

The mentor *rains* down
knowledge on the student
and bestows upon society
a gift – a trained
professional that through
continued research and
teaching reflects *some* of
the wondrous talents the
mentor possesses.

In this respect, the student
is like the rainbow. She
depends on the mentor for
Light in the same way the
rainbow depends on the sun.

And through the rainbow, we
see the sun's Light is
composed of many colors. We
know them as ROY G BIV.
                (MORE)

                    163

                    TALI (CONT'D)
                  (whispers)
          The ROY G BIV I have
          distinguished from your
          Light is: Righteousness,
          Optimism, Youthfulness,
          Generosity, Benevolence,
          Intelligence and Valor.

          Your Light will forever shine.
          Thank you, Daniel, for your
          selfless dedication. I am so
          grateful. I love you. Always.

She salutes.

                    TALI (CONT'D)
          Shema Yisroel Adonai
          Eloheinu Adonai Echad.

                              FADE OUT.

twenty-four

I received a letter in the mail from a colleague. He wrote: "While vacationing in Spain, I saw this in the newspaper and thought you would want to know that Daniel was famous all over the world. I'm so sorry he passed on. He will be missed by many."

Enclosed was a full page article in *El Pais, lunes 25 de noviembre de 2002, Necrológicas* ("Obituaries"): "*Daniel Benson, el cientifico que relaciono' el acido fólico con la anemia.*"

I was out of sorts for a few months and had fallen behind with everything. I added a footnote to Danielle Van Dam.

DATE	NAME	AGE	HOMETOWN	STATUS
Feb 2, 2002	Danielle Van Dam	7	San Diego, California	Murdered by neighbor, David Alan Westerfield, who had no prior criminal record.
*Jan 3 2003				*Westerfield sentenced to death. On death row at San Quentin State Prison.

March 12, 2003, before going to sleep I spoke out loud to Daniel:

"Hi, Sweetheart. Are you home yet? I miss you terribly. I wanted to tell you some great news: Elizabeth Smart was found alive. They arrested her abductors – it was a homeless man and his wife."

Elizabeth had been held captive for nine months. She must have had amazing coping skills. After reading about her tragedy turned to triumph, I thought I would do something celebratory, like write a poem or bake a cake. But instead I chose to do nothing. NO THING. I double-bolted my doors and drew the curtains. I was still struggling.

I soon added another name to the growing list:

DATE	NAME	AGE	HOMETOWN	STATUS
April 21, 2003	Amanda Berry	16	Cleveland, Ohio	MISSING.

I had a dream that Daniel called.

"Hello?"

"Hi, Sweetie." He sounded blissful.

"Hi." I was excited. "Where are you?"

"I'm home."

"Oh, I'm so happy for you. Do you need anything?"

"Not a thing. I love you. I'm a phone call away."

"I love you, too."

Josh Groban sang, "To Where You Are:"

"Who can say for certain

Maybe you're still here

I feel you all around me

Your memories so clear…"

Then there was silence.

I woke up. It was like a phone call from 1986. I felt like I had been kissed in the middle of the night. Daniel kept his promise; he let me know that he had arrived home.

I joined an online dating service again. Now, more experienced, I exposed the liars within sixty seconds. They would say, "You're exactly what I've been looking for." "My kids will love you." "I'm taking my profile down."

Almost all of them were one-timers over a cup of tea for me and coffee for them. I didn't make more than a thirty-minute investment in anyone. It was a perfect plan – and then I met Benjamin.

It was a freezing day in December 2003. I walked from Penn Station down to Battery Park, watching the water of the Hudson River ripple from fierce winds. My full-length down coat, hat, scarf and gloves kept me warm.

In my right hand I carried my bag with Benjamin's profile: "…inquisitive mind; drawn to independent-minded women; enjoys intimate conversations, chess, Scrabble, writing, Nutella, rainbow cookies and anything dark chocolate." I had read it a dozen times. I carried a gift bag filled with homemade rainbow cookies and Nutella-filled dark chocolates.

When I arrived at World Financial Center Three, I saw the gaping hole that had held Twin Towers. The new structures would soon serve as a memorial to the approximately 2,600 people, including eleven unborn babies who had lost their lives in New York City twenty-seven months ago.

At twelve twenty in the afternoon, with ten minutes to spare, I walked into Devon & Blakely Restaurant. There was a pinecone wreath on the door, silver and gold garland around the windows and a Christmas tree decorated with ornaments and multicolored lights. A baby grand player piano played "Silent Night." I sat on the plush leather chair and listened to the music.

I recognized his smile and his dimples: he had put a recent photo online.

This is a good sign.

He was tall with wavy dark brown hair and hazel eyes. I put my hand out to shake his, but he ignored it and kissed my cheek.

We were led past a cocktail lounge into the dining room with floor-to-ceiling windows overlooking the water. During lunch he told me he was divorced with two girls, was looking for a serious relationship and was a prosecuting attorney for special victims.

"Special victims?"

"Domestic violence, rape, child abuse, you know."

"Did you actually choose this specialty?"

"To summarize it in one sentence: I started out as a patrol cop and made one too many collars on domestic abuse – advanced in rank to detective, still dealt with the scum of the earth and decided to go back to school to study law, with the delusion that I can clean up the streets."

"That was one long sentence," I smiled.

"Yeah, well, try living it." He smiled back.

It was nearly two o'clock when he picked up the check. As we left the restaurant, I thanked him and gave him the bag of homemade cookies. He looked inside the bag and said, "Wow."

We walked up the steps to the big glass windows overlooking West Street and the new construction site. We stood there in silence; he stroked my hair.

He kissed me on the cheek. "I'll see you soon," and then he walked away. He turned around once, twice. He smiled. I smiled back. He turned around for a third time, winked and waved. I was happy.

To summarize this relationship: We dated for three months; I was comfortable with him and shared my childhood trauma; he was uncomfortable with me and shared no insight that he had learned from working with special victims; he wanted to become lovers but not exclusive; I ended it – whatever *it* was.

I didn't understand how to risk loving someone without being terrified of heartbreak. I was exhausted trying to figure it out.

There are plenty of fish in the sea.

I had to learn to be more patient. I would wait for the goliath golden tigerfish or the rare bluefin tuna. In the meantime, I wrapped myself up tightly in my blanket and lived in my cocoon.

I dreamed a lot. In one of the most memorable dreams, the main characters were fish, as in the movie *Finding Nemo*. However, the setting was not in a pool, a lake or an ocean. It took place on a stage in an auditorium.

There were hundreds of fish in colorful suits and dresses. The females wore makeup, fin-polish and toe-shoes. They were being called one by one to perform by a stage manager, also a fish, who carried a notepad in his fin and a pencil in his mouth.

"Next," called the stage manager, dismissing the fish now on stage.

"Noooooo... pleeeeeze.... gimme another minute. I can really wow ya! Look..." the fish started to tap dance as he was dragged off the stage.

"I said, NEXT."

A timid fish adjusted the microphone.

"Testing, testing, one, two, three."

I was sitting in the auditorium watching these auditions. I knew the fish who were not chosen would die.

The timid fish on stage was singing her heart out in a moving rendition of "Sounds of Silence." She was chosen.

A big bouncer-type fish carried a bucket into the director's office. The director was a tall fish in a suit with a white collar and black stripes. He smoked a cigar. The bouncer came bee-bopping in with this bucket full of minced-up fish.

The director was indifferent.

A swishing noise from the bucket got louder and louder. A little fish popped his head out from all the other pieces of fish. Somehow, he had survived this ordeal.

I was so happy for this little fish.

The director was confused. He pushed the fish back under.

The little voice screamed "Noooooo" before going down.

I cried out loud; I was furious at the director.

The little fish came up again, but the director kept pushing him down. The little voice screamed out, "Think."

The director froze.

The little fish looked just like the director: the same suit with the white collar and black stripes. Everything was the same except he didn't have a cigar.

I woke up. My bedroom was dark. It was two in the morning. I reached for my pen and notepad and jotted down some questions to think about in the morning. Are we the author of our own script? Are we the main character as well as the director? Are we the saboteur – the person to push us down? I was like a fish out of water, unable to breathe.

Yes, yes, yes.

I heard on the news that fourteen-year-old Georgina DeJesus was missing from the same neighborhood where a girl had gone missing a year earlier. I Googled her name. Amanda Berry was still missing.

DATE	NAME	AGE	HOMETOWN	STATUS
April 21, 2003	Amanda Berry	16	Cleveland, Ohio	MISSING.
April 2, 2004	Georgina (Gina) DeJesus	14	Cleveland, Ohio	MISSING.

A month later I added an addendum: Jose Antonio Ramos was declared legally responsible for the death of Etan Patz, the six-year-old boy who had gone missing on May 25, 1979 in lower Manhattan. Ramos was presently serving a twenty-seven year sentence in a State Correctional Institute in Pennsylvania for two other child molestation cases. His scheduled release date was November 7, 2012.

twenty-five

That September a new California law allowed the public to use their personal computers to view information on sex offenders required to register with local law enforcement under Megan's Law.

To celebrate the upcoming Thanksgiving, I bought myself a new handbag. When I went through my old bag, I came across a familiar business card from a conference I had recently attended. I had met a man there who was sixtyish, very tall and very slender. Maybe six six and one hundred and sixty-five pounds. He invited me to participate in a study he was conducting about personality types.

I called him.

"Hello?"

"May I please speak with Rich Faust?"

"Speaking."

"Hi, Rich. This is Tali Stark. I met you at the Mind Body Medicine conference."

"Yes, Tali. I remember. You're the registered dietitian, right?"

"That's right. Is it too late to be in your study?"

"Not at all. I'd be happy to have you."

"What do I have to do?"

"First you fill out the questionnaire, and then we do a follow-up interview where I give you your results."

"Okay, sounds good."

"I'll mail you the questionnaire. If you have any questions, give me a call."

The questionnaire arrived in two days. It was twenty-four pages with hundreds of multiple-choice questions. It said to give the first answer that comes to me and not to think about it too much.

Question 49: "How often do you remember your dreams?
    a) most nights
    b) a few times a week
    c) a few times a month
    d) less often"

I checked (a).

I wonder if Rich interprets dreams.

Question 135: "How easy is it for you to feel relaxed?
    a) not easy
    b) fairly easy
    c) quite easy
    d) very easy"

I can't imagine what (d) feels like.

I checked (a).

I felt like *I* wrote question 139: "Are you impressed by the blunt truth even though it can be painful?
    a) not at all
    b) a little
    c) somewhat
    d) very much"

I checked (d).

I'd rather be hurt by the truth than misled with a lie. That's my motto.

An hour later I stuffed the completed questionnaire into the return envelope, signed and dated it, November 30, 2004, and took it to the post office.

Two days later Rich emailed me: I received your completed questionnaire. Please let me know when you're available to travel into the city for a follow-up interview.

I emailed back: Would it be okay if we wait until after the holidays? I'll be in the city on February 22. Can we do it then?

He agreed. I chose that date because it was Daniel's birthday.

January 2005. Close to thirty million people were now living with HIV. The cumulative death toll in the U.S. exceeded five hundred thousand. Nelson Mandela announced his son had died from AIDS.

It was two in the afternoon. We met at the Café at the Angelika Theater at Houston and Mercer Street. Rich chose this place because we could stay as long as we wanted and nobody would bother us.

We sat down. He took out a folder; I took out a pad and pen.

"A little background before we begin," he said. "The theory of the six personality types is based on the work of George Ivanovitch Gurdjieff, an Armenian psychic, mystic and teacher. Gurdjieff spent twenty years traveling from Egypt to India, Tibet and China seeking the 'wisdom of the East'."

I listened. I jotted down the name Gurdjieff after asking Rich to spell it.

"The six types, in general, have the characteristics of the Roman gods and goddesses for whom the planets were named: Luna the seer, Venus the romantic, Mercury the messenger, Saturn the thinker, Mars the warrior, and Jupiter the good father and the chief God. Both men and women can be all the types.

"There are two "Feeling" types, Venus and Jupiter; two "Doing" types, Mercury and Mars; and two "Thinking" types, Luna and Saturn. As your enneagraph shows, you have high scores in both Jupiter, a feeling type, and Mercury, a doing type. This makes you a mixed type." He gave me a copy of my enneagraph.

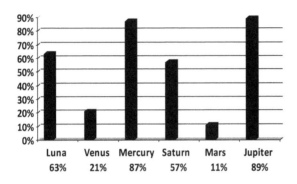

	Luna	Venus	Mercury	Saturn	Mars	Jupiter
	63%	21%	87%	57%	11%	89%

"Is that common?"

"Lots of people are a mixed type, but this is unusual because these are opposite types. Mercurys are doers first, then thinkers and then feelers. They are very quick, and are good at organizing things, both physically and mentally. Their thinking leans toward efficiency and cleverness before depth and deliberation. They tend to be unemotional."

"Well, then I'd guess that Jupiters are *very* emotional."

"Yes, Jupiters are feeling types first, then thinkers. They're the most compassionate type. They don't like confrontation or having to criticize others. They're not doers."

"I think I'm good at getting things done. I'd like to think that I finish everything I start."

"That's because you're eighty-seven percent Mercury."

"Okay. I understand."

"Your lowest score is Mars at eleven percent and that makes sense because you're not assertive, competitive and confrontational. Mars are the Warriors."

"That's really true. I'm not any of those things."

"Venus is your second lowest at twenty-one percent. You're not romantic."

"What? I am too," I said, defending myself.

"Let me explain. You want love but it's not the driving force in your life. For Jupiters, compassion for others is more important than romance for yourself. Right?"

I nodded.

That's exactly right.

And then out of nowhere I told Rich everything about my childhood trauma. Everything – the whole story. I was talking so fast that I didn't recognize my own voice. Exhausted and emotionally drained, I stopped. I was too embarrassed to look at him.

What the hell did I just say?

"It's wonderful that you're able to share this." His voice was soft and sympathetic. "I think it means that you're ready to really deal with it. You should work with someone who specializes in child abuse because it's so complicated."

"I know a psychiatrist, but I can't afford it right now because I'm looking to buy a second residence, an apartment, somewhere on the water."

"Don't you think this is more important?"

I stayed quiet.

After a moment of silence he handed me another sheet of paper. "These are your psychological scores."

I was disappointed with my self-confidence score. "Forty-nine percent in self-confidence. Really?"

"That's about average. Remember these are percentile scores. So fifty percent is exactly average."

He stared at the sheet and then at me. "I can't believe you have such a high score on trusting other people – sixty-five percent – after what you went through. I would have expected your score to

176

be about twenty percent. It's hard to imagine that anyone with that kind of childhood trauma could learn to trust people again."

"Both my husband and my mentor restored my faith in people. I was very lucky."

"Was? Are they no longer in your life?"

"I'm divorced five years and Daniel passed away four years ago."

"I'm sorry."

I could tell that he was looking at me, waiting for me to say something. I looked at my results and said, "Only fourteen percent in assertiveness?"

"Yes, fourteen percent for assertiveness is low even for a Jupiter. A reasonable level of assertiveness is necessary if you want to achieve your goals in life. So maybe you can think about strengthening that trait."

"I'm surprised to see how extroverted I am."

"Sixty-eight percent is a high score. You must get that from Mercury. Do you not consider yourself to be extroverted?"

"I consider myself to be quiet. The exception is when I'm teaching." I asked, "Which type is the happiest?"

"You really lucked out. Mercury is the happiest and Jupiter is the second happiest."

"Really?"

"Really."

At four o'clock we gathered our belongings. As we left the Angelika Café, he again suggested that I go back to therapy. "It really is a good time. You showed in the interview that you're ready to deal with the trauma. There's nothing more important in your life right now."

I didn't say anything.

He must have sensed my hesitation. "There's another way to deal with trauma," he said. "Write about it. It can be cathartic, and even transforming. I know a lot of people who benefitted from writing about their deepest thoughts and feelings about their pain and suffering. It doesn't matter if you write it as memoir or fiction. Trust your instincts. You'll know what you're supposed to do."

I had spent my entire life trying to let go of my past. Do I actually have to get closer to it in order to let it go?

A week later I laid down on my sofa with the lamp over my shoulder and a newspaper in my lap. I had extinguished all the other lights in the house and I read in near darkness:

Nine-year-old Jessica Lunsford had vanished from her home in Homosassa, Florida on February 28, 2005.

I stayed up-to-date on Jessica's case.

March 18: Police found Jessica's body buried in a shallow grave under the back porch of a mobile home one hundred yards from her home.

One hundred yards? That's just three hundred feet, the length of a football field.

March 23: Police arrested convicted sex offender John Evander Couey. He had kidnapped Jessica from her bedroom and held her bound and gagged for two days while police, search dogs and volunteers swarmed the neighborhood.

April 20: Documents released by state prosecutors show that Jessica had been raped and buried alive in two plastic garbage bags with her hands bound with wire.

June 23: Couey confessed that Jessica was still alive in his closet when police came to his door to question him about her disappearance.

I felt anguish. I could have been Jessica. Thirty years ago, when I was nine, I could have been murdered.

I was lucky.

twenty-six

After learning what had happened to Jessica Lunsford, old feelings of hopelessness began to resurface. Rich's voice continued to echo in my head that I was "ready to go back to therapy." But I didn't go. Instead, I shopped for comfort foods. I walked up and down the aisles imagining new cookie recipes, using avocado instead of butter and applesauce instead of sugar.

I was sleeping less than three hours a night. First, I tried eating kiwi, Swiss chard, and tart cherries to raise my body's melatonin levels. When this didn't help I took melatonin pills. I tried valerian root and 5-hydroxytryptophan. My sleep deprivation increased my anxiety. I tried St. John's wort. My last attempt at self-medication was *SAMe* (*S*-adenosyl methionine) and rhodiola for depression and mental alertness.

I Googled "anxiety disorders" on the Internet.

1. *Generalized anxiety disorder, which may involve physical symptoms that occur along with anxiety.*

2. *Panic disorders, which include sudden, irrational fear and*

feelings of danger or impending doom.

3. *Obsessive-compulsive disorder (OCD), which includes frequent, repeated thoughts leading to repeated or persistent behavior.*

4. *Post-traumatic stress disorder (PTSD), which involves reliving a traumatic event and feelings of numbness and disinterest in daily activities.*

I was experiencing all of the above. Exercise had helped at one time but not anymore. Nutrition can only do so much. I considered trying something new, like yoga or meditation or perhaps medication. Isn't it ironic that the only difference between meditation and medication is *one* little letter?

During the night I imagined the stars fading away, leaving only the darkness. Staring into this hopelessness, I relived the agony of my childhood trauma. My eyes were puffy and my teeth hurt from grinding. I had a recurrent nightmare that I ate shattered glass, which perforated my lungs, leaving me gasping with every breath I took.

I was too scared to do nothing.

NO THING.

Dr. Miriam Remsay's name came to me. Dr. Gottlieb had given me her name nearly seven years ago. She was the one who specialized in childhood sexual abuse.

Call her, said the voice in my head. *Call Dr. Remsay.*

She was a youthful woman in her early sixties with long brown hair tied up high. I knew that her smile and her firm handshake were sincere.

She invited me into her office, which looked like a comfortable living room. For two hours, as I sat on the couch and she sat on the matching chair, we discussed my childhood trauma, my past treatments and my present insomnia.

"For starters, we need to address your sleeping problem. It's essential for your recovery."

"I've tried every over-the-counter remedy."

"You may need a prescription, something like Ambien for sleep. Or maybe Paxil or Prozac to increase your serotonin levels. This will change your brain chemistry. It will help you to live more in the present, instead of being locked in the past, and this will help you get some sleep."

Ambien? Paxil? Prozac? I don't know.

I said, "Is there something else I can do?"

"Okay, let's see how you progress with therapy. Continue eating a balanced diet and exercising. I want you to try to have positive experiences every day to counteract your negative expectations. This can all help your brain to readjust itself."

"How can a brain readjust itself?"

"The stress of trauma changes brain chemistry. Let me show you what I mean." She reached out for my hand. "Close your eyes and try to focus."

I closed my eyes and felt her place something into the palm of my hand.

"Can you tell me what this is?"

A pen or pencil? Maybe a flashlight?

"I have no idea."

"Can you feel its weight?"

"Is it a lipstick?"

"No. Can you get a sense of its shape?"

"Sort of tubular."

"What about its texture?"

"It has texture?"

"You can open your eyes."

A spool of thread.

"Your brain couldn't recognize it because your sensory perception is off. But because your brain is adaptable, you can change it. Changing your thoughts, feelings and actions can change the actual wiring of your brain. Not right away, of course, but over a period of time."

The thought of improving the wiring of my brain was both frightening and empowering at the same time.

"Being present in the moment is the only way to bring back those brain structures that deserted you when you were overwhelmed by trauma. The goal is to *connect* with the here and now. *Now* being a forty-one-year-old woman and not a nine-year-old girl."

"Thank you. That explains why I feel so disconnected at times."

"Just because you understand *why* you feel a certain way doesn't mean that you can suddenly change *how* you feel. That takes time."

I committed to the first eight sessions. I handed her a check for twelve hundred dollars.

She said, "I'd rather be paid at the end of each session."

"Please, I feel so out of control. The one thing I can control right now is how I pay you. Please, let me pay in full."

"Okay."

I continued to fight the urge to control everything; no degree of control would permit me to turn back time. Instead, I told myself that this was my way of telling the universe that I was committed to healing myself from my childhood abduction and sexual assault, at least for the next two months.

The following week Dr. Remsay asked, "Where did you grow up?"

"In the Bronx."

"Where in the Bronx?"

"First we lived in a two-bedroom apartment on the Grand Concourse."

"Did both of your parents work?"

"Not at first. My mom was home all day with three kids, all under the age of five. Looking back, I don't know how she did it. My dad worked for a kosher meat market and left for work by four thirty in the morning. I was four when we moved to Co-Op City."

"Co-Op City; is that like a present-day housing project?"

"It's more like a complete neighborhood. It was built after the demise of Freedomland, a big American history-themed amusement park. We moved there because my parents wanted us to grow up in a safe neighborhood."

"Freedomland; safe neighborhood – how ironic. I'm sure that your parents could never have imagined that their little girl would be in danger in an *ideal* community like that." She made quote marks in the air with her fingers.

"I was so excited on my first day of school. My mom, my brothers and I would walk to the little yellow schoolhouse, only a few blocks away. My brothers and I walked home together, without Mom."

"Your mother was working at that time?"

"Yes. She took a part-time secretarial job with the local newspaper."

"What time did she get home?"

"I guess around two. She was always home when we returned from school."

"What's your earliest recollection before you moved to Co-Op City?"

I smiled. "Mom liked to sleep late so my oldest brother, Joseph, was in charge. He'd prepare breakfast for the three of us: nothing fancy, just a bowl of Rice Krispies with milk. One day Andrew experimented to see if the same "snap," "crackle," and "pop" occurred with Coca-Cola. It did. After that he swore he was allergic to milk."

She smiled.

"Anyway, one morning my mother told Joseph that she was proud of him for washing, drying and putting away the dishes. But later that week she watched him, as chubby as a cherub, lick our bowls clean before putting them back into the cabinet. No soap or even water ever touched the plates. My mother took all the bowls out of the cabinet and all of the spoons out of the drawer and dropped them into the sink."

We both laughed.

Another week I tried to discuss my trauma in the present tense. The goal was for me to be able to talk about it without getting hysterical.

"I know this is difficult for you, Tali, and I wish I could make it easier." She reached out to me with a tissue. "The very core of recovery is self-awareness. I'll teach you to be more comfortable being uncomfortable so that we can revisit your past. You'll need to experience the trauma again in the present to get to the other side. This exercise will help you to feel safe again. Your mind, body and brain need to be convinced that it is safe to let go."

Another session Dr. Remsay pushed a pillow against my chest and told me to push back.

I couldn't. Something was holding me back.

"Breathe. I'm right here with you."

I took a deep breath.

"Push," she told me again.

I couldn't. I didn't understand why not.

"I said, PUSH!"

I pushed so hard that she fell back against the bookcase. A framed photo of herself and her two kids fell to the floor.

"I'm sssor-ree." I was shaking.

She approached me, "Don't be sorry. You're fighting back."

"I know."

"You're angry."

"I know, I know."

"You're learning to release it. I'm proud of you." She took me in her arms and hugged me.

I couldn't stop crying.

She hugged me even tighter.

She recommended that I read Zelig Pliskin's *Gateway to Self-Knowledge* and answer the eighty-five questions on anger. I did. I was "easy to become angry and hard to calm down" rather than "hard to become angry and easy to calm down."

I had a lot of work to do. I committed to another eight sessions.

The following week, Dr. Remsay said, "Can you tell me about a happy event in your childhood that you know you'll always remember?"

"Although I know I had a happy childhood, aside from *that* day, it's easier for me to recall my adulthood."

"Okay. That's not uncommon with childhood trauma."

I smiled. "I was so happy the night when Daniel and I went to see *Man of LaMancha*."

"Tell me about it."

"I had my hair done and wore my new purple dress with a beautiful matching amethyst necklace and ring that Daniel had given me. He wore a suit and the red tie I had given him. We shared dinner first and then we went to the theater. The show was amazing. It was a magical evening," I said still smiling.

"Anything else?"

"I actually remember how the evening ended."

"What do you remember?"

"I told him that he reminded me of Don Quixote. I thanked him for teaching me to believe in myself."

She smiled sympathetically. "Can you notice that your story about Daniel has a beginning, middle, and an end?"

I replayed the story in my head and nodded.

"That's the difference between how people talk about positive memories versus traumatic experiences: Traumatic memories are disorganized. Only some details are remembered very clearly. Trauma has a beginning and middle, but the timeline is off, it doesn't end."

Interesting.

"Why is that?"

"One reason may be because the mind tries to create meaning out of what happened, and the meaning we make of our lives changes how and what we remember."

I thought of Viktor Frankl's equation in his book *Man's Search for Meaning*:

S – M = D. Suffering minus Meaning equals Depression.

In July, President Bush signed The Adam Walsh Child Protection and Safety Act, named in memory of six-year-old Adam Walsh from Hollywood, Florida, who was abducted from a Sears department store on June 27, 1981 and found murdered two weeks later. The Act created a national database of convicted child molesters and increased penalties for sexual and violent offenses against children. It also established Code Adam, a program that tells businesses what actions to take when a child is reported missing.

At the end of July I added a footnote in my book: Alejandro Avila was sentenced to death for the abduction, sexual assault and murder of five-year-old Samantha Runnion.

DATE	NAME	AGE	HOMETOWN	STATUS
July 15, 2002	Samantha Runnion	5	Stanton, California	Murdered by Alejandro Avila, who was previously acquitted of molesting two other young girls.
*July 23 2005				*Avila sentenced to death. Incarcerated at San Quentin State Prison on death row.

A death sentence is not enough.

On another follow-up visit Dr. Remsay said, "We are going to rewrite your trauma so that it, too, has a beginning, middle, and an *end*." She gave an extra emphasis on the "end."

She told me, "We are going to explore your past safely. You will learn to live with the memories of the past without being overpowered by them in the present."

We rehearsed how to express my anger. She taught me to say it like I meant it.

NO! STOP! I SAID NO!

The next time I walked into her office, I saw an exercise mat, a baseball bat and a box of tissues.

She handed me an index card and said, "Read it out loud."

"Holding onto anger is like drinking poison and expecting the other person to die. Buddha."

"Now, pick up the bat."

I did.

"We are going to start a dialogue, you and me. You are safe here. You are likely to get angry and you are going to express that anger, right here, right now. Are you ready?"

No. I can't pretend to be angry on call. I don't want to be angry anymore. I want to be calm.

"Tali, let's go back in time. I want you to close your eyes and go back in time with me. You are nine years old. You are walking to school in the rain. You are alone. It's raining out and you are singing and you are happy. You are a happy nine-year-old girl, a good girl. Are you with me, Tali?"

I nodded yes.

"Stay with me, Tali. You are crossing the street, walking to school. You are happy and singing in the rain. There is a man in a car across the street. The car is a limousine, a white limousine. The man asks you to help him. You are a good girl – you want to help him. He asks you for directions and you want to help him. You are a good girl. Are you still with me, Tali?"

My fear center shook. My heart rate sped up. Yes, I nodded.

"You walk closer to the man in the white limousine. He asks you for directions. It's raining hard. He tells you to come in out of the rain – he needs directions and he doesn't want you to get wet. You are a good girl; a trusting girl – you listen. You get into the car. You don't know the man is a bad man. You trust him; you sit

187

down in his car. He locks the doors and drives away. He abducts you in his car. It's not your fault, Tali. Can you hear me? It's not your fault."

I heard her but I didn't move.

"Tali, are you still with me?"

I whispered, "Yes."

"Good girl; stay with me. I'm here with you. You are not alone. You are okay and none of this is your fault. Stay with me."

I nodded my head yes.

"The man drives you to an empty lot. There is nobody there to see you, hear you or protect you. It's not your fault. The man forces you to hear things you never should have heard." She paused. "What do you want to tell the man now?"

I feel dissociated. This isn't working.

"Tali, the man is showing you things you never should have seen. What do you want to tell him?"

I'm scared.

"The man touches you. You are a good, trusting little girl. You are feeling things you never should have felt. What can you, the grown woman, do now, that you, the little girl, could not do then?"

With my eyes still closed, I gripped the bat. My heart feverishly pumped blood to my extremities. I was ready.

"Go ahead, Tali."

I raised the bat above my head.

"Give it all you've got."

I slammed the bat down onto the mat.

"HARDER."

The bat went up and slammed down.

"AGAIN."

The bat went up and slammed down again and again and again. Moments later, my nerves were shot, my tears recycled. I needed to scream. I wanted to smash The Man's face into pieces.

Again. I screamed. Again. I shouted, "NOOOOOO." And again. "NO. NO. NO."

"YES!" she said.

I no longer needed to hear Dr. Remsay's voice. A flood gate had been opened and all my rage came pouring out. Playing an active role in liberating my nine-year-old self was empowering. By rewriting the scene, I had become unfrozen.

That night I slept for ten hours straight. I didn't remember a single dream.

On my final visit Dr. Remsay said, "I'd like for you to write down as many words as you can beginning with the letter L. You will have one minute. Are you ready?"

Minute, minute, minute echoed in my head. My breathing was shallow, my eyes were open wide and my shoulders were hunched. I felt anxious. I had a stomach ache.

It felt like thirty seconds had passed before I wrote the first word. Limousine. Loser. Lure. Lousy. Liver. Link. Lose.

Crap, I already wrote that. Think!

Life. Laughing. Like. Love. Light. Learn. Leader. Ladder. Lion. Live.

"Okay, please stop."

Lucky. I sighed and looked away.

"Don't worry, Tali, this is not an intelligence test."

I was still looking away, my foot nervously tapping on the carpet.

"How many words did you get?"

I looked at my list. "Seventeen. And a half. I used part of the same word twice."

"That's okay," she smiled. "You're going to be okay. The average is about fifteen words. People with post-traumatic stress disorder average only three to four."

I looked up.

"I asked you to improvise making unfamiliar associations with a single letter so that you can see that you're okay."

My breathing had slowed down, my face softened, my spine straightened, and my eyes lifted. I wore a glimmer of a smile.

twenty-seven

I got a part-time job offer to join a team of healthcare professionals in Rockland County to work with patients living with HIV and AIDS. I scheduled my nutrition class and my private practice clients into three days a week and committed three days to the clinic ninety minutes away.

I rented a studio apartment in Nyack overlooking the Tappan Zee Bridge. My new white sofa sat elegantly on top of the plush red carpet. I bought a glass bistro table with four red velvet stools and put them in front of the big bay window overlooking the water.

Stuart stopped by to mount the big screen TV on the wall.

"Tal, the apartment looks great."

"Thank you. I really appreciate your help."

"Give me another ten minutes to hang this thing and I'll help you put the cabinet together."

"No, it's okay. The directions say I should get it done in forty minutes. I'd rather take you out for dinner."

It was eight o'clock when Stuart headed home and I took another look at IKEA's "How to Assemble" pamphlet. I went step by step and, lo and behold, four hours later I was done.

It had been over a decade since my AIDS research with Daniel. Unlike the patients at the Bronx Veterans Hospital, those at the Nyack clinic came from all the high-risk groups: homosexuals, Haitians, hemophiliacs, blood transfusion recipients, intravenous drug users, their lovers and their infected babies. Everybody received some "cocktail" of antiviral drugs.

Although I loved teaching and seeing clients at my home office, my new job provided me with a renewed sense of purpose. I started a research project on lipodystrophy – a condition associated with HIV and the medications used to treat it. It involved a loss of fat in the face, buttocks, arms and legs and increased fat in the upper back, breasts and stomach. I hoped to help these patients feel better and look better with nutrition and exercise.

The revised HIV testing guidelines for health care settings were released by the U.S. Centers for Disease Control and Prevention. On June 1, 2006, I asked a colleague in Nyack, a case study supervisor, "When can I take the rapid HIV test?" I wanted to experience the test as a patient would.

"What about today?"

"Great."

At three thirty he found an empty office. He counseled me in a calming voice, answered all of my questions, told me what he was doing, when he was going to do it, and why. After he pricked my finger, he gave me the literature: *Safe Sex; Drug Use; Taking Medication; Nutrition and Exercise.* He made it simple and nonthreatening.

After ten minutes he gave me my result.

Sometimes being negative is a good thing.

Dr. Remsay sent me a book, *Vipassana Meditation: Healing the Healer*, by Paul R. Fleischman. Her note said: "I hope all is well. Please read about 'The Wounded Healer' on pages 52-3. Dr. Fleischman, a world renowned psychiatrist, had this essay published in some of the best psychiatry journals in the world. Also enclosed is a brochure from The Healing Process. I hope you will consider attending this life-changing retreat. The address and phone number are on the back page of the brochure."

I opened the book to page fifty-two and started reading:

> *"The wounded healer functions as a high quality professional. He/she is typically well-trained, diligent, self-educating, and reliably kind and knowledgeable in dealing with patients. But, inside, known only to them, and carefully concealed from others, the wounded healer feels alone, frightened, anxious, depressed. His/her professional attainments are genuine, and form excellent compensations for experiences of deprivation earlier in life... The wounded healer is a person suffering from a deep, human, personal pain... and who is accordingly sensitive to, and activated by, a lifelong calling to heal."*

Dr. Fleischman wrote exactly what I had felt for years. In the past I had rationalized that my childhood trauma had transformed me into a more caring, compassionate person. However, since my interview with Rich Faust, I now understood that as a Jupiter I always was that compassionate person. The trauma could not *stop* me from being that person. I may be a wounded healer, but I knew with certainty that I was supposed to help people feel better.

At the July 4, 2006, office fundraiser in Nyack, I bought two dozen raffle tickets. The proceeds would buy toys for the kids at the AIDS clinic.

"Tali, they're calling your name," an excited colleague alerted me.

"Why?"

"You won something."

I won a free yoga class. I nearly gave it away, but something told me it was time to try yoga. I read it was good for relaxation.

The following week, the male instructor began, "In yoga you focus your attention on your breathing and on the sensations in your body. I invite you to pay attention to the connection between the two. Take a deep breath. Exhale slowly and notice if you feel calmer."

I did.

"Approach your body with curiosity and let go of the fear. We hold each position for five breaths to remind us that everything has a beginning and an end."

I kept telling myself that my trauma had a beginning and an end, but my occasional flashback made a liar out of me.

The class was difficult. My faulty amygdala translated the instructor's gentle touch on my back as an assault. My entire body tensed up. My breathing sped up, my face felt flushed and tears welled up in my eyes.

The next morning in my Nyack apartment, as I put my foot on the pedal to lift the lid on the garbage can, my back went into spasm. In slow motion I held onto the wall with both hands and slid down to the floor. I couldn't get up. My cell phone was on top of the kitchen counter, too far away. I could only reach the broom leaning against the wall. I used it to knock the phone down to the floor. Fortunately it didn't break. I dialed nine-one-one.

In the emergency room the doctor gave me a cortisone shot but no prescription for pain or antispasmodic medication.

Dammit.

He said, "You need to see your orthopedic surgeon. Go back to Long Island and no driving."

"I can't do one without the other," I said. "I live alone."

"Call someone. You cannot drive. I'm sorry." He left the room.

You're sorry? Shit! I have so much to do. Who am I going to call at eight in the morning to come and get me? How am I going to get my car back home to Long Island? Who is going to take care of my patients?

Finally, I called my brother, Joseph. He and his wife, Rachel, took time off from work. Joseph drove me home in my car across the Tappan Zee and Whitestone bridges. Rachel followed in their car.

The next day Aunt Kim and Uncle Lloyd took me to my orthopedic surgeon. He remembered me from my car accident six years before.

"You're pretty messed up, Tali."

I heard him but I was not able to understand.

"You're going to have to quit your job in Nyack. You can't be traveling back and forth for at least six months."

It was too much for me to grasp. Who was going to care for my patients? How was I going to get my stuff back to Long Island? I missed everything the doctor said except for "don't drive" and "bed rest."

Thank God for Aunt Kim. She stopped by every day to make sure that I had everything I needed, including a donut cushion to sit on, which took the pressure off my lower back.

One day I was moodily reflecting on my rotten luck.

"You're a fighter, Tal." Aunt Kim said. "You're strong."

I loved that she said that.

"You're too smart to waste time feeling sorry for yourself. You've got to take care of yourself. How in the world can you help people if you're ailing and stressed out?"

She always knew what to say to make me feel better.

Aunt Kim and Uncle Lloyd drove me to my many appointments: doctors, physical therapists and chiropractors. After a month, although still in pain, I began seeing clients at my home office again. I still couldn't drive long distances or get a good night's sleep.

I got a call from my friend Frank, a top fitness instructor I had known for years.

I told him, "I threw my back out a month ago after a yoga class."

"Are you taking anything?"

"I'm on cyclobenzaprine for spasms and hydrocodone for pain but nothing's helping."

"Can you drive?"

"Short distances."

"Can you come over here sometime today?"

I trusted him. I got in my car and drove the six miles to his studio.

He tested my baseline strength. With very light weights, he put me on machines for my neck, back, shoulders, torso and legs.

"Lots of people underestimate the dangers of yoga. I want you to stay away from it for now. I'll show you some safe stretches to do at home."

He showed me five exercises to do at home to strengthen my back and neck.

"Tali, your days of working sixty hours a week are over."

"I tried yoga to help me relax. I just find it so hard to relax."

"My wife just got back from a retreat that helped her focus better. She's a lot more relaxed now."

"Where'd she go?"

"It's called The Healing Process. It's in the Berkshires."

"I've heard of it before." I made a mental note to look at the brochure that Dr. Remsay had sent me.

For four months I had almost no physical activity except for training twice a week with Frank. In September I began teaching two classes at the university and I continued seeing my clients at my home office. I wrote, I read, I prayed, but most important, I rested. My back gradually improved. Frank told me I no longer needed to see him; I was strong enough to train on my own. I bought two exercise machines; one for the neck and another for the back. Frank showed me how to use them.

Soon I was off all medications and I felt better.

Please let this feeling last.

In January, 2007, thirteen-year-old Benjamin Ownby from Union, Missouri was reported missing. Just four days later, he was found alive, along with another boy, Shaun Hornbeck, who had been kidnapped in October of 2002 and held captive for over four years. Both boys were reunited with their families.

Thank God.

Michael Devlin was charged with abducting and sodomizing both boys. Seventy-eight charges were filed against the forty-one-year-old, six foot three, three-hundred pound Devlin.

Three hundred pounds is heavier than a baby elephant.

DATE	NAME	AGE	HOMETOWN	STATUS
Oct 6, 2002	Shawn Hornbeck	11	Richwoods, Missouri	~~MISSING.~~
*Jan 12, 2007				*FOUND ALIVE (now 15).
Jan 8, 2007	Benjamin Ownby	13	Union, Missouri	~~MISSING.~~
*Jan 12, 2007				*FOUND ALIVE.

I made my May reservation for The Healing Process.

twenty-eight

I opened my eyes before the alarm went off. I had a dream that I was sitting in traffic, patient but eager to find shortcuts.

According to the *Dreamer's Dictionary*: "Watching traffic in a dream suggests you're trying to solve a problem alone for which you should request help; a traffic jam predicts obstacles that will require a long and patient effort to overcome."

I had a busy day ahead of me. I saw clients at my home office from eight until two and then I drove to Berkshire County, Massachusetts. Exactly one hundred twenty-five miles as MapQuest said, I made a left turn into the parking lot of a rustic farmhouse. I saw cars but no people. According to my car's thermometer, it was sixty-two degrees out, but the steady wind made it feel cooler.

Aside from the sputtering of my car engine cooling, it was spine-chillingly quiet. There were no leaves blowing in the wind; no birds chirping, and oddly enough, even the flowing water in the creek was mute. I felt like I had just entered the *Twilight Zone*.

I walked around, passing many cottages. I loved the outdoorsy surroundings and the sound of gravel under my feet. A gray-haired man in his mid-fifties sat on the porch, reading in a rocking chair. He didn't glance up.

"Excuse me," I said, "I'm so sorry to bother you."

He looked up.

"Can you please tell me where the office is?"

He pointed right behind him.

I smiled as I walked past him. He did not smile back. They were friendlier inside. I signed in and was given the key to room seventeen. I would have preferred room eighteen, for *chai*, meaning alive, but didn't ask for it.

Everything in my room, including my queen size bed, was wooden. There were six pictures and three mirrors on the wall, not including the one in the bathroom – four mirrors and no hair dryer.

On each side of the bed was a nightstand with a hideous gargoyle lamp with bulging eyes and sharp teeth – it freaked me out. I tried the door into the adjoining room, eighteen, to make sure it was locked. It was.

A shelf held a mishmash selection of books: *Ethan Frome* by Edith Wharton. A collection of Plato's works; as Emerson once said, "Plato is philosophy and philosophy is Plato." *Under The Tuscan Sun* by Frances Mayes. I enjoyed the movie version but not enough to read the book. *India's Freedom* by Jawaharlal Nehru, published in 1936. The jacket said that Nehru, like Gandhi, was imprisoned several times before India finally became independent in 1947.

I brought two books with me: my *Dreamer's Dictionary* and *Gateways to Happiness* by Zelig Pliskin. I also brought a Hallmark talking card that Stuart had given me years ago. It was the *I LOVE LUCY* Vitameatavegamin commercial. "Girlfriend, I'm your Vitameatavegamin girl. Are you tired? Run down? Listless? Do you poop out at parties? Are you unpopular? The answer to all your problems is in this little bottle." It still makes me laugh.

I heard when my neighbors in room eighteen arrived. Two men were talking loudly about baseball. Roger Clemens signed a contract to continue playing for the Yankees and twenty-nine-year-old relief pitcher for the Cardinals, Josh Hancock, died in a car crash. He was texting on his cell phone when the accident occurred.

I promise I'll never text and drive again.

By nine o'clock I had brushed and flossed my teeth and was journaling in bed.

That night I dreamed that one of the men in room eighteen came into my room through the unlocked door. He watched me sleep, unbuttoned my pajama top and touched my breasts. I woke up before anything else happened. I wasn't scared because I knew it was just a dream.

Being desecrated by a stranger was the reason I was there.

The next morning during breakfast they gave everyone a one-page questionnaire to fill out. Three questions touched me: What was your childhood nickname? What childhood issue are you dealing with? Have you ever considered suicide?

For years The Man's voice had echoed around and around in my head and once or twice had almost chipped away my resolve to go on.

I looked around the dining room at the other twenty survivors, seven male and thirteen female, and wondered who had victimized them. Was it a stranger, a neighbor, a teacher, or maybe even a family member? How many had numbed themselves with medication, drugs or alcohol? How many of them had considered suicide?

I pictured us all as children sitting under the big circus tent watching the clowns juggle balls, the acrobats flying through the air, and the elephants, each holding the tail of the one in front. We had dreamed of becoming baseball players, doctors, teachers and mommies.

"What I've got they used to call the blues.
Nothin' is really wrong, feelin' like I don't belong,
Walkin' around, some kind of lonely clown.
Rainy days and Mondays always get me down."

I wanted to leave my past there, in Massachusetts.

I was told to fill in the blank: I feel _____.

Courageous.

I thought of Grandma Devorah. I was around four when I watched the big cockroach scurry up her kitchen wall. Grandma chased it with her black shoe, determined to kill it. The ugly thing escaped behind the clock. Another one scrambled across the linoleum floor. Grandma cornered it. *BAM!* Triumphant, she threw the ugly black bug into the garbage can. Then she went after the one behind the clock. *BAM!* "Courage lost, everything lost," she declared.

In the program I heard the words "forgiveness," "unconditional love" and "trust." I didn't feel any of them. I heard "negatively programmed in childhood through words and actions." I had no idea what that meant. "What the mind represses the body expresses…"

That's true.

"… through illnesses like chronic fatigue, migraines and back pain."

Back pain? Hello!

"We fear feeling our anger. But holding it in is even worse."

Yes, yes.

I knew I had been running away from my anger, and when I wasn't running, I numbed myself with ice cream and work.

"The goal is forgiveness, but you must learn to express your anger before you can forgive. You forgive yourself and you forgive the person who hurt you. Forgiveness will set you free."

On day two, we were told, "Go back to childhood and see what needs have not been met." I was told to give Mom and Dad back their "patterns."

What?

This program was not about overcoming childhood sexual abuse. It was about understanding all of our childhood issues and forgiving our parents. It was the best they could do at the time, even if it wasn't good enough. I had to refocus. I was all psyched up to deal with The Man in the white limousine.

I learned about my Spirit Guide – the someone or something who came from the Light to guide me.

But after a few more terms like "negative love" and "not feeling lovable," I regretted being there. I wished I were at Canyon Ranch, a well-known spa less than thirty minutes away.

I heard about how obsessive thoughts led to obsessive actions like workaholism.

That's me all right.

I heard about how self-numbing through addictions make life tolerable at the time, but at the expense of lost insight of what is going on inside your mind and body.

"A traumatized brain keeps secreting stress hormones, signaling the fight-or-flight-or-freeze response, long after the event has passed. Freezing, feeling paralyzed to move or speak, and therefore unable to protect oneself, is most detrimental in leaving long-lasting invisible scars."

That day I wanted to run but I couldn't. I froze. I tried to scream but nothing came out.

"There is some truth to the saying that time heals all wounds. But the other part, the part that is even more important, is the work that you put into healing during that time. In other words, healing is an active process. People who actively *do* something to deal with trauma use their stress hormones productively and therefore are at much lower risk of staying traumatized."

I resolved to focus on the program and gave up my fantasy of getting a hot stone massage or facial at Canyon Ranch. I knew I was in the right place after all. I had to keep going even if I was uncomfortable.

Our teachers, Brian, Barbara and Sara, were about to begin our guided meditation. Sara said, "Soon we are going to ask you to close your eyes. Obviously you won't see what's going on around you. But no need for panic. It's okay."

I shifted in my chair.

Brian continued, "If we were able to do your brain scans, each of you would probably show an increased activity of your amygdala, the fear center of your brain. One of the benefits of meditation is that it calms the fear center."

In a soft-spoken voice, Barbara said, "The purpose of today's meditation is to calm your fear center. So, when you are ready, take a deep breath and slowly allow your eyes to close."

I took a deep breath, closed my eyes, and focused on their voices and the images they were presenting. Following directions, I completed three exhales with "ishes" and a final exhale with an "om."

Breathe.

Brian continued.

Pay attention. Listen to what he's saying.

My inner voice was louder than his.

Focus. Breathe in. Exhale.

The room was quiet with the exception of heavy breathing. I opened my eyes and saw it was the girl next to me. Every three seconds she exhaled loud and clear, *whoo.*

No wonder I can't concentrate.

I tried again.

Inhale; one, two, three, four, and exhale; four, three, two, one.

Nothing. My mind wandered. *No thing.* My meaningless thoughts were deafening.

I can't be the only one having a difficult time with this. Try again.

I closed my eyes tightly. Seconds passed. My eyes stared at the empty screen of my mind. My abdomen was rising and falling rhythmically.

And then, finally – something. Unbelievably, a bright violet light appeared. I had never seen anything like it before. Was this my Spirit Guide? I fought the temptation to open my eyes again. I followed along in the visualization, watching the violet light dance. My Spirit Guide was silent but not still, continuously dancing around, changing its shape and size, but never its color.

Barbara told us that we would be climbing ten steps. We counted them together. My Spirit Guide produced an ocean of gentle but powerful waves as I floated to the top.

Sara told us to leave our Spirit Guide and walk straight ahead to meet with our Highest Power. I saw a small white light, like a twinkling star, turn to light pink. It turned into a deep pink, a pale red and finally into a fire engine red. The light was so bright that it radiated heat.

Is this real?

I thought that one of the teachers was shining a heat lamp on me. I gave in to the temptation – I opened my eyes. There was no one near me, only other participants sitting with their eyes closed. I started to cry. I closed my eyes again. I apologized to my Highest Power and prayed for it to return. It did! I raised my hands to my heart in gratitude.

Brian told us to ask our Highest Power if there was a message for us today. I heard, very clearly, "You're okay. It's time for you to let go."

I'm okay. I have to let go.

Soon after, Sara guided us back down the ten steps. My Spirit Guide was at the bottom of the steps, waiting for me.

This was the most amazing experience. Was this why people took drugs and alcohol?

The next day I met privately with Barbara.

"You do not have children?" she asked, looking at my questionnaire.

"No."

"Have you had any abortions?"

"No." Immediately I felt sick. I took a deep breath. I remembered the promise that I had made to Stuart. But keeping secrets prevented me from becoming who I wanted to be. I was there to heal and that meant telling the truth. Feeling exposed and ashamed, I placed my praying hands across my stomach. I said, "Wait, yes, I had one abortion." I started to cry. And here, for the first time, I began to mourn the loss of my unborn child.

We were divided into four groups and driven to the nearest cemetery, two miles away. It was gloomy and smelled like rain. I was given a single red rose and told to search out the grave of an infant. If dread had a taste, it was the combination of curdled milk and rancid meat. I became nauseous in the somber moments it took for me to find Marc Matthews. His birth and death day were the same, May 14, 1988. I placed my rose on his grave. I lay down and embraced the earth. I cried as if that boy, who never had the chance to live for even one day, were mine. I felt shame for extinguishing the spirit that was meant to be born into this world in May 1990.

I then had the assignment that everyone else had: to search out the graves of a man and woman who could represent our parents. We had been told that it was a lot easier to forgive the ones we loved if we remembered they would not be with us forever.

I found a woman who had a long life. Karen Pamela Stevie was ninety-eight years old. A devoted wife, mother, grandmother and great-grandmother.

"Mom, I forgive you for not seeing my pain. Why did you ask me if I was gay? I needed you to ask me if I was okay. I forgive you for all the times you forgot which foods made me sick. I forgive you that your best was not good enough. I love you."

I was sobbing like a little girl. Oh my God, I just wanted to go back to my room and bury myself under the blanket.

I walked away to find a man who could be Dad. I stopped at Victor Maddox because I didn't have the energy to go any farther and I didn't want to get any closer to my classmates. He was only seventy-two. My father was seventy-two. I just wanted to get this over with.

"Hi, Dad. I'm supposed to forgive you for something. I don't know what... I'm sorry that you had such a difficult life and had to drop out of high school to support your siblings. Thank you for telling me that we have angels watching over us. I believe you. I forgive you for not spending more time with me. I love you."

I started to walk away but then turned back. I knelt down on both knees, my hands trembling, touching the earth.

"Dad, there's something else. And this is really hard for me. Why did you tell Daniel that he couldn't marry me? I told myself that I wasn't mad at you, but I was. I loved him; he was the only man who ever understood me. You knew very little about me and nothing about him. I thought I'd find someone else, but I haven't; maybe I never will. I know you did what you thought was best, but you didn't know what was best for *me*. I'm not mad at you anymore. I forgive you."

My head was going to explode. I rejoined the group. "Does anyone have an aspirin?" A woman reached into her bag and gave me two. I thanked her and swallowed the pills without any water.

That was the hardest day of the week.

The following day we met as a group. A bundle of index cards and a marker waited for us on each of the twenty mats spread across the floor. In front of the room sat a box containing gloves and yellow plastic bats. We were told to take a pair of gloves and a bat and to choose a mat to sit on. I chose a mat near the back wall. I wanted to be as far away as I could be.

Sara said, "Today is the day to deal with your childhood issues. On each of the ten index cards you are to write down a negative feeling that you have been carrying with you since childhood. You have ten minutes."

After ten minutes we were told to put on our gloves and pick up our bats. An ominous silence saturated the room – the harmony before the madness.

"Look at your index cards and silently name your feelings, starting with 'I am'."

I am angry. I am sad. I am depressed. I am frustrated. I am lonely. I am frightened.

I looked around the room, comforted to know that this exercise was done in silence.

I am suspicious. I am anxious. I am resentful. I am lost.

Then we were told to say these words out loud, to take each index card, one by one, and scream each feeling out loud as we beat the card to shreds with our bat.

Oh shit.

I remembered the exercise I did with Dr. Remsay.

I put on my gloves. I took hold of my bat. I hit the "Angry" card and I said "I am angry." I did it again, a little louder and a little harder. I swung eight more times before the index card was torn to pieces.

I moved on to the second card. It took only six over-the-head swings to beat the shit out of my "Sadness." "Depression" was no longer readable after three swings. My heart rate increased; my back and neck grew tense. I saw "Frustration" sitting motionless on the mat until I hit it with all my might. By the time my ten cards were beaten to a pulp, I too was torn apart and exhausted.

We were given one more card. "This card is for you to write down your secret."

Oh my God.

I placed my secret face down on the mat. Just the thought of going back to that day choked the life out of me. We were reminded that we were in a safe place and told to say our secret out loud. We all did it at the same time, so I heard only my own. I was so exhausted I didn't care if anyone else heard me.

My voice rose a full octave, "I was abducted and sexually abused by a stranger I call The Man."

As I raised the bat above my head, new energy rose within me, and I slammed that card with every ounce of strength I had left. I felt blisters forming on my palms. The pain exploded to the surface. I had enough.

That night I picked at one of my blisters the way I had picked at my cuticles when I was a kid. But then I stopped. I went into the bathroom, washed it, dried it, kissed it and went back to bed.

The next, and final, morning I felt the metamorphosis within me. "Why did this happen *to* me?" changed to "Why did this happen *for* me?" On the drive home I felt that the anger, shame and fear had subsided. I had inched a small way forward.

The seasons passed. I cultivated my relationship with God on a daily basis. I started my day with the discipline of prayer. I hoped my positive thoughts would lead to positive actions. I was ready for my next big challenge.

twenty-nine

July 24, 2007: My feet stepped over the grass, moist from the morning dew.

Am I alone?

I moved steadily but not fast. I saw that I was climbing. My body leaned forward to make the ascent easier.

Where am I?

Although a winter hat covered my ears, I caught a glimpse of the diamond stud earrings that I had bought in Israel. I was wearing a mountaineering jacket over a turtleneck sweater, snow pants and hiking boots. These were heavy boots, heavier than the ones I owned. I stumbled on a tree branch; my gloved hands broke my fall.

I'm pretty sure this is me but I can't see my face.

A panoramic view of a mountainside opened up. If, in fact, this was me, it was clear that I was climbing a mountain. My sunglasses blocked the sun's strong rays.

I awoke to the natural morning light.

That was an interesting dream.

July 25, 2007: A flashlight shined in from outside my tent. "It's time to go," a man's voice said. He had an accent that I couldn't identify.

I heard many feet marching. I smelled nature's frosty air. I saw only the back of the head of the person directly in front of me. I felt my blood rush. I touched the small stone in my pocket; I knew it was engraved *STRENGTH*, the meaning of my last name. I breathed slowly; I savored each breath.

I am strong.

I know I can open my eyes and this will be over, but I don't want it to be.

"*Acuna matada,*" a man's voice said.

Acuna matada is from The Lion King. It's Swahili for 'No worries.'

"The summit is less than an hour away. *Acuna matada.*"

Summit?

"Soon we will be descending from the greatest mountain in all of Africa. Enjoy these moments, my friends. Enjoy your final ascent on Kilimanjaro."

Kilimanjaro? Really?

I woke up to the sun percolating through my bedroom blinds.

July 29, 2007: Jeffrey, age fifty-seven, was referred to me by his cardiologist to help him lower his cholesterol, blood pressure and weight. At five eight, he weighed one hundred and ninety-four pounds. He wanted to lose forty pounds. I reviewed his blood work and took his blood pressure, baseline body fat and girth measurements. I gathered his family history, food intake and exercise routine.

He said, "Last August I climbed Mount Kilimanjaro. It took five days up and two days down. I've gained a lot of weight since then."

Kilimanjaro?

After Jeffrey left with his nutrition plan and a follow-up appointment, I went on the Internet to gather information about Mount Kilimanjaro. Many different companies offered tours. The prices were confusing; not everything was included. The trip could cost between five and seven thousand dollars.

Jeffrey helped me plan my trip, based on his experience on Mount Kilimanjaro.

"The Travel and Immunization Center at North Shore University Hospital will tell you what shots you need to take and when. You should also ask them about Cipro and Diamox."

"I know Cipro is an antibiotic. What's Diamox?"

"Diamox is for altitude sickness. Mount Kilimanjaro is just over nineteen thousand feet high. Even on Diamox I got sick."

"Do you mean you were throwing up?"

"Yes, but I had all sorts of symptoms leading up to that: headache, nausea, dizziness, shortness of breath. I'm sure I was dehydrated, that's one of the side effects of taking Diamox. I should've drunk more water."

Jeffrey said the best time to climb Mount Kilimanjaro was between February and May when it's not as cold.

I would love to be on the mountain February 22, Daniel's birthday.

"You'll hit every season on the mountain. You'll start out in shorts and tank tops, but it gets colder as you climb higher. By summit day, you'll hit twenty to thirty degrees below zero."

He had followed a low-fat diet on the mountain and said I could ask for a lactose-free diet. He said for an extra sixty bucks I could order both a firm mattress for my back and a down sleeping bag. The porters would carry my luggage and I only had to carry a backpack.

I booked my seven-day mountain climb, from February 21 through March 2, for a total of twenty-seven hundred dollars plus another two grand for the round trip flight.

All this because of a dream. I wonder what I'll learn on the mountain.

John Evander Couey, a repeat sex offender whose crimes against Jessica Lunsford led to new, tougher laws across the nation, had been sentenced to death. I updated my book.

DATE	NAME	AGE	HOMETOWN	STATUS
Feb 28, 2005	Jessica Lunsford	9	Homosassa, Florida	~~MISSING.~~ Murdered by John Couey, a convicted sex offender, who kidnapped Jessica from her bedroom.
*Mar 18, 2005				*Police found Jessica's body buried in a shallow grave under a porch 100 yards from her home.
**Apr 20, 2005				**Jessica was raped and buried alive.
***June 23, 2005				***Couey confessed that Jessica was alive in his closet when police came to his door to question him about her disappearance.
****Aug 24, 2007				****Couey sentenced to death.

On September 16, the doctor at North Shore University Hospital wrote out two prescriptions: ciprofloxacin HCL or Cipro and acetazolamide, which is Diamox. She also handed me a single foil package containing four pills.

"This is oral typhoid fever vaccine. These four pills need to be refrigerated and taken every other day the week before your trip." She gave me a sticker with the dates 2/10 (day 1), 2/12 (day 3), 2/14 (day 5) and 2/16 (day 7) circled. I was given a follow-up appointment for two vaccines: hepatitis A and Tdap for tetanus, diphtheria and pertussis.

On the news, Michael John Devlin pleaded guilty to all seventy-eight charges filed against him in the abductions and molestations of Shawn Hornbeck and Ben Ownby. He was sentenced to three life terms plus an additional one hundred and seventy years for producing child pornography of Shawn Hornbeck and transporting him across state lines to engage in sexual activity.

I trained every day. Some days I weight trained; other days I climbed "hills" on the elliptical machine. Twice a month I walked ten to fifteen miles on the sand at Long Beach, twenty miles away. Jeffrey said the sand was similar to the ash which comes from the volcano on Mount Kilimanjaro.

I ate a variety of foods to ensure that I got all of the vitamins and minerals that I needed. Once a week I went into the health food store and ordered a shot of wheat grass juice. I chased that nasty green stuff down with ten shots of cherry seltzer.

That December, the New Jersey Legislature abolished the state's death penalty, resulting in Jesse Timmendequas' sentence being commuted to life in prison without the possibility of parole. He had been on Death Row since 1994 for raping and murdering seven-year-old Megan Kanka.

Son of a bitch.

DATE	NAME	AGE	HOMETOWN	STATUS
July 29, 1994	Megan Kanka	7	Hamilton Township, New Jersey	Raped and murdered by neighbor, Jesse Timmendequas - received death sentence. (MEGAN'S LAW)
*Dec 17, 2007				*NJ abolished death penalty. Timmendequas to serve life in prison without parole.

I was on my way to Africa wearing the Star of David necklace that Daniel had given me and a ring that my sister-in-law, Rachel, had just given me for good luck. I was carrying two quotes. From the Talmud, "Three things restore a person's good spirits: beautiful sounds, sights and smells." And from Hemingway's *The Snows of Kilimanjaro,* "I wonder if there'll be another time as good as this."

February 21, 2008. E-mail to my family:

Hi Loved Ones:

The eagle has landed! It's 2 P.M. in New York and 10 P.M. here in Africa. Everything went smoothly. I made friends on the flight so the 15 hours went fast, found my bag immediately and my driver was waiting for me. I met one guy in my group, Karsten from Denmark. We drove together from Kilimanjaro Airport to the lodge in Arusha. Tomorrow I rest and early Saturday we head up the mountain. I am happy, healthy and VERY much at peace! Thank you all for your love and support.

All My Love, Tali

February 22: *Happy Birthday, Daniel! You are eighty-one years old today.*

At our morning pre-climb briefing I met up with Karsten and the other hikers: Annemarie, Maura, Todd, Kent and Ron all from California; Craig and Ronnie from Johannesburg; Geoff from Australia and Robert and Erik, both gastroenterologists, from Holland. Annemarie was a gynecologist and Craig was a plastic surgeon. Four physicians on board – I was in good hands!

Meke, our group leader, introduced us to Charles, James, Joseph and Peter, our summit porters.

"Welcome to Tanzania. We appreciate that you are all first-timers. Kilimanjaro is not only the highest mountain in Africa, but it is also one of the highest walkable mountains in the world. The park itself extends over the entire mountain. Our group will be hiking up the Shira route. The route down will be different to

213

control the traffic on the mountain. We will be on the mountain for eight days and seven nights.

"Every evening there will be a briefing for the next day's climb. We will tell you exactly what to expect, what to wear and what to pack. Only the summit porters will climb with you. The other hundred porters are trained to carry your luggage, tent, food, water and everything else you will need on the mountain. Bottled oxygen will be available for emergency situations. The porters will have your tents up with your luggage inside before you arrive at each camp. Ted, the cook, will have your meals ready on time so you will not be hungry. Anything can happen on the mountain, even if you are healthy. It is our responsibility to get you off this mountain safely. If we think you are in any kind of danger, like pulmonary or cerebral edema caused by hypoxia, you don't have a choice; you are getting off the mountain."

"What's hypoxia?" Ronnie asked.

"It's a condition that can happen to anybody, young, old, healthy and fit people, at high altitudes. Your hands, feet, brain and lungs are deprived of oxygen. Signs you can see may be your fingers turning blue. Signs you cannot see may be fluid buildup in the lungs or brain. This can lead to fatal complications and that is why we have the last word on who climbs and how high. Am I clear?"

We all nodded our heads.

Todd asked a question about acclimating, a mountaineering term.

Meke told us, "After each climb we will rest, eat, drink water and allow our bodies to adjust to the higher elevation, lower temperature and less oxygen in the air. We never sleep at the higher altitude. We always return to base camp at a lower altitude."

"Do you recommend that we take Diamox?" I asked.

"Diamox can prevent altitude sickness, but it increases dehydration. It is your responsibility to drink plenty of water, especially if you take Diamox."

I'll take the Diamox and drink lots of water.

My hotel room had a bathroom with an above ground flushing toilet and a shower, a luxury for this part of Africa. The towels were stiff and coarse. The walls were painted white. There were no pictures. The twin bed had a mosquito net. A copy of the Bible sat on the nightstand.

Before dinner I lit the *Shabbat* candles, said the prayer and sang "Happy Birthday" to Daniel. I hoped to feel his presence on the mountain.

I woke up many times in the night with muscle spasms in my left leg. I thought I was dehydrated. I paced around. When I returned to bed I had a dream of a nine-year-old girl dancing. "Congratulations on your effort to discover your authentic self," said the male teacher in the dream.

I thought of Daniel. His last words to me were something about dancing. I was very lucky to have him in my life (even now). He was strong enough, secure enough and brave enough to love me through some pretty dark days. I trusted him to protect my soul while I tried cementing fragments of my childhood back together. Daniel was the perfect anchor for me then and I was thrilled to think he was here with me now.

After breakfast, the twelve of us piled our stuff into three trucks. Sharing a truck with me was Karsten, age forty-eight, Erik, sixty, and Robert, fifty-nine. Robert sat in the back row with Karsten, coughing and sneezing. I rolled down the window.

This can't be good.

Driving two hours to base camp, we passed Mount Meru and saw the snow-capped peaks of Mount Kilimanjaro in the distance.

Oh my God, it's beautiful. Absolutely beautiful.

Kilimanjaro Park smelled like pine. There was dust everywhere. We climbed fifteen hundred feet. We acclimated at Shira Camp, resting, eating and drinking water. I used the bathroom: a big bucket in a tent. The porters came around with hot water. I washed the caked-on dust off my face, changed clothes, snacked on Lorna

Doone cookies and drank lots of water and hot tea. I was happy to be on the mountain where I didn't have to think about anything else.

My back hurt. I had to pack smarter and lighter for the rest of the journey. At the end of the day, my pedometer said we walked eleven thousand steps – five and a half miles.

By seven in the evening we sat in the mess tent with a kerosene lamp. We were all doing well except for Robert, who was having a hard time breathing. We wondered what he was going to do for the rest of the trip.

Chacula bomba! (The food is fabulous!) Onion and leek soup, bread and butter, vegetables and beans, spinach, fried fish and potatoes, mango for dessert, lots of tea and water. *Asante sana,* Ted. (Thank you Ted, our cook.) By nine I was in my tent under my sleeping bag saying my prayers.

I woke up to the aroma of hot mint tea just before six thirty. We were told to pack rain gear and light gloves in our backpacks. The porters carried the rest of our stuff. An hour later we gathered in the mess tent for porridge, bacon and eggs. We filled up our water bottles and headed *poli-poli,* slowly-slowly, to Shira Cathedral, a prominent rock formation, about two and a half hours away. They told us to do a scramble, that is, to climb hand-over-hand up the rocks. We did all this together except for Robert, who stayed behind. They were testing our ability to climb more difficult terrain. I loved this.

We rested for thirty minutes and then continued to Shira II (12,598 feet). The walking was peaceful; there was little talking. When I squatted to use the bathroom I felt my intestine pushing out from my left side. I thought it was a duodenal hernia, but I knew that I was not in any immediate danger. I pushed it back in and gently massaged my left side.

Nothing is going to bother me today.

Later I spoke with Erik, the surgeon from Holland. He touched my side and said that he could still feel it and agreed that it was a duodenal hernia and most likely congenital, but not immediately dangerous. I'd take care of it when I got home.

The next three hours were hard because we were climbing higher. We hiked to Moir (13,780 feet) where we ate lunch with spectacular views of Mount Meru's dramatic crater and Ol Donyo Lengai's active volcano. Some hikers in the group got altitude sickness, but I was fine. The Diamox seemed to be working. My pedometer, on the other hand, had stopped working, so now we all guessed that we had walked about six miles in five hours. We returned to our lower-altitude base camp for dinner. I slept from ten until midnight, used the bathroom and then easily fell back to sleep. I woke up at six thirty feeling well rested.

The next day we climbed even higher and it got harder. Altitude sickness came to me at 14,000 feet. My breathing became shallow and my fingers got numb and started to tingle. These were side effects from the Diamox, which I was taking twice a day.

My bowel movements were great despite the changes in diet, altitude and activity. For the first few days my tent was very close to the make-shift bathroom. Sometimes nature called while we were hiking and we had to pee on the mountain. I would go behind a bush without distending my colon again. I received a standing ovation from my fellow hikers who knew I had a hernia.

There are no secrets on the mountain.

I rested in my tent with my eyes closed. I prayed to my Spirit Guide. The violet light appeared, disappeared and then reappeared. I felt the marvelous light energy travel through my body. I hadn't seen it since attending The Healing Process last May.

I made myself drink lots and lots of water because I knew Diamox was a diuretic: two cups before breakfast, six cups with breakfast (water and tea), six cups during the first hike, maybe four cups during the second hike, another two cups before dinner, six at dinner and another two before bed. That's twenty-five to thirty cups of water every day. I was happy to be close to the porta potty.

It was cold and icy at the higher altitude. We wore our down jackets for the afternoon climb to Lent Hills (15,617 feet). I was winded. I had a headache and tingling in my fingers, mostly my left hand. I was in a good mood and none of this bothered me.

The big problem came when we descended to base camp. I developed a crippling headache which wouldn't go away. Dr. Craig gave me medication, a combination of ibuprofen, Tylenol and codeine. It worked quickly.

Charles did the briefing for the next day: "You will wake up at six thirty, pack your snacks, rain gear, gloves and sunscreen. Breakfast is at seven. By eight we will hike to the next camp, Lava Tower, about four hours away. We will have a hot lunch and rest. Around three we will begin another hike, close to 16,000 feet. Remember the summit is 19,341 feet."

I was in my sleeping bag by nine. I got up twice in the middle of the night to pee. I woke up around six in the morning and my headache was completely gone. I had enough time to stretch out my back and to thank God for how far I had come. I prayed that I would be able to climb even higher.

I walked into the mess tent for breakfast with a smile and an enthusiastic, "Good morning, everyone!"

Without missing a beat Craig said, "What the fuck are you so happy about?"

Everyone laughed.

We hiked four and a half hours with two short breaks. We were higher and it was harder to breathe. By twelve thirty in the afternoon we arrived at our third base camp. My gear was waiting for me in my tent where I rested on my air mattress with my legs over my rolled-up sleeping bag. I listened to the symphony of hail on top of my tent. It sounded like the thunder of applause.

The altitude was affecting my appetite. For the first time I did not feel hungry, but I ate lunch anyway, even though I couldn't taste anything. I added lots of salt to the chicken soup and two pieces of fried bread. Finally I could taste something.

I enjoyed the afternoon hike. We were disappointed when we arrived at our destination because there were too many clouds to see anything. Before bed I washed up with the baby wipes I had brought from home. It was the best one could do on the mountain. There were just two and a half days to summit.

I woke up with my eyes swollen shut. I couldn't see but I remained calm. All four doctors said it was from my salt intake but not to worry; it would go away within an hour.

Stay away from the salt.

This was a long and extraordinary day. The best part of the trip was the scramble up the Barranco Wall. It took ninety minutes of hand-over-hand rock climbing to reach the top. We took thirty minutes for lunch while we looked at the snowy peaks of Mount Kilimanjaro.

I loathed the three-hour descent back to base camp. It was slippery and took longer than expected because one of the porters had slipped and sprained his ankle. Craig bandaged him up and gave him pain medication. Now, at a lower altitude, my decreased appetite, tingling fingers and confusion had subsided. I felt good.

Before dinner I rested in my tent under my sleeping bag. I closed my eyes and thought of Daniel. I was at peace.

They told us the summit day, day seven, would take ten to twelve hours.

Can I actually do this?

In my dream eight months ago I never saw myself summit. I was more relaxed after I stopped making the summit my goal. My goal was just to be on this mountain. I was already successful.

It was three in the morning. After sleeping five hours, I had to pee.

The terrain at this camp was like no other – rocky and dangerous. I stepped out of my tent into complete darkness. Even with my flashlight I was confused; I didn't see the bathroom. At the other camps I was in the tent closest to the bathroom. I was not going to risk twisting my ankle looking for it. I turned around to go back to my tent, but now I was confused again.

Which tent is mine?

The altitude was affecting my mind. They all looked the same. I took a guess, I looked inside and I was right. I peed outside my tent. I slept another three hours for a total of eight hours.

Daniel appeared in my dream. He said, "*Shema*, listen. You can travel great distances, but still stay where you are. To grow you've got to learn the lessons, make the changes and move on." A single tear streamed down his left cheek. I told him that I loved him. I felt him say, "I am very proud of you."

During our morning climb I picked up two small heart-shaped rocks to put on the gravestones of Grandma Devorah and Daniel. I knew he was there with me.

By one thirty in the afternoon we arrived at our final campsite. I couldn't believe how good I felt; I had no symptoms at all. I wasn't even tired.

Karsten didn't come to lunch and Ron was led down to a lower altitude because he was sick. Even thirty minutes farther down made a difference. Robert, who was doing awfully the first few days, had somehow recuperated and was doing well.

We planned to leave at midnight so that we could reach the summit by sunrise. I was packed and resting in my tent. I wore my down coat and lay under my sleeping bag. I listened to the hail hit the canvas. I hoped it would not hail at midnight.

The terrain was far more risky than the previous day. Even in the daylight it took me ten minutes to walk the sixty feet to the bathroom. If I had to pee at night I would do so outside my tent.

My eyes were tired so I rested before dinner at five. My Spirit Guide appeared on its own. It danced around, got larger and then smaller again. This happened four or five times. When it faded away I opened my eyes.

After-dinner summit briefing: "We will wake up at eleven and meet in the mess tent by eleven thirty for tea and porridge. We will leave for our final ascent at midnight for two reasons: first, so we can arrive at sunrise, and second, because seeing what we are climbing in daylight would be too scary."

We were told to pack for temperatures that would be below freezing: a heavy hat and face mask, hand warmers and heavy gloves. Also in our backpacks would go sunglasses, sunscreen, headlamp, extra batteries, three liters of water, medicine, snacks, camera, toilet paper, money and passport. We were told to start with a light hat and gloves, three upper body layers, a windbreaker, our down coat, two pairs of thermal socks, boots, gaiters (for traction) and our walking sticks.

I checked off every item. I felt ready. The rest was out of my control.

Meke, our group leader, told us that Stella Point at 18,885 feet, the first summit, was about six hours away. We should arrive in time to watch the sunrise. We would rest only ten minutes to eat and take photos.

He said that those who could hike another hour would go on to *Uhuru* (Freedom) Peak at 19,341 feet, the rim of the volcano, the highest summit. Once back at camp we would eat, drink and rest for one hour before descending to final base camp, about three hours away. Estimated round-trip time: ten to twelve hours. Temperature at the top: -4 to -22 degrees Fahrenheit.

After the summit briefing we slept four hours until it was time to go: Thursday, eleven thirty at night, "Blessed are You, King of the universe, Who guides us on our journey." I was ready.

The climb up was very grueling. I felt my ears pop from the change in altitude. It was dark, and as in my dream from so many months ago, I couldn't see anything except the back of the head of the person in front of me. I trudged through the darkness, hardly aware that I was moving.

"*Shema...*" I cried out the first word of the prayer, but the fierce winds blew the word right back into my face.

After the first two hours of the climb, I had trouble catching my breath. I couldn't focus on my breathing because one of the porters was singing effortlessly in Swahili.

How does he do it?

Finally he stopped and I was able to concentrate on inhaling and exhaling through my nose again. Soon I got my breath back.

By the fourth hour we were divided into two groups. I was placed in Group One, with Karsten, Todd, Kent, Craig and Ronnie. Annemarie, Maura, Robert, Erik and Geoff, in Group Two, reached Stella Point an hour after us. Ron, who had complications earlier, was led down to a lower altitude base camp.

It was very cold but I was dressed for it. The darkness outside lifted and I breathed through my nose with no problems.

In my head I heard one voice telling me, *I'll never make it,* and another voice telling me, *I'm already there.* I had to let go of both voices in order to remain present in the moment.

We reached Stella Point, the first summit, at six-forty in the morning. I couldn't believe I was standing on top of Mount Kilimanjaro, with a panorama of mountains and sky in all directions. I collected lava rocks, took photos and drank hot water. I was too excited to eat.

We stayed there for ten minutes and then "*twenda, twenda*" (let's go, let's go), off to *Uhuru* Peak. I started off with energy but then became lightheaded. I saw flashes of light.

Are people taking photos of me?

I had to sit down.

Meke pulled off my gloves to see if my fingers were blue from a lack of oxygen. They were. He asked me a question which I couldn't understand. I heard him say, "She has hypoxia. Run her down the mountain."

Her? Is that ME?

I observed everything around me but I was not participating. I heard Meke's voice again, "James, run her down the mountain."

Her is ME!

I was no longer lucid. James seemed to be speaking in gibberish. He brought me down quickly, arm in arm. I was not in control and I could not stand it. After an unknown amount of time had passed, I asked him to show me how to get down the mountain by myself. He showed me how to ski down in my boots with one hiking pole for balance. He led. I followed. I swallowed a lot of his dust. I looked and felt the dirtiest I had ever felt in my life.

After the first hour it was not as steep and we just climbed down. I caught my breath and was able to talk with James.

"How many times have you climbed this mountain?"

"Too many to count."

"Do you climb every trip?"

"We rotate. Many need money to pay rent."

"How much is rent?"

"Thirty dollar rent and more for school."

"What are you studying?"

"Design. I graduate soon."

"And then what would you like to do?"

"I marry you and move to America."

"Thanks, James, but I'm old enough to be your mother." I said blowing out a gust of air.

"No. I say you twenty-eight."

"Plus fifteen years."

He laughed, "No believe."

At the end, I tipped James a month's rent: one dollar for getting me down safely and twenty-nine dollars for his charm.

I returned severely dehydrated. Everyone was back for lunch at noon. We packed up and headed to our final base camp, two hours away.

I lit the *Shabbat* candles in the mess tent before anyone came in for dinner. They glowed in the Kilimanjaro beer bottles. Everyone loved it.

I started the dinner conversation about *Uhuru*. "What was Freedom like up there?"

Kent: "It was quick."

Craig in his South African accent: "And fucking cold."

Todd: "It must have been -40 degrees with the wind chill."

Ronnie in his South African accent: "My legs were heavy and I couldn't breathe."

Craig, rolling his eyes: "She doesn't care about your fucking legs. She wants to know what *Uhuru* looked like."

We were all laughing.

I really want to know what Freedom felt like.

Craig: "It was fucking glorious."

Karston: "I snapped my photo by the sign, looked out into the heavenly skies, and then turned around. It was fast."

Todd: "It was intense. An indescribable paradise."

Ronnie: "The descent down was grueling. My knees will never be the same. I think I lost a couple of toenails."

We all caught Craig rolling his eyes again.

More laughter.

Karston decided to end on a high note: "Freedom is within reach if you just keep climbing."

I slept nine hours straight. Nothing hurt. I felt great. Today was all downhill, literally. We had the usual breakfast: porridge, toast with peanut butter, omelet and lots of tea.

On the way down, we were all taken aback by the beautiful waterfall display. Meke told us that it was natural, not man-made.

The source of the water were the glaciers at the summit. We passed through the changing vegetation zones and tropical rain forest at the bottom. We looked for monkeys but didn't see any.

We were off the mountain by three. It was an hour's ride to Kilimanjaro International Airport Lodge where we stayed overnight. My morning flight to Nairobi, Kenya, took off on time. From my seat I watched the sunrise behind Mount Meru. We flew at 18,000 feet. It was hard to imagine that I had climbed higher than that. The snow-covered plains grew farther and farther away.

I have to let go. In order for me to touch down again, I have to let go.

We landed safely in Nairobi. I had two hours before boarding the flight to Amsterdam. I bought lots of Amurula (African liquor), chocolates and tea as gifts for family and friends. I bought amethyst earrings for Mom.

Nairobi to Amsterdam was about four thousand miles. We arrived eight hours later, where it was two hours earlier. Lunch was served at twelve thirty on the plane. The food on the mountain was better.

After eating, I tried to sleep but I felt there was something wrong with my body. In Amsterdam, prior to boarding for New York, I felt nauseous and feverish. I made it to the bathroom in time. I knew the blood was not from my period.

As I waited to board the plane back home, "Bright Sunshiny Day" by Jimmy Cliff played over the speaker. I sang the first verse barely above a whisper:

"*I can see clearly now the rain is gone.*
I can see all obstacles in my way.
If you look high above the clouds are gone.
It's gonna be a bright, bright, bright, sunshiny day."

I sang to plant these words into the universe. *Kabbalah* says that speech is closer to spirituality than action. When we say positive words, we bring Light into this world.

thirty

After a full day of sunshine there come the inevitable clouds, and sometimes rain, followed by, God willing, a beautiful rainbow.

When I returned home, one of my phone messages was from my oncologist. "Tali, it's Dr. Kent. I hope you had a great trip. Please call my office. It's time to climb another mountain."

I loved that he remembered my trip. I called his office. They squeezed me in the next day.

Last September, my gynecologist had diagnosed my routine Pap test as abnormal. Another test, a colposcopy, was scheduled. She used a magnifying device resembling binoculars to look at my cervix more closely. After the exam she told me to get dressed and meet her in her office.

Office?

In the years of knowing her we hardly ever had a face-to-face conversation. I couldn't tell you what color her eyes were. I'd fill her in on the latest nutrition trends and she'd catch me up with her family.

"You tested positive for HPV."

"What's HPV?"

"Human papillomavirus. It's very common and most likely it was sexually transmitted."

Sexually transmitted? What?

I now saw her eyes were brown.

"Abnormal cells were detected in your cervix. I want you to see Dr. Warren Kent, an oncologist."

An oncologist? Oh my God.

Dr. Kent told me that I needed to have a biopsy, done in a hospital under sedation. It required a minimum of one week of bed rest afterward.

I didn't like the idea. "But I'm climbing a mountain in a couple of months," I said.

After negotiation, we decided that I would continue to train for the climb. Surgery would be after the trip. From that day forward I had blocked out the fact that there were abnormal cells growing inside me.

I had decades of training at blocking negative things out. I was an expert.

Now, it was Tuesday, March 4, 2008, two days after I had returned from my trip. Dr. Kent arranged for my pretesting and surgery. He performed the LEEP (loop electrosurgical excision procedure), in which a wire loop is electrified and cuts through the cervix like a scalpel. This biopsy removed all the areas of abnormal growth and doubled as treatment.

Dr. Kent said, "You have cervical dysplasia, which is an abnormal growth of cells in your cervix. Your abnormal cells were confined only to the surface of the cervix. When caught early, like yours, it's easily treated, but later stages can progress to cervical cancer."

I was supposed to be on bed rest for one week after this procedure, but I felt incredible. I was back to work in two days.

Richard, that is, Big Dick, called out of the blue. It had been six years since I last saw him.

"How are you?"

"Great. I just got back from climbing Mount Kilimanjaro."

"La-di-dah. You're self-aggrandizing."

"Excuse me?"

"It's more effective if you let someone else discover your strength." He said, "It's like a man on a first date bragging about his charitable contributions."

"You know me for almost ten years. Do you think I'm trying to impress you?"

Asshole!

No answer.

That was the moment it occurred to me that perhaps he had given me HPV. "I have a question for you and please remember I'm a truth-seeker."

"I know, Tali, that's one of the things I love about you. What's the question?"

"During the time we were together did you sleep with other women?" Even though we always had protected sex, he knew I was monogamous.

"That's none of your business," he said in a dismissive voice.

That revealed perfectly who he really was.

I squeezed the phone. I imagined crushing it like an empty soda can.

He was still talking; I hung up on him in mid-sentence. I took a deep breath.

Relax.

In the spring I hired landscapers to build a pond with three cascading waterfalls in my backyard. The sound of the running water was peaceful and healing. It would serve as a reminder of the waterfall on Mount Kilimanjaro. I reintroduced my hands to the earth and planted; around the pond, azaleas and tulips that would reincarnate every spring, and in the new terracotta pots, pansy and yellow trillium flowers.

That summer I watched an episode of *Cold Case Files.* "Innocence Lost" was the case of a young girl who had been abducted and raped in the South Bay area of Los Angeles in May 1996. Her abductor then drove her back to the place where he had kidnapped her. Within six months five other young girls were also abducted, raped and then driven back to their initial abduction sites. Despite thousands of leads, the cases went cold.

Two years later, Billy Lee Mayshack, a fifty-three-year-old convicted sex offender from South Bay, was matched by his DNA to all six crimes. At that time he was in jail for sexually molesting his two young grandsons. One of the many questions he was asked was why he returned his victims.

He said, "In a sick way I cared and that's why I took them back. I didn't want anything else to happen to them."

Caring is not sick. I can't imagine that my abductor cared about me.

These were the only other stranger abduction cases that I knew of where the children had been brought back as I had been.

I am so lucky he took me back.

I added these cases to my notebook. I knew the number of unknown victims was far greater than I could imagine and the number of unreported cases was greater still.

DATE	NAME	AGE	HOMETOWN	STATUS
May-Nov 1996-1998	6 girls and 2 boys	7-10 ?	South Bay, Los Angeles	All abducted and raped, but returned ALIVE hours later to abduction site.
*July 2008				*According to Cold Case Files, in 1998, Billy Lee Mayshack was charged with 6 counts of rape and 2 molestation charges of his 2 grandsons.

thirty-one

It was a raw November morning, colder than usual, only thirty degrees at eleven thirty. Rabbi Levine was having a fundraiser at the Temple for children with life-threatening illnesses. There was a clown making balloon animals for the kids and, for the adults, there were specialists volunteering their services: doctors, psychologists, physical therapists and me, the registered dietitian.

I was there alone, in a small room off to the side, answering questions about the role nutrition plays in cancer. I had plenty of downtime to study the poster on the wall. The Tree of Life had ten branches, each with a Hebrew word that I did not understand. "Learn *Kabbalah* Today" was all that was written on the bottom.

I remembered my *Kabbalah* class in Israel: The rabbi said, "We are responsible for the amount of Light we receive and reveal in our lives."

I wanted more Light in my life.

By three in the afternoon, when everyone had gone, I asked Rabbi Levine if he taught *Kabbalah*.

"No. But my colleague, Dr. Avigdor Wilson does."

"A doctor?"

"He has a Ph.D. in Jewish philosophy and he's a professor at Stony Brook University. He's also a spiritual advisor who is well-versed in *Kabbalah*."

He pulled out a business card from his wallet and handed it to me. "Here. His office number and email address."

I chose to send him an email: Dear Dr. Wilson: My name is Tali Stark. Rabbi Chaim Levine suggested that I contact you. I am interested in learning more about *Kabbalah* and I am hoping that you can point me in the right direction. I look forward to hearing from you when time allows.

He quickly responded: I recommend that you first read some of Rabbi Areyh Kaplan's books, guaranteed to be filled with insight and wisdom. *Kabbalah* must be approached with basic understanding of Torah knowledge. It is a wonderful and meaningful study and I am happy to hear that you are interested. I'd like to invite you to Barnes and Noble in Great Neck on Thursday at 3:00 P.M. I will be discussing my new book, *Understanding Kabbalah in Today's World*. If this is of interest to you, we can talk afterward.

I Googled his name. His book came up. I scrolled down until I saw his picture. He was very handsome. He had a full head of brown wavy hair, blue eyes and a clean-shaven youthful face. I wondered how old he was.

I replied: Thank you for your quick response. I'll see you at Barnes and Noble. Congratulations on your book.

The store was jam-packed; I couldn't even get past the standing crowd, mostly women, to see if there were any available seats. I listened to what others were saying: "I studied with Dr. Wilson. He's great." "I came all the way from Philadelphia to see him." "I'm not surprised at this turnout."

Dr. Wilson was introduced as "the author of the hot-off-the-press book, *Understanding Kabbalah in Today's World.*"

"Hello." His voice was soothing. I could tell he was smiling. He opened with a question: "How many of you would volunteer to visit sick people in the hospital?"

Many hands went up, including mine.

"It's nice to see that you have charity work in your heart, especially the *mitzvah* or commandment of *bikur cholim,* meaning visiting the sick. When we help others and try to cheer them up, God takes note. Our actions become spiritual entities that contribute to the building blocks of *tikun olam,* or fixing the world."

Even when I tried to catch a glimpse of him, I could not see past the many heads in front of me.

"Tell me, will the view be more meaningful if you get airlifted up a mountain or if you hike five days to climb it?"

People laughed because the answer was obvious.

"We are in this world to climb life's mountains. The times when we feel our best are when we overcome obstacles, when we experience discomfort. These moments are opportunities for us to bond with God. In the middle of life's difficulties lies an opportunity for personal growth."

I like that. If only I could have understood it years ago, I might not have felt so alone.

After his presentation, he received a standing ovation. Every person there wanted him to sign his book. I picked up a copy and began idly thumbing through it as I waited patiently at the end of the line.

Thirty minutes later, it was my turn. "It's nice to meet you, Dr. Wilson. I'm Tali Stark."

He stood up. He was about six feet tall. He was more handsome than his photo. "Tali," he shook my hand. "Nice to meet you. I hope you learned something today."

"Yes, I learned a lot. I look forward to reading your book."

"Do you have any questions?"

"Am I allowed to take your *Kabbalah* class?"

"I'm sorry. You would have to be a full-time enrolled student."

"I understand. Can you recommend anyone else I can study with?"

"Why don't I take your number and get back to you."

As I searched for my business card I said, "I appreciated your comment about climbing a mountain in five days because that's exactly how long it took me to climb Mount Kilimanjaro."

"Wow," he smiled. "Did you summit?"

"I made it to the second highest summit, Stella Point, but not to the highest summit, *Uhuru* Peak."

"*Uhuru?* What does that mean?"

"It means freedom in Swahili."

"Congratulations – that is quite an accomplishment."

I handed him my card. "You had mentioned reading Areyh Kaplan's books – I've been reading his book, *Innerspace*. I have a lot of questions but I just don't know where to start."

"The first step to *Kabbalah* is the understanding that we *don't know*. This humility is essential before embarking on any pilgrimage. We don't have to travel far to gain humility; simply stare into the night sky and realize how small we are in comparison to the endless space that exists in the far reaches of the heavens. Asking the right questions is just as important as discovering their answers."

Daniel taught me that I didn't need to have all the answers; I only needed to know where to find them.

My missing Daniel must have inspired my next question. "How long does the soul in the spiritual world need to sleep or rest before starting a new lifetime?"

"Only the physical body needs sleep, the soul only needs spirituality. Do you own the Jewish spiritual book, *The Chumash?*"

"Yes. Yes I do."

"Good. We can use it to begin our Torah lessons. You need to have basic understanding of Torah before going on to *Kabbalah*."

"*Our* Torah lessons?" I was smiling, "But, I thought…"

He laughed, "We can meet outside of the classroom. It would be my pleasure to spend time with a student as enthusiastic as you."

"Thank you. Thank you so much."

"How about one day next week we meet at the coffee shop next door?" He held up my business card, "I will call you."

"I'd like that."

"Remember to light the *Shabbat* candles tomorrow, they are one of the biggest instruments of spiritual significance we have."

"I light candles every Friday."

"Good. *Shabbat* gives us the spiritual light to carry us through the week, and the candles light the way for the *Shabbat* to enter into our homes. The *kabbalistic* writings tell us that the *Shabbat* should not be viewed as merely a *day* of the week, but it is a living spiritual entity that we can embrace. *Shabbat* is the perfect time to study and pray because our capacity to understand and appreciate all things spiritual is doubled."

"It was really nice to meet you, Dr. Wilson."

"I enjoyed meeting you too, Tali."

At the coffee shop, he stood up and waved me over. He was dressed casually in a sports jacket over his jeans. After a little small talk, and after ordering our beverages, he said, "We need to recognize the gifts we have even if they are few and especially if they are many. We must take into account the restrictions that God commanded us to follow. Following a restriction is a *mitzvah* – a commandment. For example, your husband might have cravings for food that are forbidden by the Torah. Yet you might not be tempted by this same craving at all. The world is filled with physical cravings, all of which relate and directly connect to a spiritual aspect of our *nefesh*, our soul.

He glanced at my left hand where my wedding ring had once been.

"I'm not married," I said. "I'm divorced."

He nodded his head and smiled.

I noticed he wasn't wearing a ring either. "Are you married, Dr. Wilson?"

His eyes focused on his coffee mug, "I'm divorced. And, please, call me Avi."

Okay, Avi.

He referred to several passages in *The Chumash* in an attempt to answer my questions: "Is divorce a sin?" "What happens if a divorced woman marries a *Kohayn*?" "Is it a sin for a healthy woman to not have children?"

Nearly two hours later, he paid the check and kissed my cheek. "I look forward to seeing you again."

"Yes. Me too."

When I got home, there was an email from Avi: Thank you for making the time to meet. I enjoyed discussing your thought-provoking questions. I look forward to more of them.

Me: I have two more questions. Although thought-provoking in a different way, I hope they still make you smile.

1. If you could be anyone other than you for one day, who would you be?

2. What would you do if nobody could find out?

Avi: 1. Definitely Superman or Popeye. "I am what I am, and that's all what I am." Except my muskuls are smaller... Arrg ug, ug, ug, ug, ug ug. ☺

2. I have to invoke the Dr. Professor oath on this one. If people only knew...

I laughed. He's handsome, smart and funny. He reminded me a little bit of Daniel.

That night I had a vivid dream: I was cleaning Daniel's apartment. Daniel was helping me. "We're still a great team, Sweetie," he said and then disappeared. His youngest daughter, Lara, arrived and sat down on the sofa while I moved cans of food from the living room to the kitchen. She said, "I miss him." "I miss him too," I said. She started to cry. I was calm as I hugged her. That was the end of the dream.

I had a flashback. Years ago, soon after Daniel passed away, Lara and I got together at her apartment – she wanted to give me back the Don Quixote paperweight that I had given Daniel.

She sat down on the sofa next to me. Her voice was soft, "I had a dream about my father. I would like to share it with you.

"My dad was sitting in the back seat of a white limousine with a little girl. The car was surrounded by reporters. Dad rolled down the window and told them, 'She's going to be okay. The man was caught.' That's it; that's the dream."

I was crying.

The man. The Man. THE MAN.

"What's wrong? Why are you crying?"

"Were you the little girl?"

"No. I don't know who the little girl was."

"Did your dad tell you anything about me?"

"Like what?"

"Did he tell you anything about my childhood?"

"No. Nothing."

No thing.

"When I was nine years old, I was abducted and molested by a man driving a white limousine. Your dad was the first person I told. He helped me in so many ways."

Lara started crying. We hugged and held each other for a long time. Perhaps each of us longed to reconnect with the special soul we loved and lost.

My missing Daniel was not just a thought; it was a sensation – an actual ache in my body. Even though six years had passed, I still felt as if a piece of my heart had been cut away, resulting in phantom pain. Like a physical injury, it hurt. If only you could see the internal bleeding you would understand. It really hurt.

thirty-two

It was January, 2009. A new year, a new friendship and a new diner.

I asked Avi, "Reviewing history, Jacob and the love of his life, Rachel, were not buried in the same place. Is it believed that their souls reconnected?"

He said, "There is a specific purpose for Rachel to be buried in Bethlehem. The Torah tells us that when the Jews were exiled to Babylon, they would pass her resting place and would ask her to pray for their quick return. It says 'Rachel weeps for her children.' Rachel never faltered the entire time that the other wives of Jacob were having children and she wasn't able to. But she continued to pray until finally God granted her children. So she gets the title of our 'Mother.' Do not confuse the fairytale endings of souls being together if they are buried together. There is one heaven and Rachel is there with her family looking down and trying to protect us, as mothers do."

"Truly a lesson that speaks to my heart."

"Why is that?"

"Maybe because I never had children. Do you have children?"

"I have a son, Raphael. He's twenty-two. He's attending the Sackler School of Medicine in Tel Aviv. He graduates this May."

"You must be very proud of him. You look young to have a twenty-two year old."

How old are you?

"Thank you. If you don't mind my asking, did you want children?"

"Yes." I smiled, "I would have been quite the birthday party planner."

He laughed. "Great spiritual *Rebbe* Menachem Mendel Schneerson encouraged celebrating birthdays as the anniversary of the soul's reentry into the physical world."

"That's a beautiful thought. Did you celebrate your birthday as a kid?"

"Yes. It was a family affair. The birthday boy – there were five of us – got to choose from a camping trip, an adventure park, the circus or a couple of other options."

"That sounds like lots of fun, but, *five* boys? Your poor mom."

"She was certainly never bored. I always chose the camping trip. I loved roasting marshmallows. Even today, I can easily eat a bag." He exhaled noisily before changing the subject. "I'll be in your area on Monday, around noon. Are you available?"

"Yes."

"Can you think of a quiet place where we can meet?"

"Let me think about it and I'll call you on Sunday. *Shabbat Shalom*." [Good Sabbath].

"Have a spiritual *Shabbat*."

He picked up after the first ring.

After the polite dialogue of "Hello" and "How are you?" I said, "I know of this quaint restaurant; it's a perfect atmosphere to discuss *Kabbalah*. The food is good even if the menu is limited."

"Don't worry about the menu; it's all about the company and the sharing of spirituality."

"It's called The Rainbow Café. On special nights they have Andrea Boccelli, Barbra Streisand and even Allan Sherman singing "Hello Muddah, Hello Fadduh!""

"I love Allan Sherman. Who's Barbra Streisand?" He said laughing.

I emailed him the address to The Rainbow Café.

I tossed and turned throughout the night.

I sent Avi an email at seven in the morning: It just occurred to me that I may be deceiving you – not in a malicious way. I would never want you to think that I knowingly lied or misled you. The café where we are supposed to meet for lunch is my home. If you prefer, I can send directions to a local restaurant of your choice. Please accept my apology.

He quickly responded: Good morning! I hope you didn't go to too much trouble. I knew we were talking about your home. I look forward to seeing you there around noon.

Now relieved, I felt happy and excited to see him.

thirty-three

Avi arrived with eight roses, the seven colors of the rainbow and one white one. "Hello. These are for the chef."

"Thank you. They're beautiful. I've never received a rainbow bouquet. Very original. Please come in."

I led him upstairs. "This is the kitchen, the genesis of my culinary creations." I put the flowers on the counter, walked a few feet to open the cabinet above the fridge, moved a few items aside and reached for a glass vase.

He said, "I love the red sink. How brave."

I walked over to the sink. "Brave? I like that." I filled the vase with water, added a few drops of red food coloring – for a more vivid presentation – and placed it on the counter. I then opened a drawer and removed a pair of scissors.

He tapped the porcelain sink like he was testing for wet paint as he gazed out the window. "That's some pond you got out there."

I smiled as I cut the stems on a slant.

"I can see the fish from here. They're mammoth."

I laughed. One by one, I placed the flowers in the vase.

"And beautiful."

"Thank you." I carried the vase into the dining room.

"You're not serving koi for lunch today, are you?"

I laughed again as I set the vase on the table.

He moved into the living room, looking at the white leather sofa, matching loveseat and the Venetian plastered walls that framed the television screen. "Lovely."

"Please sit down. Make yourself at home."

He sat down in the dining room and laughed when I handed him the menu.

Welcome to
<u>The Rainbow Café</u>

Monday, January 12, 2009

THE BEGINNING
Fresh brewed hot coffee/tea

THE MIDDLE
Bagels
White fish salad
Spinach salad

THE END
Fruit salad
Roasted marshmallows ☺

During lunch we talked about the The Tree of Life, also known as The Ten *Sefirot* (Universes). Avi gave me a copy of a diagram. Crown, *Keter*, was at the top and Kingdom, *Malkhut*, was at the bottom.

"It is impossible to study *Kabbalah* without a grasp of the *sefirot*. Let's start with the basics. These ten *sefirot*, starting with Crown, are the ten utterances or attributes of God. The endless Light of God continuously flows downward to nourish creation, Kingdom, which is the physical universe."

I looked at the diagram. "Can you explain each *sefirot*?"

"I will briefly explain each *sefirah* – *sefirot* is plural. Crown is God's will, the highest *sefirah*. And emanating from Crown, from right to left, are the remaining *sefirot*: Wisdom, Understanding, Kindness, Justice, Beauty, Dominance, Empathy, Foundation and Kingdom. These ten *sefirot* refer to the various concepts, qualities and attributes that God uses to create His universes. They are the basic ingredients of creation."

THE TREE OF LIFE

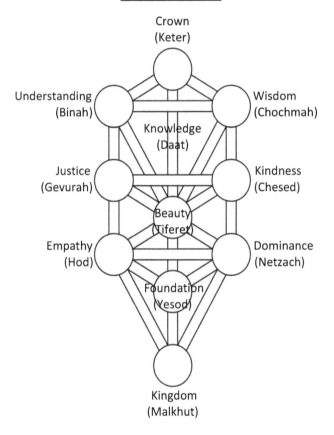

"What about Knowledge?"

"Knowledge does not emanate from Crown. It is the result of man's experiences in the physical universe, Kingdom. So, in counting ten *sefirot*, if Knowledge is included, then Crown is not, and if Crown is included, then Knowledge is not. Understand?"

"I think so. There are never more than ten *sefirot* because you count either Crown, God's will, or Knowledge, man's experiences, but not both."

"*Malkhut*, Kingdom, is our physical universe. This universe has the ability to receive everything from above; it is the ultimate receptacle or vessel. Can you see that Foundation connects the spiritual world of Beauty to the physical world of Kingdom*?*"

I nodded.

"Spirituality isn't something you learn. It's something you experience. Perhaps one day I can show you how it's used in meditation."

"I would love that."

Before he left, I gave him a Superman card that played the theme music. He did not open it in front of me.

Avi called me when he got home. "First, thank you for being such a wonderful barista."

"You're welcome."

"Second..." He started laughing. He said something, but I couldn't understand what – he was laughing so loud.

"What?" Now I was laughing too.

"I just opened the card." He was still laughing. "This is so funny."

I was laughing so hard that I couldn't talk.

"I'm embarrassed that you recognized me. No one is supposed to know who I am." He was still laughing, "Now I will have to put away my cape and tights."

"Your Superman secret is safe with me!"

"That's good to know." He was now serious. "I enjoyed reviewing the *sefirot* and I hope you got something out of it. There is more that I can teach you if you're interested."

"Of course, I'm interested."

"Do you have any questions now?"

"Yes."

"Okay."

"How long have you been divorced?"

"Oh, a personal question," he laughed. "To be honest, my life is very complicated."

"I'm sorry. I didn't mean to get too personal."

"No problem. Let's get together soon, okay?"

"Okay. Good night."

"*Layla tov*, Tali."

Three minutes later he called me back, "You have a wonderful soul, Tali."

I loved that he called me back. I was worried that I had made him uncomfortable.

"It gives me joy to be able to share spirituality with you."

"I'm sorry about the personal question. I was just hoping to get to know you better."

"I appreciate your candor."

"I had to be honest even though I was afraid of what you might say. I think that's a natural phenomenon; it's like a fear of falling."

"The reason many people don't open up their hearts is because they're afraid they're flying without a net. But, you don't have to worry. I'm not like the Keystone cops. I won't move the net when you decide to jump again."

"Jump again?" I laughed. "I don't want to make your life more complicated."

"We'll see what happens. Sweet dreams."

thirty-four

A vi called the following night, "Seriously, once I take off the spiritual hat and the Superman cape and then put down the analyst notebook, I am still a very complicated man. I don't know of too many people who can handle a personal relationship with a complicated person and then after all is said and done still see him and respect him as the spiritual advisor again."

"We are all complicated."

"Yes, we are all complicated, but we are not all spiritual advisors. To unravel me and then try to wrap me up again and see me as a spiritual advisor would be as difficult as trying to put a kitchen appliance back in its original box the same way as it came out... can't be done."

"If you sense that our friendship would change because of your complications, then I'll respect that. But I want you to know that I once put an appliance back in its original box. Not easy, but very rewarding when the job was done."

He laughed but then grew serious. "Trust me, my personal side is very different from my spiritual side. On the other hand, if you want a spiritual advisor, then you don't want to stray far from the professor me."

"Speaking of straying, I'll be visiting my parents in Florida. Is it okay if I email you?"

"Just because you are farther away geographically doesn't mean we have to stop our lessons. Don't forget to read the traveler's prayer before takeoff and give to charity."

Although I had left for Florida, I kept the correspondence going via my smart phone:

Dear Avi: I hope you don't mind helping me piece together the life that you've been living. So, for your convenience, and my entertainment, I have composed a brief questionnaire. Interestingly enough, it was just approved by the *Kabbalah* University. You'll be getting a letter soon from the higher authorities. They're making it mandatory that you fill this out. Weird, huh? Please check the answer that best describes you.

1. The inner me is mostly
    ___ quiet
    ___ hyper
    ___ wild
    ___ high on over-the-counter meds, drugs and/or alcohol

2. I think people would be most surprised to learn that I
    ___ am *not* Superman, but I wear tights
    ___ sing back up for Bon Jovi
    ___ belong to a Jewish mob
    ___ frequent OTB

3. My secret desire includes but is not limited to
    ___ flying over the ocean
    ___ diving under the ocean
    ___ walking on the ocean
    ___ peeing in the ocean

4. If you were to "unravel" me, you would discover
   ___ a well-lit, deep, introspective vessel
   ___ a very hungry core
   ___ a bag of marshmallows breaking down from sugar to
   glucose molecules
   ___ what the %$#&@!

Avi: LOLOLOL! I would like to know what your reaction would be if you found out I have a past life of being a food addict, womanizer, cross-dresser and/or sexual deviant. Would you, for example, not want to study with me anymore? Would you report me to the Superheroes Society? :x)

Food addict makes the most sense – I've seen him binge on marshmallows. But I can't rule out womanizer – he is very charming. Cross-dresser? Sexual deviant? Is he joking?

I wrote him back: You will know the right time to tell me your truth.
Avi: Within the choices I shared are my demons.

Demons? More than one? Again, I'm thinking food addict, but now intuitively, I'm sensing cross-dresser.

Me: I prefer "life challenges" instead of demons. So, put down the marshmallows and go buy a pretty new dress. LOL.
Avi: You are a true friend. Maybe you will shop with me at Bloomingdales?

No LOL. He's serious. What can I say?

Me: Thank you for sharing.
Avi: Thank you for listening! With respect and admiration.

While playing Scrabble with my mom, my phone indicated that I had a new email.
Avi wrote: When do you return to the balmy ten degree New York area? I am sure you have had time to digest our conversation. What are you thinking?

"Who's that?" Mom asked.

"It's a client." I said, typing Avi my response: I return to New York on Sunday afternoon. I have thought about our conversation. And you said it best in an earlier email, Popeye, you are what you are! And the sooner you embrace your "self," the happier you will be. I wish that for you.

"You need to go out more, Tali. Should I go back on the dating sites for you?"

"Absolutely not." I put down seven letters: D-E-V-I-A-N-T.

"Nice." She added up the seventy-two points. "How are you going to meet someone if you don't go out?" She rearranged her letters as quickly as she shuffled her tiles when she played mahjong. "I'm telling you, it's not normal to spend so much time alone." She put all seven letters down vertically, A-B-E-R-R-A-N, above the T of DEVIANT. "Interesting board, huh?"

We both laughed.

Perhaps the universe is trying to tell me something?

It was a close game. Mom won, 307 to 298.

That night I dreamed that I was walking through the Bronx, where I grew up. I had nothing. No money and no identity. I was not wearing a bra underneath my dress. I couldn't turn back because I didn't know where to turn back to, so I kept going. I wound up at my old elementary school. I went to the principal's office and told her my name. She said, "Get on the elevator and go up. You'll know when to get off." I did. There were many people there waiting to help me get back on the road to my destination. A younger version of me was lying on her back with her hands across her chest. I asked her, "Are you the sacrifice?" She said, "Yes." I asked, "Can I be the sacrifice?" She said, "No."

The more I looked at this dream, the more I thought that I was on a difficult journey and I was not clear where the final destination was, but I thought I was going in the right direction (up). At times I lacked support (no bra), but there was help along the way. I would eventually get there without sacrificing myself (again).

I called Avi the next morning and asked him if dreams had any deep meaning.

"Let's see what the Zohar has to say about dreams."

"The Zohar?"

"Zohar means radiance in Hebrew. The book is a collection of commentaries on the mystical writings of the Torah.

"It says, 'When a person goes to sleep at night, their soul leaves them to soar above, each soul according to its own way. When we sleep, a major portion of our soul leaves our body in the one percent (physical) world to plug into the ninety-nine percent (spiritual) world. Sleep is not just a time for the body to rest; it is also a time for the soul to access the source of its power. Dreams are a way that our soul reminds us of our spiritual work.' So before you go to sleep, close your eyes, say the *Shema* prayer and ask the Light to continue to show you messages in the form of dreams."

"I'll definitely do that. Thank you."

"My very jaded past has seeped out and I'm sure has given you some insight into the complications that reside in my psyche."

"A little bit."

"Part of my past still remains buried deep inside me. I'm not sure if I can, want to or need to work any of it out. But much of what I've experienced, and I've experienced a lot, has been dissected, discussed and analyzed. I'm comfortable with who I am but it doesn't bode well for relationships with others."

"I understand."

"I've been analyzed professionally and told that I am like an astronaut on a roller coaster or a race car driver in rush hour traffic. I've been exposed to so much unusual behavior that anything normal is mundane. The problem is partially genetic and partially of my own doing."

Ropes bind us all. I did not know what else to say.

"Tali, do you have someone picking you up at the airport tomorrow?"

"No. I usually call a car service."

"It's Sunday. I don't have any pressing plans. Please let me pick you up."

"I would love to see you. I just don't want to inconvenience you."

"Not at all. Email me the flight info and I will check for delays."

"I really appreciate it."

"We can relax when we get back to your place. I will even take my shoes off." I could tell he was smiling.

"Is there a certain dress code for this? Shoes off? I don't know – are you sure that you're ready for me to see your socks?" I laughed.

His voice was serious. "There is no official dress code, but unfortunately, one of my problems is that I imagine a proper dress code for different occasions, but we won't go there yet. I do wonder, at times, how it is that you know so much about the subculture worlds. I am very curious just how open-minded you are."

I had no idea what he was talking about.

thirty-five

It was one thirty in the afternoon. My plane had landed on time. Avi had me meet him at *departures* rather than *arrivals* because there was far less traffic. I found him immediately. The ground was wet from light snow, with the snowflakes melting as soon as they touched down. During the forty-minute ride home we talked about Torah, mostly about the *sefirot*.

We picked up some Chinese food and brought it back to my house. Later on, around sixish, as we sat on the couch, Avi began to shift his weight as if he were getting up, but he stayed there and glanced over at me.

He looked so handsome, more tempting than the chocolate-covered strawberries he had brought over. In that second I wanted to kiss him but quickly pushed it out of my mind.

Still looking at me, he brushed his hands across his forehead and through his hair. He ran his tongue along the outside of his bottom lip, "Come here."

I quickly moved over to him.

His fingers touched my lips, tracing my smile. In slow motion he kissed me.

I returned the kiss. The deep, passionate one that had been secretly hibernating since I first met him.

WOW!

Endorphins ricocheted around my brain.

Is this really happening?

He left after one more kiss and called me twenty minutes later. "It didn't take me long to get home." I could tell he was smiling.

I was too. I was enthralled by his unwavering confidence and magical power to arouse.

Can this go anywhere? Am I strong enough to protect myself from getting hurt?

"You are a special soul, Tali, and you have occupied my thoughts since we first met. You are a very erotic woman with extraordinary sexual desire. It makes me feel good being with you."

I was suddenly nervous. "I enjoy being with you too."

"I can tell that something is bothering you. Did I overwhelm you with information about my internal struggle?"

"I'm feeling anxious because although I know you have an internal struggle, I'm not exactly sure what it is. I like you a lot. I'm afraid of getting hurt."

His voice was soft, "I had hoped to communicate to you the style in which I need to live my life. I would be honored and excited to introduce you to the physical and spiritual activities and knowledge that reside inside me. There are only a few people who know this side of me; as much as they were like-minded, they still lacked the soulfulness and erotic desire that you have."

Erotic desire?

"If you're open to a different kind of sexual experimentation, then it would make me very happy to lead you on an extremely erotic, sexual and fantasy-filled adventure that is guaranteed to make tonight's wonderful and exciting kiss boring by comparison.

You will need to trust me implicitly and have an open mind and an insatiable appetite, all of which I believe you have in abundance."

Oh my God. What kind of sexual experimentation?

I was sure he thought I was more open-minded than I really was. I said, "I really enjoy your company and it's been a long time since I felt this happy. But I have good reasons to be cautious. Perhaps we can talk about it when we get together?"

Avi arrived wearing a suit, tie and an excited grin. He gently kissed my lips. I felt a rising feeling in my chest. When he placed his hand on the small of my back, and kissed me again, a powerful surge of energy flowed through my body.

He whispered in my ear, "So, tell me."

These three little words were the rumble in the distance before the storm.

"Tell you what?" I whispered back.

He sat us both down on the couch, caressed my hair, and said, "It sounds like you have your own demons?"

And there was the lightning that made the hair on the back of my neck stand up.

"I don't know if I'd call it a demon."

"Okay. Surprise me."

"Surprise you?"

"You appear to be very put together – dotting your i's and crossing your t's."

"I'm still a work in progress."

"Aren't we all? So what's your demon?"

"I was abducted and molested when I was nine years old."

"Oh, I'm sorry," he was caught off guard. "Did they catch him?"

"I never said anything."

"To anybody?"

"Not for fifteen years."

"I don't know what to say. I'm sorry for your pain. This might sound silly, but I feel the need to do something to undo what has been done."

The storm subsided.

"You are a strong woman. Help me understand what scarring this has left you with."

"I'll think about it. Thank you for asking."

"Thank you for telling me your secret."

Later that week we discussed what scars had been left from my childhood trauma.

I said, "I don't like to feel out of control."

"Okay."

There was a pause. "I had a lot of anxiety."

"Do you still?"

"Yes. But it's not as bad." Another pause. "I had trust issues and a lot of anger."

"Do you still?" He half-smiled.

"Yes. But it's not as bad." I half-smiled back. "So, you asked about how you could share your desires. What are you looking for?"

He flashed a big smile.

I wanted to taste that smile.

He said, "There's a lot I would love to share with you and teach you. Perhaps in the beginning I could give you complete control. As you get comfortable with the game, then I get to make the rules."

Game? He thinks this is a game? And then "rules" echoed in my head.

"I want to experience the fun, but a part of me is scared. The old me would run away, but the new me wants the experience, the romance and the adventure. I don't know what to do. I don't want to ruin our friendship."

"Let's not plan. We'll see what happens."

The next night, for the first time, we went into my bedroom, my safe haven. Decorated in mauves and lavenders, it captured the energy of love and serenity. At the foot of my bed was a Max Turner bronze sculpture of a life-size girl and boy sitting on a bench reading a book. On the wall was an Italian mosaic of two cherubs gazing into each other's eyes. The room was dimly lit. I wore a buttoned-up white shirt, jeans and red toenail polish on my bare feet.

He kissed me gently on the lips, placed me on the bed and studied my face. He traced my lips with his finger, and said, "Right now, my lips are the only thing I don't want to take off of you." He kissed me again. Despite the central heating unit clicking on, I got goose bumps. He looked profoundly into my eyes and said, "Would you mind wearing more makeup?"

I laughed. He knew just what to say to calm my nerves. He moved a wisp of hair away from my eyes. I loved his soft touch. I was smitten.

"You would look even more erotic with eye shadow on."

Erotic? Wait a minute. He's serious. He doesn't know me at all. I don't even own eye shadow.

He kissed me again. This time my tongue wrestled with his. I had never been asked to wear *more* makeup. Stuart didn't even want me to wear *any* makeup on our wedding day.

Avi put one hand on my chest and started to unbutton my shirt with the other.

His provocative words from the past pierced my prefrontal cortex: *demons, secret, womanizer, cross-dresser, deviant, subculture, internal struggle, demons, demons, demons.*

In the end, only one word protected me, "Stop."

He did.

During a moment of silence, the sexual tension unraveled. I got up and headed for the bedroom door.

He said, "I'm sorry I upset you. Are you okay?"

"I'm okay." My back faced him as I walked from the bedroom to the kitchen.

He followed, "I feel as though I may have rushed you."

"You didn't rush me. You surprised me. I can't be *that* girl for you."

"I don't want you to be Marlo Thomas." Although I still wasn't looking at him, I could tell he was smiling.

Despite the obvious tension, I smiled too.

Out the living room window, reflecting off the street lights, snowflakes plummeted from the darkness above.

Avi joked, "Hey, you're a dietitian – you must know what a snowman eats for breakfast."

I laughed. "It's got to be frosted flakes."

"That's grrrrreat."

"Very funny."

A minute later, he put on his coat. "I hope we can continue our studying."

I was conflicted.

He touched me gently on the arm, "I know I have issues. My thoughts and actions don't always support the fact that I teach spirituality. Maybe on a bad day you eat junk food, even though you teach nutrition."

I nodded, mesmerized by the falling snow. A sudden gust of wind stirred the bare tree limbs.

"The work that we do does not represent the totality of who we are. We are human beings. We are fallible."

"Yes we are," I nodded again.

I want to study Kabbalah. I want to study with him.

I said, "If we continued our studying I'd want to barter in some way."

"Okay, how about my lessons in exchange for your delicious home-cooked meals?"

I turned, smiled and shook his hand. "Deal."

Valentine's Day fell on a Saturday. Avi visited me after *Shabbat* was over. He gave me a *Shabbat* Cookbook, a funny card and a single yellow rose.

"I would like to share *Shabbat* with you. You would find it very meaningful."

"I would love that."

"I'm visiting my son in Israel in two weeks. Are you available next weekend?"

"Yes." And with a big smile, holding up my new book, I said, "I'll use this to help me plan the menu."

thirty-six

I prepared for our first *Shabbat*. It's traditional to cover the table with a white tablecloth. The white conveys purity and is the color of transformation. On the table were a dozen white roses and a bottle of wine from Avi and two *Shabbat* candles. Just before sundown, after I lit them, I followed tradition to welcome the Sabbath – I closed my eyes and waved my hands over the candles toward my face three times before singing the blessing in Hebrew. The translation is: "Blessed are You, Lord our God, King of the universe, Who has sanctified us with His commandments, and commanded us to light the lights of Sabbath."

Avi said, "Amen."

I opened my eyes and looked at the candles – this completed the *mitzvah* of lighting the candles. The combination of the white tablecloth and the lit candles transformed the ordinary weekday into a *Shabbat* complete with a sanctuary and altar.

Avi opened the wine. He had brought his own *kiddush* (sanctification) cup which had belonged to his grandfather. It was a five-inch silver goblet decorated with a geometric pattern. It rested on a small matching plate. The purpose of the plate was to catch the overflowing wine. The *kiddush* cup was used only for this ritual purpose. Avi held the cup in the palm of his hand as he filled it with wine, intentionally allowing it to flow over the top and onto the plate: as in the *23rd Psalm,* "my cup runneth over."

After he recited the *kiddush* blessing, I went into the kitchen and filled a large cup with water for the blessing over washing of the hands.

Avi followed me into the kitchen. Standing over the sink he said, "Remove your ring so that your entire hand, from wrist to fingertips, gets wet."

I removed the amethyst ring, the one Daniel had given me, from my left hand and then poured the water twice on my right hand and twice on my left.

He lifted my hands up before I recited the blessing and then he repeated the same blessing as he poured water over each of his own hands.

We dried our hands and he uncovered the two challah loaves that I had made. It's a ritual that there be two loaves to serve as a reminder that when the children of Israel fled Egypt and wandered through the desert they were sustained by the *manna*, food that fell from heaven each day. But, the Torah explains, on Friday enough *manna* fell for two days so that the children of Israel could rest on *Shabbat*, and honor the commandment not to work that day.

He lifted both challahs, "Blessed are You, Lord our God, King of the universe, Who brings forth bread from the earth."

I said, "Amen."

He ripped apart one challah and put the first piece in his mouth. "Very good." He gave a piece to me.

The *Shabbat* meal began.

We talked while we ate. I asked, "What was the meaning of lifting my hands after washing them?"

"The actual blessing refers not only to *washing* the hands but to *lifting* them. It's to symbolize lifting one's intentions during the Sabbath."

"Why the hands?"

"Our hands are particularly susceptible to spiritual impurity. Washing and lifting our hands was the ritual that the priests performed at the altar in the Holy Temple in Jerusalem. It's our way of connecting with the Holy Temple from afar."

"Can I ask you another question about the *sefirot*?"

"Of course."

I showed him a new diagram that I had named "The Ten *Sefirot* and Man," in which I superimposed the ten *sefirot* over the figure of a human. "Is this correct?"

"Emanating from Crown is Wisdom, representing the right side of the brain. And Understanding represents the left part of the brain. The six *sefirot* are external attributes. Kindness is the right arm and hand that gives freely and Justice is the left arm and hand that holds back. Beauty is the center of the *sefirot*. Dominance the right leg, represents the urge to accomplish a goal, and Empathy is the left leg, representing the persistence to follow through. Foundation is the sexual organ responsible for making connections, hence, the penis. Kingdom is represented as the feet. It is the ultimate vessel and has the ability to receive everything from above as well as send energy back upward from below. Yes. This is correct."

I smiled.

"This illustration can be used during a meditation to help the mind become completely present in the moment."

"Do you think we can meditate together sometime?"

"More likely, I will guide you. What about tomorrow?"

"I would love that."

"Okay. Any other questions?"

"Yes. I've read that from a *kabbalistic* perspective speech is closer to spirituality than action. What does that mean?"

Avi turned the diagram in my direction and pointed to the bottom of it. "The physical universe, Kingdom, represents action." He pointed to Kindness, Justice, Beauty, Dominance, Empathy, and Foundation, and said, "The six *sefirot* are considered another universe and represents speech." He moved his finger up toward Understanding, "thought," and next pointed to Wisdom, "and mind." He drew my attention to the top of the diagram. "And Crown, the highest level, or universe, is God's will."

I nodded my head.

"So now do you see how speech is metaphysically located in a higher universe than action?"

"Yes."

"Can you also see that action, which takes place in the physical universe, is farther away from the Light of God's will than speech?"

"Yes," I replied, nodding my head. "So our positive speech can bring Light into this world? It's not just a superstition?"

"Everything – our actions, speech and thoughts affect our mind and our will. It is not a superstition."

For the first time, I was starting to get it.

It was after midnight and I could hardly keep my eyes open. I said, "Thank you for the wonderful evening."

"*Layla tov,* Tali."

"Good night."

We went to sleep; me in my room and Avi in the guest room.

In the morning we took a walk and ate brunch. During the afternoon, Avi guided me through a meditation.

I sat down on the sofa. Avi told me to close my eyes, uncross my legs, and turn my palms upward. I emitted a long breath, *whoo*. I was relatively calm and very aware of my surroundings. I heard the soft music playing in the background and saw the blank screen in my mind's eye.

He spoke slowly and articulated every word. "Become aware of your breathing. Inhale. And exhale. Observe how your breath comes in and goes out effortlessly. Take a deep breath to relax your body. Exhale fully. Take another deep breath to relax your mind, letting your breath out with a sigh as you go even deeper. Become aware of your spirit within filling you with energy, with love and with Light. This energy, love and Light of your spirit is here for you in every moment. It is always present in your body, quietly living and quietly being."

I am very relaxed.

"Now imagine yourself outdoors, in the wide open physical universe of *Malkhut*, Kingdom. You feel energy flowing through your feet which ground you to the earth. This energy now travels upward to *Yesod*, Foundation, and continues to flow into your left leg, *Hod*, Empathy, and into your right leg, *Netzach*, Dominance. Feel this energy as it travels even higher into your torso, *Tiferet*, Beauty."

I can feel my chest expand and then deflate. I see a kaleidoscope of colors.

"This Light energy moves into your left arm, *Gevurah*, Justice, and into your right arm, *Chesed*, Kindness, and up toward your face."

My face feels flushed, like I am in front of the sun. Hello, Purple Spirit Guide!

"Take a deep breath as this energy floods into your left brain, *Binah*, Understanding, and into your right brain, *Chochmah*, Wisdom. Breathe in as this energy summits the highest universe, *Keter*, Crown. You bathe in this glorious, bright white Light. Like a helium balloon, you float higher and higher and even higher."

I am weightless, the world is now beneath me. I am engulfed in a cloud of safety. I see the white Light; a glowing flame; a candle. DANIEL! Hi Daniel. He smiles. He makes a wish – I can't hear it. He blows out the candle, but the magnificent Light remains. Of course – it's his birthday tomorrow. There are many balloons. I let go. Of what? I don't know. But like a helium balloon, I float upward.

Avi's voice returned, "You are grateful. Express this gratitude silently to yourself."

Thank you, God. Thank you, Daniel. Happy Birthday, Sweetheart.

In the reverse order, he slowly guided me from Crown back down to Kingdom and said, "When you are ready, take a deep breath, slowly exhale, relax your body and gently allow your eyes to open."

I slowly opened my eyes and sat in silence for a moment.

"How do you feel?"

"That was amazing."

I was present in the moment. I felt that I was growing spiritually. I was transforming.

After dinner the *Havdalah* ceremony marked the end of *Shabbat*. It included four blessings intended to use our five senses – to taste the wine, smell the spices, see the flame of the candle, feel its heat and hear the blessings.

We waited for sundown and the first three stars to appear in the sky. Avi told me that we needed three things for this ritual: a glass of wine, my special *havdalah* candle, the one I had brought back from Israel, and fragrant spices of cinnamon and cloves.

He recited the first blessing over the wine, the second blessing over the sweet spices, a gift to make up for the end of *Shabbat*, and the third blessing over the *havdalah* candle. Avi held his hands up to the flame with curved fingers and looked for the shadow of his fingers on his palms. This was done to give the lit candle a purpose before the flame was extinguished. He put a few drops of wine on his fingers and extinguished the flame from the candle.

After he recited the final blessing, we said goodbye to the Sabbath.

thirty-seven

It was a mild and luminous Sunday in March. While I was taking a walk in my neighborhood, I saw a dog, without a leash, sitting at the corner of Liberty and Clemency. He had so much hair that I couldn't see his eyes. His sweet face, with a distinctive underbite, and his tail, which looked like a long straight blond wig, told me he was most likely a Shih Tzu. When he wagged his tail, he reminded me of Cousin Itt from *The Addams Family*.

As I got closer, this precious little dog walked toward me. I squatted down and picked him up. He was so cute. I brought him back to my office. I read his tag – his name was Java – and got the phone number to call his home. I fed him dry cereal and lots of water. He ate and drank everything.

I brought him into the backyard. The paper airplane that I made for him barely flew in the breeze. With his paw, he patted the air as he sat and watched me repeatedly fetch it. But nothing interested him more than having his hair brushed. I told him about Grandma Devorah, whose long beautiful hair I also brushed. I felt very maternal. With each stroke I imagined what it would be like if I had had a baby. I would have loved, provided and protected.

Four hours later his family picked him up. The return of solitude triggered a three-hour crying binge; my entire body heaved with convulsing sobs. Java's little paws left footprints on my heart. My soul yearned for companionship, devotion and love. How had I avoided it all these years?

I visited the local pet stores looking for a dog to call my own, but I didn't feel a connection with any of them. Maybe I'm not supposed to *buy* a dog. I tried North Shore Animal League, but I still didn't find what I was looking for. I wanted to rescue them all but I left heartbroken and alone. Looking for a dog was so personal.

Even though I had never had a dog before, Java seemed familiar to me – as if I had spent time with him before. Maybe in a past life? Was there such a thing as reincarnation? I would ask Avi.

thirty-eight

A vi returned from Israel at five in the morning and came to see me at five in the afternoon. I saw the red string around his left wrist, similar to the one I had gotten when I was in Israel. I remember it had lasted three months before it frayed.

"What exactly does the red string mean?"

"It started in Ancient Israel by the sages of *Kabbalah*. Rachel is known as our mother and mothers are known to protect their children from evil. So after the red string is wrapped around her tomb several times, it is cut into pieces and worn on the left wrist."

"Why the left wrist?"

"The left arm and hand represent receiving justice and any negative force that comes our way enters through our body from the left side. The red string acts to intercept it."

I looked at his red string more closely. "I don't remember mine having so many knots."

"There are a total of seven knots. Each knot represents a color of the rainbow. Together they all represent the white Light of mercy which influences the physical world."

I did not know that.

I told Avi about Java and asked him if he believed in reincarnation.

He said, "*Kabbalists* use the Hebrew term, *gilgul ha-nefesh*, meaning recycling the soul. There is a reference to this belief in the prayer said before the bedtime reading of the *Shema*, in which we declare forgiveness for all who have wronged us '*bein b'gilgul zeh bein b'gilgul acheir*,' that is, 'whether in this incarnation or another incarnation.'

"The Zohar reveals that Jethro, who became Moses' father-in-law, was Cain reincarnated and Moses was the reincarnation of Abel."

"Wow. I never heard that."

"So, Jethro and Moses – Cain and Abel – were able to resolve age-old karmic obligations when Jethro gave Moses his daughter's hand in marriage. In their original incarnation, Jethro (Cain) took Moses' (Abel's) life. In the later incarnation, Jethro provided Moses with a wife. This rectified Cain's original sin of fratricide. Yes, I believe reincarnation is real.

"The belief is that God creates our soul which enters our body forty days after conception. Each soul has a mission to repair itself and a part of the world. If the soul does not complete its mission through life's trials and tribulations, then it gets another chance by being reincarnated."

"How many chances does a soul get?"

"That depends on where the answer comes from. According to the Zohar, a soul is reincarnated until he gets it right. Other *Kabbalists* have said that if the soul adds damage to the world instead of repairing it, it gets no more than three chances to get it right."

"So if a person commits a serious crime and receives two consecutive life sentences, will he be reincarnated to pay off the second one?"

"That's one way to look at it. But remember, God is the ultimate Judge. He knows everything. We are responsible to pay our debts whether we are found guilty in this physical universe or not. And of course the opposite also applies. When a person continuously performs *mitzvot* yet experiences what appears to be misfortunes, it's believed that his soul will receive its rewards in *Olam HaBah*, the World to Come."

"How do we know that for certain?"

"We don't. We can't. That's where faith comes in."

"What about animals, can they be reincarnated?"

"I've read in some cases where the animal was exceptional, it can be reincarnated into a human body."

"And what about the other way around? Could a human soul be reincarnated as an animal?"

"According to Rabbi Isaac Luria, the sixteenth century *Kabbalist*, a *nefesh* can be reincarnated in a lower state if it behaves badly during a particular lifetime. So it is possible for an evil person's *nefesh* to be reincarnated as an animal as a form of punishment."

"Even if that's the truth, it can't be proven."

"No, it can't, but speaking of *emet,* meaning truth, I'm sure you'll find its meaning very interesting. The word *emet* is spelled *aleph*, the first letter of the Hebrew alphabet, *mem,* the middle letter, and *tuf,* the last letter. The second 'e,' *aleph*, is silent. *Emet*, truth, is the beginning, the middle and the end – everything that is real. *Em* means mother and represents the beginning – giving life. *Met* is death – the end of life. Life is all about discovering your truth."

thirty-nine

Avi and I shared many discussions about the upcoming Passover, the holiday that commemorates the freedom of the Israelites from slavery in ancient Egypt. One conversation triggered a change in me.

"I hope this Passover sets you free," Avi said to me.

"Sets me free? What do you mean?"

"You're one of the most self-aware women that I know, which means that you have the freedom to do whatever you want to do. And yet you're trapped by stifling parameters and paralyzed by forces you can't see. You're afraid to take risks because you're unable to break free from your decades-old bondage. After all these years, after all of your life experiences, you still have not realized how strong you are. And because of this, you're still a slave."

Tears accumulated in my eyes as I felt the deep-rooted chain jerk around my ankle. Avi was right. There was a juxtaposition of commemorating the history of my ancestors with the history of my childhood. The excuse of my past had kept me shackled for thirty-five years.

I know the message of Passover is to attain freedom in mind, body and soul and to rise above our inner limitations.

"Thank you, Avi," was all I could say.

He posed a riddle from Paul Harvey, a legendary radio commentator: "What is greater than God, more evil than the devil, the poor have it, the rich need it, and if you eat it, you will die?"

I closed my eyes to ponder the question. "Nothing!"

Absolutely nothing.

The following week, Avi and I shared dinner in my backyard. We sat on the glider bench over flagstone pavers surrounding the pond. I watched the top basin pour out a generous amount of water to both the right and left waterfalls. It reminded me of The Tree of Life with Crown at the top continuously flowing down to Wisdom and Understanding.

He saw a copy of the book I had just bought, Lisa R. Cohen's *After Etan:The Missing Child Case that Held America Captive.*

He picked it up, flipped through the pages and, avoiding my eyes, said, "We're all held captive by something. What's this about?"

"It's the true story about a little boy who was abducted thirty years ago."

"Did they ever find him?"

"No."

The expression Avi wore – one of reassurance, hope and faith – was mismatched to what I felt – distrust, fear, and abandonment.

A cloud passed in front of the setting sun. For a moment it seemed several degrees colder.

I wanted to tell Avi that Etan Patz would be thirty-six years old now, but he didn't ask. I also wanted to say that Jose Ramos, a convicted pedophile serving twenty-seven years for two unrelated child molestation cases, had been a suspect but there wasn't enough evidence to charge him.

Dusk had arrived and Avi had clearly disconnected. In the illuminated pond, the underwater spotlights created an illusion. The red-, ginger- and auburn-colored koi triplets now appeared to be battery-operated toys.

Avi had another conversation brewing in his mind. "I'm moving to Israel." He was blasé.

I heard him, but it took a while for the news to sink in. I stared at the tall *Iris pseudacorus* on the windward pond edge.

"Raphael graduates next month and he's decided to practice medicine in Israel."

I had planted them to help protect the calm-loving water lilies from strong winds.

"My wife is already there and I'll be joining her next week."

My amygdala sounded the alarm.

He was smiling but it wasn't real. It was as deceptive as his words in the coffee shop, *I'm divorced.*

I felt vulnerable. I wanted to run.

The moon spilled soft light into the yard.

My wife?

I rubbed my arms; I was suddenly chilled. I said, "*Mazel tov.* That's great news; you'll be a family again. That's great news." The repeated sentence was for me – to calm down.

Soon after he helped me bring the dishes back inside the house, he left. In the distant glow of the porch light, his walk to the car seemed vigilant and contrite.

I felt my cheeks getting wet. My hands trembled as I closed the door.

I prayed: "Dear God, please give me strength to keep believing that miracles do exist and they flow down from Your Light above giving birth to miracles below. Please help bring closure to Etan's family and renewal to Avi's."

I wiped my tear-drenched face as I denied my feelings for Avi. I would miss his stimulating discussions and his keen wit. To mask the silence, I turned everything on that made noise – the television, the radio, the KitchenAid mixer. Nothing softened the sound of his goodbye.

I attempted to nurse my broken heart with an old-time favorite accessible drug – ice cream. But not even that comforted me. Loneliness returned and the old voice of negativity crept in from all sides, *What are you, stupid?*

Stop. My soul whispered, *Careful, Tali. Be mindful. Search for meaning.*

I practiced this self-talk. It made me feel stronger. Soon enough my soul would drown out my negative thoughts at the seed level, before they began to grow.

Under a blanket, I drew my knees up toward my chest and wrapped my arms around them as I, once again, returned to my cocoon.

My dreams continued: I was in a bathroom, water dripping from the shower. Aunt Kim entered and said, "The man of wisdom has passed away." I held out my right hand, palm up, and put it into the shower. It was now flowing with warm water. At the cemetery I was in charge of the funeral.

When I woke up I meditated on a verse from the Talmud: "Holy One of Being, I am yours and my dreams are yours. I have dreamed a dream and I do not know what it means." After consulting some books on dreams, I tried to piece the dream together to make sense to me.

The flowing water in the shower represented Torah and my right hand reaching in, palm up, was my *chesed*, my love, to receive it. Drops of water symbolized a rebirth. I would mourn the man of wisdom, Avi, but I would discover something new for myself.

It wasn't until that evening that I grasped the word "cemetery" had the word *emet* (truth).

forty

I was on the elliptical machine watching Rachel Ray, the television cook, when the phone rang.

"Hello?"

"Hi, Tali, this is Neha. I don't know if you remember me, but you returned our dog to us three months ago."

"Hi. Is Java okay?"

"He's fine. We were wondering if you were in a position to take care of him."

I got off the elliptical machine to check my date book. "I would love to watch him. When were you thinking?"

"Well, we were actually wondering if you wanted him."

Oh my God, I must have done something right.

"Is he okay?" I asked again.

"He's fine." Neha was crying. "It's just that we have two young boys and things are overwhelming. When we saw you with him we thought you were a great team."

The last time I was part of a great team, it was with Daniel.

We decided that Java would move in with me on the first of July.

forty-one

Even with my new housemate, I was jittery for weeks after Avi moved. I loved Java, but I hated missing Avi. I remembered his generosity in sharing *Kabbalah*. He also taught me to be present in the moment and to "let go." It's so hard to let go. I wish I were better at it. In hindsight I also saw that this relationship was an opportunity for me to grow.

Feeling uncomfortable can be a sign that I am on the right path.

I knew that I needed to go out, perhaps start dating again, but instead, I went back to searching the newspapers for information about missing kids.

On August 26, 2009, Jaycee Lee Dugard was found alive.

ALIVE!

She was the eleven-year-old girl who had been abducted walking to her school bus stop eighteen years ago.

Eighteen years ago!

Fifty-eight-year-old convicted sex offender Phillip Craig Garrido, of Antioch, California, and his fifty-four-year-old wife, Nancy Garrido, were arrested. I added the footnote in my notebook.

DATE	NAME	AGE	HOMETOWN	STATUS
June 10, 1991	Jaycee Lee Dugard	11	South Lake Tahoe, California	~~MISSING.~~
*Aug 26, 2009				*FOUND ALIVE. Husband and wife, Phillip and Nancy Garrido, were arrested.

A month later, September 30, 2009, John Evander Couey, the repeat sex offender who raped and murdered nine-year-old Jessica Lunsford in 2005, was reported to have died of natural causes at fifty-one.

That October, I saw a photo of the adult Jaycee Lee Dugard on the cover of *PEOPLE Magazine*. She had become pregnant twice by her captor. She gave birth to her first daughter when she was fourteen and to her second when she was seventeen.

I loved that Jaycee Lee Dugard moved on after eighteen years of her life had been stolen. I was lucky – I was robbed of just three-and-a-half hours.

In April 2010 The National Alert Registry began e-mail notifications to help families learn of sex offenders in their neighborhoods.

There had to be a way for me to help people who had been sexually abused – children or even adults like me, who were still living with the shame. I heard how pets improved thousands of lives. Java had already improved my life in just nine months. It was time for me to get back to doing what I did best - helping people. But this time I wasn't going to do it alone.

I Googled "pet therapy" and looked at images of dogs in hospitals and nursing facilities putting smiles on people of all ages.

Java could do this.

I called one certification company. They mailed me paperwork and told me to get Java a dog license, update his vaccines, take his photo and mail everything including forty dollars for membership. Java was soon invited to be tested as a pet therapist. I was given the place and time of testing.

On Sunday, April 25, 2010, Java obeyed every command given and earned his certification as a therapy dog.

DREAM: Java and I were together in a big room with high ceilings and big windows. The windows were covered by thick curtains that allowed absolutely no light to come in. Java pulled back the first curtain only to reveal another. He barked, "Look, Mommy, another curtain." He pulled back the second curtain, exposing a third. He pulled back the third curtain, exposing a fourth. Finally we saw light shining through. Java pulled back the fourth curtain and barked, "Mommy, come see what I've found!" Behind the last curtain was a white dog. Java said she was a Havenese. Her name was Binah (the second *sefirah* of The Tree of Life, meaning understanding). "Can we keep her, Mommy? Please!" The light was so bright I couldn't see if Binah had a dog tag. She kissed me. Java was thrilled. I wanted "understanding," but I didn't know what to do.

On the evening of May 19, 2010, I added a second addendum for Elizabeth Smart. Wanda Barzee was sentenced to fifteen years in federal prison after pleading guilty to kidnapping conspiracy.

Fifteen years? I pray that the Smart family is more forgiving.

That July, Jaycee Lee Dugard was awarded twenty million dollars for the mistakes made by the California Corrections Department that prolonged her eighteen years of captivity.

On December 10, 2010 I made a third addendum for Elizabeth
Smart:

DATE	NAME	AGE	HOMETOWN	STATUS
June 5, 2002	Elizabeth Smart	14	Salt Lake City, Utah	~~MISSING.~~
*March 12, 2003				* FOUND ALIVE 18 miles away from home. Homeless man, Brandon David Mitchell who did odd jobs in the Smart home, and his wife, Wanda Barzee were arrested.
**May 19, 2010				** Barzee was sentenced to 15 years in federal prison after she pleaded guilty to kidnapping conspiracy.
***Dec 10, 2010				*** Mitchell was found guilty of kidnapping and sexual assault. He was sentenced to two life-terms in federal prison.

*Two life-terms? Brandon Mitchell will have to reincarnate to pay
off his debt.*

my new beginning

"From the Darkness,
through the fire,
and into the Light."

forty-two

I had lunch with some friends who were talking about a psychic named Gloria who lived upstate. For an hour, they shared their "Oh my God, can you believe it?" stories. One girl had been told she was pregnant before she knew it herself. I asked for her phone number before I said goodbye.

I called Gloria that night and made an appointment. She said, "You won't be coming alone?"

How does she know that? I don't want to leave Java alone for most of the day.

"No, is that okay?"

"It's okay. Please keep him in a carrier because I have five cats roaming around."

President's Day fell on a very cold Monday. The front door to Gloria's house was open, but the outside glass door was closed. I knocked.

"Coming."

The thermometer on the window read twenty-three degrees outside.

"Come in. Come in." Gloria was an attractive woman in her fifties with long blonde hair. She wore no makeup. She told me that she had moved her cats downstairs and that I could allow Java to roam about. She had put out a bowl of water for him.

In the kitchen a steaming dish sat on the counter top.

"That smells amazing."

"It's homemade lasagna. Everything is fresh – meat sauce, mozzarella, even the pasta."

"Wow. I'm impressed."

"Would you like some?"

"Oh, no thank you."

How sweet.

We sat down at the dining room table. There was a note pad and pen for me and tarot cards for her. She told me to shuffle the cards and then pull four out. I did.

"Are you ready to begin?"

I laughed nervously.

She turned the first card over. "Who's the doctor?"

Daniel?

I said, "Can you be more specific?"

"It's someone from a very long time ago."

Daniel.

"It's a love relationship."

It has to be Daniel.

I whispered, "Is it someone who's passed on?"

"No, he's still living."

I said nothing. I had no idea.

"You'll be in a meaningful relationship soon." She nodded with pleasing premonition. "You'll reconnect with someone from years ago. Or maybe it'll be a new project. It'll be big, you'll see."

From her mouth to God's ears.

She turned over the second card and said, "Your mother has a ring that belonged to your grandmother – an engagement ring. Nothing fancy, but you should have it."

"I have no idea."

"Call your mother and ask her about it. Your house was robbed?"

"Yes."

"They got an expensive watch?"

"My Movado."

"But they didn't get something else – something more important to you."

She didn't ask it as a question so I kept my answer to myself.

They didn't get the amethyst necklace or ring that Daniel had brought back for me from Korea.

"They took something of your grandmother's. That's why she wants you to have the engagement ring. Ask your mother."

"I will." I jotted down "Grandma's ring" and "Call Mom."

She turned over the third card. "Java's not a reincarnation of someone that you knew from a previous life. The family gave him to you simply because they couldn't afford to keep him. He does belong with you, though."

How can she know my question about reincarnation?

She turned the last card over. "There's an older gentleman."

I said nothing.

"Perhaps you worked together?"

I was listening.

"He loved you." She looked into my eyes. "He loved you very much."

I couldn't say anything.

"He wants you to wear the ring."

Oh my God!

"Last night I went to a wedding and wore the amethyst necklace that he gave me, but I decided not to wear his ring."

"Who's *he*?"

"Daniel, the love of my life."

"He's thanking you for the dance."

The dance?

"He wants you to listen to the song 'The Dance.' Do you know the song?"

"I've heard of it, but I can't remember the words."

In a soft voice she sang, "'*Looking back on the memory of the dance we shared beneath the stars above. For a moment all the world was right'* – Da da da da da dada da da da. There's a message in there for you. Look up the song when you get home."

"Okay. This was amazing. Thank you."

"One more thing." She was looking behind me.

I turned around to see what she was looking at, saw nothing, turned back around and said, "What?"

"There is someone here with you. He's sitting in that chair behind you."

I thought of Daniel – his birthday was the next day. I said, "Can you be more specific?"

She paused to look at me. "He's calling you *Mommy*."

I felt a chill. I turned back around and still saw nothing.

"Do you have a son who passed away?"

I shook my head no.

"Do you know of a young man in his early twenties who passed away?"

I turned to face her, still shaking my head.

"He's tiny. His face looks twentyish, but his body is small, like an infant."

Java circled my chair and sat down by my feet. He appeared to be staring at something behind me.

For the third time, I turned around. And, again, I saw nothing. But I felt something. I winced as I clutched my chest.

"What's the matter?"

"I have chest pain."

"Get up and stretch."

I did.

"Now I feel tingling. It's traveling to the middle of my back."

"Take a deep breath and hold it."

I did.

"Now let it out very slowly."

I felt some relief.

"Better?"

"Yes. Thank you." I continued standing. Java settled on the carpet but was still staring at the chair.

Gloria said to the spirit, "Do you have a name?" After a moment, "He doesn't have a name. Do you have any idea who he is?"

"Maybe." I was emotional. "Can an aborted fetus come back as a spirit?"

"Oh, yes."

"I had an abortion twenty-something years ago."

"That explains why the infant looks twenty years old."

She leaned toward the chair behind me. "Honey, are you Tali's son?"

She looked at me, nodding her head. "He's nodding yes."

And then I felt it. I felt *him*. I know I felt him. I cried with regret and shame that I had not known better back then. I placed my arms across my chest as if I were holding him.

"Your son came here to get help to move on because he can't do it himself."

Is this really happening?

"He's saying, 'It's okay, Mommy. I forgive you.' That's what he's saying."

I cried.

Mommy's here with you now. I am so sorry. Please forgive me. I know that I made a big mistake – the biggest mistake of my life. If I could do it over again, I would choose you. Oh, God, I feel you hugging me. I love you. Please forgive me.

"He's saying, 'I forgive you. It's okay. I learned what I needed to learn while I was here.' Do you understand, Tali, that he'll have another chance in another lifetime?"

My heart felt so heavy I couldn't breathe.

Please, please, please forgive me. I didn't know what I didn't know. I made a terrible mistake.

"Tali, he's ready to go. Are you ready to let him?"

"Of course."

She pointed up, "I'm going to open a portal." After a moment, "The light is there but it's too far away. He needs help to go to it."

"What can I do?"

With her hands extended out, palms upward, Gloria said, "Lift him from the chair and then up toward the light." She extended her arms and slowly lifted them up.

I moved toward the chair. I did exactly what she did. I visualized myself holding my baby for the first time.

"It's okay, Tali," Gloria said. "I'm here with you. Your son is moving up into the light. Everything is happening the way it's supposed to. '*I love you, Mommy. Don't be afraid.*'"

Seconds later I felt something brush my cheek. Less than a minute after that, with a heavy heart, I said, "He's gone, isn't he?"

"Yes. He made it. He's through the light. I can't see him anymore."

The pain traveled away from my heart. It lifted.

To where?

"Are you okay? Do you need anything?"

"I'm okay." I reached down to pet Java. He licked my hand. I couldn't stop crying. I sat back down, my thighs over my hands to stop them from shaking.

Gloria said, "You did great, you helped him go. I saw it happen. I saw that you felt it, even though I know you didn't see it. It was meant to be a healing for you as well as for him."

I was stunned. "How can this be? My son was not even born. How can he appear as a twenty-year-old?"

"In the higher universe there is no time or space. This is why they can appear anywhere, at any time, at any age. Spirits connect with us any way they can to get their message across. Also, when a soul is preparing to reincarnate it chooses parents who will be able to provide it with a specific opportunity to evolve and transform, even if it is not born into this world."

She pointed up again.

"What are you doing?"

"I'm closing the portal."

What an unbelievable day.

On the way home, the Steve Miller Band sang "Abracadabra" on the radio. I hadn't heard that song since college. I waited until I got home before I called Mom.

"Hey Mom."

"How are you?"

"Great. Listen, this is going to sound bizarre but just humor me, okay?"

"What are you up to now?"

"Do you have Grandma's engagement ring?"

She laughed.

I knew that meant yes.

"Why? Did you have a dream?"

"No, I went to see a psychic."

"Oy vey is mir s'verht auf mir nisht git (Oh pain is me and the world is weighing on my shoulders)."

We both laughed.

Mom said, "I gave you Grandma's pin instead of the ring."

"The pin was stolen when my house was robbed. The psychic said that Grandma wants me to have her ring."

Mom, probably out of fear of spirits, agreed to give me the ring.

I searched the Internet for "The Dance." It was written by Tony Arata and recorded by Garth Brooks. At the beginning of his music video, Brooks explained the song's double meaning: the end of a passionate love story and the end of a person's life. Daniel's last words to me were something about a dance. Could they have been, "Don't miss the dance?"

I put Daniel's amethyst ring on the fourth finger of my left hand.

forty-three

Before I went to bed that night, I opened the Artscroll Siddur, the traditional Jewish prayer book, which has a set order of daily prayers. It's customary for religious Jews to recite the *Forgiveness Prayer* right before the bedtime *Shema*. This prayer tells us to forgive those who have wronged us. Even though I was not religious, I was ready to forgive The Man, especially because my son forgave me.

It's all about forgiveness.

"Master of the universe, I hereby forgive anyone who angered or antagonized me or who sinned against me – whether against my body, my property, my honor or against anything of mine; whether he did so accidentally, willfully, carelessly, or purposely; whether through speech, deed, thought, or notion; whether in this incarnation or another incarnation – I forgive. May no man be punished because of me. May it be Your will, my God and the God of my forefathers, that I may sin no more. Whatever sins I have done before You, may You blot out in Your abundant mercies, but not through suffering or bad illnesses. May the expressions of my mouth and the thoughts of my heart find favor before You, my Rock and my Redeemer."

I wrote a letter to The Man.

Our lesson of personal responsibility goes back to Adam and Eve. After the original sin of eating the forbidden fruit "...and the eyes of both of them were opened..." Adam blamed Eve, Eve blamed the serpent and neither accepted responsibility.

For years my finger pointed to you whenever anything went wrong in my life. But after a long journey, I have finally discovered the truth: God gives each of us free will and lessons to learn to be responsible for our own actions. Sin is not only what one does, but also what one does not do, such as not speaking out when witnessing cruelty.

I choose to believe that you are not totally evil. You are not beyond redemption. You are not without a spark of Light. You can be forgiven.

This does not free you from responsibility – but it no longer concerns me. This sin of yours is now between you and God. I forgive you.

I forgive you for the wrong choices you made on that day. More important, I forgive me for blaming myself – it was not my fault.

You and you alone are responsible for your actions. I am responsible for not speaking out and for my thoughts and feelings on the days and years that followed.

Even though you did not ask for my forgiveness, I forgive you. And even though, at times, your voice and your actions still bother me, I forgive you.

Perhaps you had no intention of hurting me. If you did, I will never understand why – nor do I want to. Either way, I no longer care. I forgive you.

I will no longer let myself fall into an emotional trauma over what you did. I want to be without anger, distrust and hatred. Therefore, once again, I forgive you.

Forgiveness is the only way forward for me. I forgive you totally.

I choose to let go of the darkness to make room for the Light.

I choose to stop running away from my past, focus on the present and believe in the future.

Tali Stark

I fell into a deep sleep...

I wanted to wipe my face. It felt wet, like I was crying. I tried to move my right hand to wipe away the tears, but I couldn't. My left hand wouldn't move either. All of my senses were dulled except for smell. I smelled urine. I thought I heard the muffled cries of a child.

Java licked my face and nuzzled his nose against mine. I heard banging on the front door. Java began barking. If chaos had a sound, this was it. At first the banging and the barking were too loud, but then the sounds softened and I saw Java's mouth move in silence. The noise became a steady sort of drone, like the static when the television shuts down in the middle of the night.

Gusts of wind moved around me. Three Hebrew letters floated around, bounced off one another and made new combinations: *tuf-aleph-mem, mem-aleph-tuf and alef-tuf-mem*. Then *aleph-mem-tuf* appeared. This meant something – *emet* – truth.

I entered a bright red light and floated up into the clouds. A few seconds passed and I was in a double helix of orange and yellow clouds. I floated higher into an emerald green cloud. I arrived at a beautiful blue ocean that turned into indigo and then into a vibrant violet. I was standing on the moon. Next to me was a lioness. She kissed me. I watched the words "courage" and "strength" transfer from her mind and body into mine. I slowly began to move my fingers and toes, my hands and feet and my arms and legs. I hugged the lioness and together we stood tall and proud on the moon, bathing in a brilliant white light.

I knew I was going to be okay.

As the light slowly faded, I felt the racing of my heart, heard the exhalation of my breath and smelled Cheetos. Java smelled like Cheetos: he needed a bath. I became aware of his furry little head beside mine as I awoke. I reached for the pen and pad on my nightstand. I needed to write down all of the thoughts in my head in an effort to understand the dream.

Being paralyzed represents my past as a traumatized nine-year-old. Now, having regained my senses, I can see and hear more clearly. The truth has always been all around me. Although it's camouflaged by a rainbow of colors, I must search out the truth.

And then I had a vivid flashback to college.

The Wizard of Oz told me, the lion, "You're a victim of disorganized thinking. You're confusing courage with wisdom." He hands me a medal.

"COURAGE. Ain't it the truth? Ain't it the truth?"

I blotted my eyes as I stared out the window at the falling snow. Like a snow globe that had been shaken, I watched the fragments of that day – that rainy Monday in April of 1974. In the past, I would inevitably shake that globe again and again because I wasn't ready to see that day clearly. Now the snow had settled. I could finally see clearly.

forty-four

The snow changed to rain and both the weather and my heart grew warmer. The delicate, fragrant petals of the magnolia tree decorated my neighbor's front lawn, the azaleas and tulips were reappearing around my pond and the neighborhood runners were shedding their layers. In celebration, I got myself a mani-pedi.

It had been thirty-six long years since I had lost my spirit. By the grace of God and the love from special people in my life, I had rediscovered it.

My precious Java was nearly twelve and we had just rescued a puppy from North Shore Animal League. She was a two-month-old white Havanese – an eight-pound loaf of bread. Just as in my dream, I named her Binah, Understanding.

I was doing well. "In the midst of winter, I finally learned that there was in me an invincible summer" (from *Return to Tipasa* by Albert Camus).

Three years ago my Mount Kilimanjaro buddies had asked if I wanted to join them in their climb to Everest Base Camp. I said no. Last year they asked me to consider climbing up Cerro Aconcagua, Argentina's highest mountain. Again I said no. My desire to train to exhaustion was gone.

Now I sat in my backyard by the pond, listening to the waterfall while reading, meditating or simply watching Java and Binah run around. Before, I couldn't sit still long enough to hear the sounds of nature or to see that the water lilies, surrounded by the moistened stones and the shimmering koi, had opened.

And so have I.

I was inspired to redecorate my home in pulsating colors – reds, yellows and blues. I was recreating my outer world to reflect my new inner efflorescence.

My favorite time of day had become very early morning, when dusk introduces daylight. The rain didn't bother me anymore; I looked forward to finding the rainbow.

One night I dreamed about my twenty-fifth high school reunion. The auditorium was full of forty-three-year-olds. Barry White appeared on stage. In his deep sexy voice, he spoke the lyrics:

"There's that look again.

You know what I'm talking about.

That insecure, that unsure, that wondering look.

It's all in your eyes, baby."

A tall, handsome man wearing a blue suit and red tie jumped off the stage and walked toward me.

"May I have this dance?"

I looked around. Nobody was dancing.

"Absolutely!"

He pulled me in close. "It's been a long time, Tal." He whipped me out and twirled me right back into him.

I said, "You look great."

"You feel great," Alex said. He flung me out, crossed our arms over the backs of our necks and slid our hands back together. "I can't tell you how much I've thought about you over the years."

Applause. Applause. Applause.

"Thank you. Thank you," Barry White said into the microphone.

Alex kissed my hand. I noticed he was not wearing a wedding ring. He looked into my eyes. It was perfect!

Applause. Applause. Applause. Pause.

Applause. Applause. Applause. Pause.

That wasn't applause – that was my alarm clock. I reached over and shut it off. I lay back down and closed my eyes.

Alex, come back, please.

forty-five

I couldn't get Alex off my mind. It had been a lifetime since we saw each other in Daniel's lab. I Googled his name and found that he was a physician living in Connecticut. I typed his name in the search engine of Facebook. Zero. I clicked on some of our mutual high school acquaintances to see if he was listed as a friend of a friend. He wasn't.

I wrote to Toby, our mutual friend from high school, to see if she had been in contact with him. She told me that he was recently divorced and gave me his email address.

Dear Alex: After all these years I find you again via a medium that didn't even exist when we last knew each other. I must tell you that I searched for you on Facebook and didn't find you. I got your address from Toby. I wanted to share with you that I saw you in my dream at our twenty-fifth high school reunion. I didn't go, did you? How are you? I look forward to hearing from you when time allows. All the Best, Tali Stark.

He did not reply.

I updated the status of Jaycee Lee Dugard's captors:

DATE	NAME	AGE	HOMETOWN	STATUS
June 10, 1991	Jaycee Lee Dugard	11	South Lake Tahoe, California	~~MISSING.~~
*Aug 26, 2009				*FOUND ALIVE. Husband and wife, Phillip and Nancy Garrido, were arrested.
**July 2010				**JLD gets 20 million dollars for CA Corrections Department's mistakes that prolonged her 18 years of captivity.
***June 2, 2011				***Phillip Garrido was sentenced to 431 years at California State Prison for 18 years of kidnapping and sexual imprisonment. His wife, Nancy Garrido, was sentenced to 36 years to life at Central California Women's Facility.

I received a letter in the mail from the Superintendent of Schools of my local school district:

Dear Parents/Guardians and Residents,

The District has been informed by the Nassau County Police Department that a registered sexual offender is residing in the proximity of your School District. The District received this information in accordance with the Sex Offender Registration Act [Megan's Law]. The individual is a fifty-year-old Level Two [moderate risk] offender. His name is ----.

This information will be circulated to appropriate District staff: building principals, staff who issue visitors' passes, playground monitors and security personnel. The staff has been directed to report any suspicious persons or activity to District administration immediately.

The District is dedicated to the safety of our children while they are in school. We are notifying you so that you can remain alert to make sure that you enhance the safety of your child. Please be advised that all of our schools have sign-in/sign-out procedures and all visitors must report to the school's main office. In addition, our K-12 curriculum includes teaching personal safety and stranger awareness skills.

Please be assured that the District will continue to take responsibility and appropriate measures to protect our children.

I called the Superintendent of Schools to inquire about how I could help. I was directed to The Long Island Alliance Against Child Abuse. Their main office was close by.

Amelda Sethica, the volunteer coordinator, said, "We handle volunteers as if they are employees."

"I understand."

"I'll email you the application. Please send that back to us with your resume."

"Okay."

"If you're still interested after orientation, we do a thorough background check."

"Okay." I expected that.

"There is a one-on-one interview, which includes drug and alcohol testing."

"No problem."

"Then there is training, depending on what program you are volunteering for."

"Okay. Thank you. I'll wait for the application." I gave her my email address.

"Thank you, Tali. Good luck."

On July 7, 2011, I finally got an email from Alex.

Dear Tali: After all these years, it's really nice to hear from you. No, I did not go to the reunion. As far as my making an appearance

298

in your dream – I think that's pretty cool. I say that because I must now tell you that several months ago, several weeks ago and, okay, I admit it, several days ago, I found myself looking at your Facebook page. It wasn't by accident or from noticing you on a list as a friend of a friend, because as you now know, I'm not on FB (yet). I actually typed your name in the search area in a direct attempt to find you. And when I did, I couldn't believe you looked the same!

I wondered if you would appreciate hearing from me. I'm not in the best place – trying to recover from the end of my marriage. I've been spending a lot of time alone with my thoughts – trying to slow things down and keep things simple.

Just like the good old days, Tal, I'm still comfortable "talking" with you. I'm very happy that you reached out. Please stay in touch and tell me how you are, aside from another year older. Wishing you a Happy Birthday! ☺ Alex

How long do I wait to respond? My intuition told me to be authentic. I responded immediately.

Dear Alex: It's GREAT to hear from you. I admit I Googled you once or twice (okay, three times), hoping to see that you became the doctor that you wanted to become. Congratulations on all of your success. I hope that your professional journey has been a meaningful one with few regrets.

I'm sorry to hear that you're not in the best place. I've been there. I understand. Spending quiet time alone to discover who you are and what you need is essential. Thank you for the birthday wishes. Perhaps one day we'll get together for another Scrabble game.

He sent me a friend request and an e-mail on Facebook. I accepted his friendship. I saw his updated photo. He was very handsome with a big smile and a goatee. He looked like Jeremy Sisto, the tall, handsome, Detective Cyrus Lupo on *Law and Order*, and George on *Suburgatory*. I opened up my mail:

Hi Tali: Communicating with you again makes me very happy. One day, soon, I'd love to take you out for dinner and continue this in person. Maybe you can talk me into a game of Scrabble. Who knows how and why things work out the way they do. Let's stay in touch. By the way, I know you were very close to Dr. Benson – I was sorry to learn that he had passed away. Alex

I got an email from Amelda Sethika at The Long Island Alliance Against Child Abuse. It was an invitation to attend their Orientation on July 19, 2011 at 6:30 P.M.

I replied, "Yes, I will attend."

On July, 11, 2011, I listened to the evening news while preparing dinner. Eight-year-old Leiby Kletzky was reported missing after he walked home alone from his day camp in the Hasidic neighborhood of Boro Park, Brooklyn. This was his first time walking home alone.

Two days later, BREAKING NEWS: Video from surveillance cameras along Leiby's route showed he stopped to ask a man for directions and then got into the man's car. Parts of the boy's dismembered body were found in the Kensington apartment of thirty-five-year-old Levi Aron and other parts in a dumpster in nearby Sunset Park.

DATE	NAME	AGE	HOMETOWN	STATUS
July 11, 2011	Leiby Kletzky	8	Boro Park, Brooklyn	Abducted and murdered by Levi Aron.

This horrific story made me think of Etan Patz, who walked *to* the school bus stop alone for the first time; Leiby walked *from* it. Neither boy made it back home.

I cried for Leiby and Etan and for all the young souls: those murdered and found, those never found and those abducted and still living in captivity.

Will it ever end?

forty-six

I walked into the main entrance of the building and took the elevator up to the eighth floor. The girl at the desk had me sign in and then led me to the conference room.

As I entered, a tall, attractive African-American woman in her late thirties greeted me, "Come on in. I'm Amelda Sethika, the volunteer coordinator."

"I'm Tali Stark. It's nice to meet you." I looked around the room. There were five people, four women and one man, seated around a rectangular table. They each had a red folder, a cup of coffee and a couple of store bought chocolate chip cookies. I sat down.

"I'd like to welcome everyone to The Long Island Alliance Against Child Abuse. We've been in existence since 1974. With non-profit organizations, we all wear a lot of hats, and we still can't do it all. That's why we have many opportunities for you as volunteers. We're grateful for whatever time you can give us. Your help will allow us to continue to provide hope for victims of abuse. We're certain you will find the work rewarding."

After we went around the room and introduced ourselves, she began. "Please open up your folders and let me go over the paperwork.

"On the left side, you will see a preference sheet. I'll go over all of the positions available. We ask that you circle three that you feel most compatible with. We will try to match your number one selection. I want to remind everyone that there will be an extensive and *expensive* background check on you. Of course, there is no charge to you, but we ask that if you have a criminal record of any kind, you not waste our time and money." She paused and looked down at her notes. "Okay. Now, if you look on the right side of your folder, you will find a full description of the positions available.

"Let's begin with the Hospital Advocacy Program. If you volunteer for this you will undergo an intensive forty-hour training program. We are looking for advocates for child victims of sexual abuse as well as adult survivors of sexual assault or domestic violence. You need to be available to be on call at least twice a month for twelve-hour shifts. This means that we can call you at three in the morning and send you to one of the thirteen hospitals throughout Nassau County."

I'm interested. I'm comfortable in the hospital setting.

"Okay, let's move on. The Child Victim Advocate Program utilizes your skills to reduce the trauma to the child victim and their non-offending family members. You will spend time with the families from the start and remain involved if their cases go to Family or Criminal Court. For this reason, you need to be available during Court hours."

The room was quiet.

"Then we have the Safe Home. It's not likely that you will be chosen for this program unless you are with us for years. The Safe Home is an eighteen-bed facility in Nassau County in an undisclosed, top-secret place – I don't even know where it is – and only the most loyal get to work there. The families arrive with nothing, only the clothes on their backs. They're there for a maximum of ninety days or until they transition to a safer location, sometimes with family in another state.

"We also have Court Advocacy, where you spend one day a week at Family or Criminal Court offering assistance, support and information to individuals seeking Court Orders of Protection."

I am not interested in being in Court.

"The Community Education Program is very important. You could represent us at seminars providing information on child abuse and sexual assault."

I love teaching.

"You can also volunteer for Special Events, which includes fundraising throughout the year. And finally, we need help with everything from filing to mailings to copying and answering phones."

The male volunteer raised his hand, "Excuse me, how long before we hear from you?"

"It will take about a month to complete everyone's background check. In the interim, we'll be looking to match your preferences with the positions available.

"Are there any other questions?"

The room was quiet.

"Okay, thank you for your time and attention. While we realize there are many places for you to volunteer, we'd like to thank you for choosing us. We think you made the right decision. We'll be in touch soon. Please turn in your preference sheet."

On my preference sheet, I wrote:
1) Hospital Advocacy
2) Child Victim Advocate
3) Community Education.

Before going home, I checked my cell phone messages. Aunt Kim had left a message asking me if I could stop by. She said that she had something for me and wanted me to have it right away.

Ten minutes later I rang her doorbell. Uncle Lloyd was watching something on television and laughing; it sounded like *The Big Bang Theory*. Aunt Kim and I sat in the kitchen, drinking tea and talking about the orientation. After ten minutes she gave me a wrapped gift.

I knew it was a book. "What's this for?"

"No special occasion."

"May I open it now?"

"Of course you can."

It was Jaycee Lee Dugard's memoir, *A Stolen Life*. She and her therapist, Rebecca Bailey, had written it as part of her treatment.

"Thank you, Aunt Kim."

"She wrote the book to help other survivors. I hope you get something out of it."

I hugged her. "Thank you so much. I love you."

"I love you too."

On August 29, 2011 Levi Aron was sentenced to forty years to life in prison. He faced the possibility of a life sentence but pleaded guilty to one count of second-degree murder and one count of second-degree kidnapping, which reduced his sentence. He will be eligible for parole in 2051.

DATE	NAME	AGE	HOMETOWN	STATUS
July 11, 2011 *Aug 29, 2011	Leiby Kletzky	8	Boro Park, Brooklyn	Abducted and murdered by Levi Aron. * Aron sentenced to 40 years to life.

In early March of 2012, I was at the supermarket checkout counter thumbing through a copy of *PEOPLE Magazine*. Elizabeth Smart was on the cover. The twenty-four-year-old had just gotten married. Elizabeth, now president of the Elizabeth Smart Foundation, serves as an advocate for children's safety.

I was reminded that there are two kinds of survivors – those who move on from trauma quickly and those who take longer. I was happy for Elizabeth, who now wore a ring on the only finger connecting a vein to her heart. I, on the other hand, had experienced a much slower recovery.

It was April 19, 2012. Aunt Kim called, "Did you hear the news?"

"What news?"

"About Etan Patz."

"No. What's going on?"

"The FBI and the NYPD received a tip in the case. A man who had worked as a carpenter, one block from Etan's bus stop, had revamped his workshop shortly after Etan disappeared. He put in a cement floor to replace the dirt floor. So the police are tearing apart the place looking for human remains."

"Oh my God."

Four days later I called Aunt Kim to tell her that no human remains were found in Othniel Miller's workshop.

On May 24, 2012, my phone rang at eight in the morning. It was Aunt Kim. "Good morning, Tal. Turn on the news."

"What channel?"

"It doesn't matter."

Every station covered the breaking news. New York Police Commissioner Raymond Kelly was announcing that fifty-one-year-old Pedro Hernandez was in custody for the disappearance and murder of Etan Patz.

What?

While Kelly was adamant that there was probable cause to arrest Hernandez, who had no previous criminal record, he admitted there was no physical evidence tying him to Etan's death.

I was too disgusted with the news to keep listening but too obsessed with it to listen to anything else.

Hernandez had told investigators that on May 25, 1979, the day that Etan had disappeared, he was an eighteen-year-old stock boy at the bodega located across the street from Etan's school bus stop.

He had never seen Etan before that day, but once he saw him, "I knew he was the one... I just felt the urge to kill." He had lured Etan to the basement of the bodega, promising him a soda. Once inside, he choked the boy to death, stuffed the body into a bag and carried it a block and a half away, where he left it out in the open with the trash.

WHAT?

It was reported that Hernandez was schizophrenic, bipolar, had a history of hallucinations and was on medication for his illnesses. He was transferred to Bellevue Hospital and arraigned on a charge of second-degree murder, meaning the killing had not been premeditated.

As of September 27, 2012, it wasn't clear whether there was enough evidence to convict Hernandez for killing Etan Patz. The Patz family, New York City and the rest of the world awaited the final resolution of this case. Trial was scheduled.

Oh my God. This is crazy.

November 7, 2012, was the day of release for Jose Antonio Ramos, the original suspect in Etan's disappearance. After serving twenty-seven years for molesting two young boys, Ramos was released from jail but quickly rearrested for failure to follow Megan's Law. (Sex offenders must provide a legitimate residence upon release from jail.) Ramos had given the address of a family member who was no longer living at the address provided.

Some people thought it was a set up. I was just happy that he was off the streets.

May 6, 2013, I was glued to my television again. After a decade, three missing Cleveland girls were found alive after a neighbor, Charles Ramsey, heard screaming. Amanda Berry, Gina DeJesus and Michele Knight were all found in the home of their long-term captor, forty-two-year-old Ariel Castro. I did not know of Michele, who was twenty-one when she vanished on August 22, 2002, because I only kept track of missing children, not adults.

DATE	NAME	AGE	HOMETOWN	STATUS
April 21, 2003	Amanda Berry	16	Cleveland, Ohio	~~MISSING.~~
*May 6, 2013				*FOUND ALIVE in the home of long-term captor, Ariel Castro.
April 2, 2004	Georgina (Gina) DeJesus	14	Cleveland, Ohio	~~MISSING.~~
*May 6, 2013				*FOUND ALIVE in the home of long-term captor, Ariel Castro.

DNA tests confirmed Castro was the father of Amanda's six-year-old daughter. In exchange for the death penalty being taken off the table, Castro pleaded guilty to nine hundred thirty-seven counts, including the kidnapping of all three girls and the murder of Michelle's unborn fetus. He received a life sentence plus one thousand years.

September 3, 2013. Ariel Castro was found hanged by a bed sheet in his prison cell at the Correctional Reception Center in Orient, Ohio. He left no suicide note.

So much for a life sentence plus one thousand years. Oh, God, please don't let him be reincarnated.

I had been volunteering for over two years as a child victim advocate and one year with the community education program. After attending many public seminars as a volunteer, I wanted to give one myself. I was comfortable with public speaking but terrified of coming out as a victim of child sexual abuse. It occurred to me that there was one thing I could do to reduce the fear.

Late September, nearly three months after many emails and phone conversations, Alex and I agreed it was time to get together.

forty-seven

It was a drab Saturday in October. I took the Long Island Expressway to the Cross Island Parkway, where traffic slowed because of heavy rain.

A flashing sign reminded me to bear right for the Throggs Neck Bridge. The rain lifted after I crossed over the bridge into the Bronx, toward Co-Op City. I signaled right at Exit 11: Bartow Avenue.

I hadn't been back since my parents moved to Florida two decades ago.

Located right off the exit was a new shopping center ten times bigger than Shopping Center One, as it was known to us kids in the 1980s. I saw Checkers, Staples, and PC Richard and Son.

Bartow Avenue turned into Baychester Avenue. I passed a sign that said "Welcome to Co-Op City." I passed my old high school; even though perched atop dozens of steps, it looked smaller than

I had remembered. I passed my old elementary school where I had curled up on the floor of the girl's bathroom.

That was the day I tried to convince myself that it was just a horrible dream.

I made a right turn at the light, down my old street, Donizetti Place. The cars were now parked diagonally along the street, not straight, the way I remembered. I slowed the car down as I glanced up at the twenty-six-story building on my left.

I made another right turn into the school parking lot. I took the first available spot, shut off the engine and got out. I looked across the street to my old building and counted the windows from the ground floor up:

One, two, three, four, five, six, seven, eight.

There it was – my old bedroom window.

"There it is," he said.

I recognized his voice immediately. When I turned around, I saw that, although twenty-five years older, he still had a full head of hair and the infectious grin of a boy. There was concern in his hazel eyes.

"Alex! It's great to see you." We hugged for a long time. "You look great."

"Look at you. I can't believe it. After all these years, tell me, why come back here now?"

I was looking at where the white limousine had been parked. "Do you mind if we take a ride?"

"Sure. Where to?"

"Dreiser Loop."

"Okay, Dreiser Loop it is. I'll drive." He had parked right next to me.

"You watched me pull in, didn't you?"

He smiled.

"I can't believe I didn't see you."

"You were distracted." He opened the passenger door of his polished black sedan.

"Nice car," I said, as I slid down onto the black leather seat.

He closed my door and walked around back while I reached across the steering wheel to open his door.

"Thank you," he said as he got in. "Do you remember the red box car that I drove back in the day?"

"Yes, I do. And somewhere in a folder I have a picture of it."

"Really? You have a picture of my 1989 Hyundai XL?"

"Yup."

"It was the cheapest model they made." He was laughing. "Whenever I turned on the air conditioner, the car would slow down to twenty miles an hour."

His laughter was contagious.

"I also remember your Benzi Box car radio."

Still laughing he said, "Whenever that car drove over a bump, that radio would switch stations."

We were both laughing like a couple of high school kids.

He started the car. Playing on the radio station was the song "Abracadabra."

"Wow, this is an old song. I remember it from college," he said.

"Me too. But I still don't know what it means. *Abracadabra* – do you think it's just a magical incantation?"

"I know that *abra,* means 'I create,' and *cadabra,* means 'as I speak'."

I create as I speak. Very kabbalistic.

"Really? How do you know that?"

"I studied Aramaic in college."

Of course he did. He was the smartest one in school.

He drove up Donizetti Place and turned right onto Baychester Avenue. We passed the little yellow schoolhouse, now a private school. He made another right turn onto Co-Op City Boulevard.

"Do you want me to turn onto Dreiser Loop?"

"Yes, please."

He turned right onto Dreiser Loop. We passed his old apartment building. I asked him if he wanted to stop.

"The only reason I came back to Co-Op City was to see you." He pulled over and stopped the car. "What happened, Tal? I mean, one day we were hanging out and laughing and the next day, well, there was no next day."

"I'm sorry, Alex."

"No, no, I'm not asking for an apology. It's just that I always wondered what happened."

I hesitated.

"Why are we here, Tal?"

"Dreiser Loop."

"Yes," he pointed, "There's the sign, Dreiser Loop."

"It looks different to me. I'm confused. Can we drive farther down on Co-Op City Boulevard?"

"Sure." He turned the car around and drove back to Co-Op City Boulevard.

"I think that's it." I pointed to a four-story brick building.

Alex pulled into the parking lot. We got out.

"Tal, where are we going?"

"This is my Chapter One."

"What do you mean, your Chapter One?"

"Forty years ago a man in a white limousine asked me if I knew where Dreiser Loop was."

"What?"

"When I was nine years old, a man in a white limousine asked me for directions to Dreiser Loop. I was so happy that I knew where it was. It was pouring out and he told me to get into his limo so I wouldn't get wet. And when I did, he drove off..."

"He drove off with you *in* the car?"

I nodded.

"You were kidnapped? What happened? Did he rape you?"

"Shhh." I gestured with my chin toward some people getting out of their car. "I'm okay now. He drove me here. Well, not *here*, but to a construction site before this building went up."

I looked around. The building was a rehabilitation center.

312

How nice. A place of healing.

I told Alex the story. He watched with both trepidation and captivation as the memory crept back into my eyes.

"I wanted to come back here to prove to myself that I'm really okay."

Abracadabra. I create as I speak.

"Tali. I'm sorry. I wish I had known. Things might have turned out differently."

"I'm sorry that I didn't tell you. I couldn't. Nobody knew."

"Come here." He hugged me. I waited for the tears, but they didn't come. He hugged me tighter.

This feels so right.

"Thank you, Alex."

"No need to thank me, Tal. Now I understand."

He drove me back to my car, his hand caressing mine.

"What are you doing tonight?" he asked.

"I'm going to write my seminar."

"That's great."

"Will you come?"

"Of course."

As I drove back over the Throggs Neck Bridge, the sun came out and I saw a double rainbow emerge over the water.

Two rainbows. Two.

From Genesis 6:19: "And from all living things, from all flesh, you are to bring two from all into the ark, to remain alive with you."

This is when I knew that I didn't want to be alone anymore. I wanted to share my life with Alex.

forty-eight

The seminar was jam-packed. My entire family was there, Alex was there, even Rich Faust was there. I wore my amethyst ring for luck. I was anxious at first but I got over it. I had learned to use my anxiety as a barometer to measure my potential for spiritual growth. My goal was to conquer this anxiety by transforming it into Light, into fulfillment. Amelda Sethica, from The Long Island Alliance Against Child Abuse, was impressed with my going down to the audience rather than staying on stage behind the podium. I felt both restored and energized.

That night I had a wonderful dream: For my tenth birthday Grandma Devorah took me to The Moscow Circus at Madison Square Garden. I felt the elephants were in distress. They all had ropes tied to their ankles.

I ran down to the elephants. The matriarch looked at me and said, *"Uhuru."* I untied the rope around her ankle and then one by one untied all the others.

They shook themselves, raised their trunks and roared in triumph.

The matriarch turned to me and said, "You have a first name, Tali, which refers to blessings, prosperity and redemption, and a last name, Stark, which means strength."

She lifted me up with her trunk and put me on her back. Madison Square Garden dissolved into a Tanzanian landscape with Mount Kilimanjaro in the distance. The elephants started marching toward the mountain.

The sun was beginning to rise. Beyond the morning mist I saw a rainbow above the mountain. The matriarch led the elephants up the mountain all the way to the first summit, Stella Point. She waited until the last one arrived.

I gazed up at the clear, cobalt sky, pointed to the final summit and called out, *"Uhuru!"*

From everywhere and nowhere, I heard, "Atta girl!"

Although my memories of the innocent nine-year-old girl remain incomplete and fragmented – *inhale* – now at forty-nine years of age, I choose to move on – *exhale.*

Every time I engage fully in what I am doing, I take a step forward. When I am mindful of my breathing – *step.* When I am calm and focused – *skip.* When I remain calm and focused despite any images, thoughts, sounds, or physical sensations that remind me of the past – *jump.* When I choose to share secrets, especially secrets about the ways that I have managed to survive – *soar.*

Later that week, on Thanksgiving Day, I took out my notebook, the one that Aunt Kim had given me over a decade ago. On the cover there was a photo of a young girl crying, picturing in her mind's eye a white limousine.

I opened it to the last page and wrote the final entry:

DATE	NAME	AGE	HOMETOWN	STATUS
April, 15, 1974	Tali Stark	9	Bronx, New York	
*Nov 28, 2013				* FREE from ***The Ropes That Bind***.

forty-nine

May 25, 2014

Every child deserves to feel safe; every lost child deserves to be remembered. On National Missing Children's Day, I invited Aunt Kim over to honor the tens of thousands of missing children.

We lit a candle and closed our eyes.

I prayed, "For all the children who were murdered, may their families find closure for their unfathomable loss.

"For the thousands who are still missing, may they and their loved ones never give up hope that their journey back home is possible.

"And for all children who have experienced physical, emotional or sexual abuse, may they be guided to a place of forgiveness and self-acceptance; may abundant sunshine provide restoration and new beginnings as they continue their journey so cruelly interrupted."

"Amen."

appendix

CHILD SEXUAL ABUSE

Please use this information to become more mindful and proactive about child sexual abuse.

STATISTICS

- Child sexual abuse is an underreported crime. The vast majority (86%) is never reported.[1,2]

- As many as 1 in 4 women and 1 in 6 men report being sexually abused before the age of 18.[2,3]

- Disabled children are 4 to 10 times more vulnerable to sexual abuse.[4,5,6]

- 90-93% of the perpetrators are known to their victims.[2,7]

- Children rarely make up accusations of sexual abuse.[8]

citations

1. U.S. Department of Justice (2003). According to a national phone survey of adolescents (ages 12-17) conducted in 1995, 86% of sexual assaults experienced by these youth were not reported to any authorities (police, child protective services, schools, or other). Retrospective studies done with adults have found similarly low reporting rates for childhood sexual victimization.

2. Finkelhor D, Hotaling G, Lewis IA and Smith C (1990). Sexual abuse in a national survey of adult men and women: prevalence, characteristics, and risk factors. *Child Abuse & Neglect*, 14(1):19-28.

3. Felitti VJ and Anda RF (2010). The relationship of adverse childhood experiences to adult medical disease, psychiatric disorders and sexual behavior: Implications for healthcare. *The impact of early life trauma on health and disease: The hidden epidemic*, 77-87.

4. Hershkowitz I, Fisher S, Lamb ME and Horowitz D (2007). Improving credibility assessment in child sexual abuse allegations: The role of the NICHD investigative interview protocol. *Child Abuse & Neglect, 31*(2): 99-110.

5. Hibbard RA and Desch LW (2007). Maltreatment of children with disabilities. *Pediatrics*, 119(5): 1018-1025.

6. Kvam M. (2004). Sexual abuse of deaf children. A retrospective analysis of the prevalence and characteristics of childhood sexual abuse among deaf adults in Norway. *Child Abuse & Neglect, 28*(3): 241-251.

7. Sedlak AJ, Mettenburg J, Basena M, Peta I, McPherson K and Greene A (2010). Fourth national incidence study of child abuse and neglect (NIS-4). *Washington, DC: U.S. Department of Health and Human Services*.

8. Mikkelson EJ, Gutheil TG and Emens M (1992). False Sexual Abuse Allegations by Children and Adolescents: Contextual Factors and Clinical Subtypes. *American Journal of Psychotherapy,* 46: 556-70.

interview with the author

by Jennifer Gans Blankfein

I had the wonderful opportunity to ask award-winning debut author, Tracy Stopler, a few questions about her incredible book and her very full life.

Q. It is hard not to question the possibility that your main character, Tali Stark, might be you, Tracy Stopler. Was Tali's abduction and abuse experience your reality?

A. The simple and honest answer is yes. *The Ropes That Bind: Based on a True Story of Child Sexual Abuse*, is based on an event that happened to me when I was nine years old. I first wrote this story as a memoir, but I had to create some scenes to move the story along and I felt it was more honest (and easier to write) once I called it fiction ("based on a true story"). With this being said, the majority of names have been changed but mean something to me as the writer. There are two exceptions: One, the names of the missing children; and two, the name of Tali's colleague, Rich Faust, who was my dear friend, colleague and editor. Prior to Rich's passing he told me that he wanted his real name to be used. Because he never got to publish his work on personality types, I was thrilled to honor his request. Some of the other characters are actually two or more combined personalities of people I know.

Q. What part of Tali's story is fiction? The relationship with her mentor, Daniel? The failed marriage to Stuart? The relationship with the smart but slightly deviant Avi? Her ultimate reconnection with Alex? The car accident, the hernia, the trip to Israel?

A. The relationship with her Daniel is a true story and a true blessing. Interesting how the term "failed marriage" still stings. This is mostly true and mostly a blessing. My own demons got in the way of more blessings, but I'm so happy that our friendship continues today. The relationship with the (very) smart, (very) funny) and (very) deviant Avi is also based on someone I know, but there is a lot of creative writing in this section. Here is where Tali learns to trust her intuition and chooses to walk away from love rather than stay in an unhealthy relationship. I was very proud of her ☺! The reconnection with Alex is unbelievable, not only to me, but also to anyone who knows the story. In real life I had not been in contact with "Alex" in over 30 years. I wrote that entire section of the book as fiction with the exception of Tali's dream of going to the 25th High School Reunion and reconnecting with Alex. (FYI: All of the dreams written in this book were real dreams of mine). After the book was complete, but prior to publication, "Alex" called me (in real life). The only thought that came to my mind in that moment was the quote from *The Ten Commandments*. "So let it be written, so let it be done." I thought this real life reconnection was a beautiful coincidence. Not to ruin a happy ending for the readers, but, "Alex" and I were never romantic. Don't be sad; we are each in a healthy relationship with other people. The car accident, the hernia on Mount Kilimanjaro and the trip to Israel are all true, but some the dialogue on the mountain was creative writing and I did not take the *Kabbalah* class in Israel; I took it in NY.

Q. Tali doesn't talk much about her relationship with her mother. It seems like maybe her mother chose not to, or was not able to be as supportive as Tali needed. Can you tell me more about that relationship?

A. Many mother-daughter relationships are complicated. Growing up, my relationship with my mom was no different. What I can say now is that we have a wonderful relationship. I know with 100 percent certainty that we both did the best that we could with the knowledge that we had.

Q. In many ways the childhood trauma made Tali more productive and focused. The obsession with keeping a list of abducted children was time consuming and I wondered if that made Tali feel she wasn't alone or did it perpetuate her feelings of helplessness?

A. There is no right answer here. I want the reader to have their own opinion as to why Tali kept track of other missing children and whether or not it helped her to move forward.

Q. Often people who experience trauma turn to drugs, alcohol or other addictions to escape the pain of the memories in an attempt to forget. Why do you think Tali was able to focus on school?

A. Tali may have passed the test of avoiding drugs and alcohol when she was in college, but she certainly had other obstacles. As the writer (and as a survivor), I wanted Tali to *be* in control. Tali wanted Tali to *feel* in control. But *being* and *feeling* in control are two different things. Hopefully the reader was able to follow Tali's transformation.

Q. People often do big things to overcome inner struggles and climbing Kilimanjaro would be one of them. Was this accomplishment helpful for Tali in terms of moving forward?

A. Overcoming obstacles may require several steps. Climbing Mount Kilimanjaro was huge for Tali. Finishing this book was huge for me ☺.

Q. I enjoyed all the references to Judaism (you sparked my interest in *Kabbalah* and the ability to receive light and share it), I remembered much of the news you mentioned regarding the missing children and realized my knowledge of AIDS/HIV in the 80s was limited. Did you, Tracy, study *Kabbalah*, keep a list of the missing, research HIV/AIDS and what was your research process for the book?

A. I did study *Kabbalah*, but not in Israel (as mentioned in the book). I took classes in NYC and on Long Island. Although I kept a list of missing children, I was not as thorough as Tali was. I think if I were actually keeping track of how many missing children were murdered, I would have been devastated. As a registered dietitian I was very fortunate to have the opportunity to work with patients living with HIV and AIDS. I did this twice – as portrayed in the story – once, right out of college when I worked at the Bronx VA Medical Center and then again, years later, when I took a position in Rockland County. The research for this book was never ending. Just when I was about to publish the story (for the first time), Jaycee Lee Dugard's captors, Phillip and Nancy Garrido was sentenced to 431 and 36 years respectively; another little boy, eight-year-old Leiby Kletzky from Boro Park, Brooklyn, went missing and was found murdered; on a happier note, Elizabeth Smart who had been missing for nine months was now on the cover of PEOPLE Magazine – she had just gotten married. And then there was the BREAKING NEWS; the craziness: Pedro Hernandez had confessed to murdering Etan Patz. This was followed by the three missing Cleveland girls found alive. It was such an emotional time and I couldn't sleep. I just wanted the world to stand still for 24 hours.

Q. Your calling seems to be helping others who experienced childhood trauma and teaching, and you have done so much personal work to get to the place of comfort in having your voice be heard publicly. Do you have any plans to tackle climbing another mountain or are you content with your current contributions to this world?

A. Thank you, Jennifer. Like Tali, I have had many opportunities to physically climb other mountains and I have declined. I choose to channel my energy by paying it forward in helping others to find their voice. In doing so, I have truly summited.

Q. Finally, was this book written solely as catharsis to help with healing, and do you have any plans to write another one?

A. I started journaling from the time I was ten years old. A lot of my writing from the past was adapted for this book. Finishing the story was a therapy assignment. At the time, it was part of the healing journey. I continued writing long after therapy and although it wasn't always cathartic, I can honestly say that now that it's done, and it's helping others find their path to heal, nothing hurts! I am writing another book, ***My Brother Javi: A Dog's Tale***. Although Tali is a character in the book, the main characters are her two precious dogs, Java and Binah (who are both mentioned in *The Ropes That Bind*). This light-hearted story is a memoir written in the voice of both Java and Binah. Unlike writing ***The Ropes That Bind***, this book is so much fun to write. I truly love being inside the head of the different dog characters. Although this is a completely different book than my first, it still has life lessons for both parents and children.

The Ropes That Bind by Tracy Stopler received the 2017 Independent Press Award and the NYC Big Book Award for "Distinguished Favorite" in the category of Women's Fiction.

To watch the book trailer go to: https://youtu.be./bXDSIQOUWIU and to watch Tracy's TEDx Talk, *Break Free From The Ropes That Bind, go to:* https://youtu.be/lowLwYXdhR4